Ho Ho Homicidal Maniac

Murder & Mistletoe Anthology Series

K.A. Merikan

http://kamerikan.com

Cover design by

MiblArt

https://miblart.com/

Editing by No Stone Unturned

https://www.facebook.com/NoStoneUnturnedEditingServices/

Contents

CHAPTER 1

BLAKE

IT'S JUST MY LUCK that my first-ever evening at a gay nightclub ends like this.

My head is a snow globe filled with tar. Scattered thoughts whir without rhyme or reason, but as I wake up and open my eyes, the world falls back into place.

I don't like a single thing about my new reality.

The musty smell of the stained mattress I'm on reaches my senses first, but as everything comes into focus, my muscles calcify with terror.

A camera mounted on a tripod is pointing straight at me, and when I look around, I realize I'm in a real-life horror movie.

The X-shaped frame of a Saint Andrew's cross, complete with wrist and ankle restraints, towers over me and casts a long shadow on my legs. Knives and saws hang on the wall, lined up by size, and the smell of dried blood is barely covered by the overwhelming stench of bleach.

Once I'm certain there's no one else here, I lift my head and attempt to dart toward the camera, but a tug on my waist pulls me right back onto the musty bedding with a loud *clang* of the chain attached to the steel belt sitting around my midsection. I narrowly avoid hitting my head on the wall, but as my temples pulse from the onslaught of fear, I grab the ring digging into my tender flesh. It's attached to the wall with links that refuse to budge when I pull.

I have always considered myself smart. I've consumed so many true-crime documentaries, I started my own podcast, and yet, when a guy dressed up as a sexy Santa bought me a shot at the club, I didn't even blink twice before downing it. He complimented my dark curls, whispered a sweet word about my green eyes, and I fell into his trap.

After all, it's my eighteenth birthday, and I left my house for the first time in weeks. I was supposed to have the time of my life, and my brother got me a fake ID so I could enter a gay nightclub. I even dressed up in a dumb Christmas elf costume in hope of attracting someone willing to take my V-card.

I glance down at the ridiculous green shorts and candy cane-patterned stockings.

If I'm so smart, how could I have been so stupid?

I would have texted my friends about where I was going, or even been there with them... if I had any.

Instead, I'm knee-deep in my worst nightmare, because the last thing I remember is Sexy Santa helping me walk when the spiked drink started working, and now I'm in a sex-and-murder basement, surrounded by raw concrete walls and furniture I don't even want to name.

They all bear traces of much use, and as I imagine this stranger strapping me to one of them to inflict torture, panic blurs all my thoughts. I helplessly pry at the lock of the steel belt around my waist.

Maybe my abductor made a fatal mistake that might just save my life? I am quite slim and have the slightest chance of pulling out of this contraption. But as I wrestle the chain with my bare hands, close to having a panic attack, a door opens somewhere above. My gaze travels beyond the camera, to a staircase leading out of this place.

Before I even see the dark shadow on the steps, some-one whistles 'Deck the Halls With Boughs of Holly'.

I'm stunned into silence as I back out into the dark-est corner of my prison without making a sound, hiding behind a cupboard like the little mouse I am. I'm not someone to act impulsively, especially not while in the vulnerable position I found myself in.

The whistling man's silhouette is tall, with wide shoul-ders, and a trim waist. He's dressed in a fitted black top and dark jeans, but I end up focusing on his balaclava which features... ears. Cute, round teddy bear ears.

My stomach clenches, but I'm soon distracted by the resounding *thud thud thud* created by the limp body he's dragging behind him slamming against the stairs again and again. He pulls it all the way down with a final tug that reminds me of a figure skater spinning his partner in a death spiral. The corpse slides over the floor, and from the shadows of my hideout I see a dark shape eject from his pocket and roll toward me.

I'm so frightened even breathing feels like too much of a risk, but when I recognize the fallen item to be a small gun, determination floods my veins. Despite my guts coiling as though they're full of snakes, I hold the chain attaching me to the wall, to keep it from clinking, and lean forward, trying to make myself as small as possible. The man in black still has his back to me, so I need to move fast.

Sweat beads above my lip as I stretch my arm. I'm about to put my hand on the firearm when my gaze slides over the dead man's face, and I realize this isn't the first time I've seen him.

It's the Sexy Santa who drugged me at the club, and while I'm relieved to see that he won't be able to hurt me in this godforsaken dungeon, I might have escaped the frying pan only to end up in the fire. Or a whole fireplace doused with gasoline for that matter. I stiffen when the whistling killer takes a saw off the wall.

I pull away from the gun and retreat into my prison of dark shadows before he can spot my hand. The weapon that could save my life is so close, but I can't risk being discovered.

The man stops whistling the jolly tune with a huff and pulls off the balaclava.

I'm dead. I'm so dead.

Even if he never meant to show me his face, even if he doesn't know I'm here, he *will* find out, and by then it will already be too late, as I know from every true-crime story I ever read.

My only hope is to remain silent as a mouse, and maybe, just maybe, thanks to a freakish amount of luck, he doesn't spot me.

I try to memorize every detail of his face. Victims are often too frantic when confronted with an attacker, and can't describe or even recognize the criminal at a later time.

That won't be me. If I survive, that is.

In the light coming in from above, his profile couldn't have been sharper. He's pale, with messy dark blond hair that barely reaches his chin. Some strands are of a lighter color. I don't see that well from afar, but his eyes are bright. Either green or blue. Maybe gray?

Big nose. Golden stubble. Must be over six feet tall. Is that a tattoo on his neck? His face is flushed, and his smile widens as he assesses the dead body. I'd describe that grin as either cheerful or predatory. Or deranged. As though he's just come back home through a snow-storm and is about to bite into a warm cookie.

Details, Blake. Details.

Just as I'm about to log his dark eyebrows into my memory, he leans down with that cheery grin and puts the saw to work on the dead man's neck. Blood splashes his face, but he just... licks his lips.

The rusty teeth of the saw bite deeper into flesh, and the sudden faintness in my head dives straight into my stomach. I'm retching, and the freak looks my way, his gaze diving into my corner behind the cupboard. I no longer have anything to lose so I dash forward, grab the gun and point it at the stranger with acid still burning my throat.

"Stay back," I demand, and when my hands shake, I pull them close to my chest, hoping that will make me appear much less intimidated than I am. The chain attached to my waist rattles, as if it has a mind of its own and wants to make it clear to him that my whole body is trembling.

I don't want to die. My life was supposed to finally be-gin next week. I was supposed to inherit half a fortune, gain new freedoms, explore the world, and suck my first dick.

The man isn't frightened, and that doesn't bode well. His eyes (blue, definitely blue) pierce me, and he doesn't even blink, like he's not even human, but a sexy lizard man.

"You're not supposed to be here," he says and cocks his head as he steps closer. Blood drips from his chin.

I'm not a crier, but right now I want to wail. I'm only eighteen, with a whole life ahead of me. What did I do to deserve this?

"H-he spiked my drink. I don't care what you do with him. I just want to go home," I mumble as my head throbs, making rational thinking impossible. Maybe my older brother was right when he said I don't have the personality to deal with stressful situations. Then again, who the hell could easily handle this kind of situation?

He takes another step closer, and I wonder if I ought to shoot yet, but I've never even *held* a gun before, and I'm less likely to miss from up close.

The man's expression turns curious as he eyes me from head to toe, and I'm all too aware that the Christmas elf top I have on is split all the way to my belly button.

"You should have shown yourself while I still had the mask on," he says with a sigh and runs his leather-clad hand through his hair. If the situation wasn't so surreal and terrifying, this could be a perfume commercial and he'd fit right in, with those looks. "What do I do with you...?"

He's holding something, and I'd recognize the thick vintage ribbon in my sleep, because I've read all the articles, books, and watched every documentary about the Christmas Killer. Hell, I even publish a special December podcast about him each year.

"Oh shit... shit," rips out of my mouth before I can stop myself, but facing the bogeyman of New England while being chained to the wall is too much to handle. "Please, just let me go. I won't even remember you. It's science."

His nostrils flare in a long inhale. He's thinking. Maybe I *do* have a chance. I wasn't his target after all. If I get out of here and report him, I could probably go into witness protection.

It should be the last thing on my mind, but I'm excited that I could be the one to crack the case of the Christmas Killer.

"Calm down and put the gun away. We will sort this out. I did save you from him after all, did I not?" He points to the dead guy whose neck is partially severed now but doesn't look back. All of his attention is on me.

He did save me, by accident. Still, he wants me to stroke his ego, so I nod and attempt to steady my voice. "Yes. I am so, *so* thankful. Please, can you just toss me the keys to those chains? I'll show myself out," I add but grip the gun more firmly when the muscular form moves closer. He's still a few paces away, and I already feel crowded, a mouse hiding from the mountain lion.

He's young, too young to be the Christmas Killer. Some historians believe he claimed his first victim in 1912, but the person I'm seeing can't even be in his thirties. Is this man a copycat?

The monster makes a sad pout. "I can't let you go, I'm afraid. But I see you appreciate the Christmas spirit." He points to my costume, in which I wouldn't have been caught dead in if I hadn't been trying to get laid at a nightclub. "I'm sure we'll get along just jolly."

He moves so fast I yelp and step back, but pull the trigger anyway, only for it to... do nothing.

I freeze, and he pulls the pistol out of my hands with a soft sigh. "Next time pull the safety off first," he says and demonstrates, as if I haven't just tried to kill him. Despite the terror sinking deep into my body, all I can focus on is that there might be a *next time*, and that surely means he doesn't plan to leave my head wrapped in the same ribbon as Sexy Santa's.

I open my mouth, ready to face him again, but before I can make any noise, a sharp sting makes me glance to my arm, where a small needle is embedded in my flesh. My eyes meet the killer's blue gaze, he smiles at me, and then everything blurs.

The last thing I hear is his soft murmur.

"Sleep in heavenly peace..."

CHAPTER 2

Nico

"Welcome in December, you know what time it is…" says my favorite true-crime podcaster, Cryptic Boy Wonder, and since I know exactly what's coming, I finish the sentence with him.

"It's time for the Christmas Killer!"

I hang a big red bauble on the Christmas tree to replace the one a customer broke earlier today. I don't mind. It happens. People rush around when December starts, eager to get decorations and gifts from my shop. If anything, I'm surprised this Tuesday evening is so slow and I might get to close on time for once.

It's for the better, because I do need to work out what to do with my prisoner downstairs.

For now though, I will indulge in the soft, warm voice of the podcaster who is very excited to talk about *me*. Is it a little self-involved to listen about crimes I know better than he ever could? Yes, but it's my little indulgence when I'm alone in my Christmas kingdom. And aren't the holidays all about being *gay*?

"But you know what I always say: There's no sugar-coating murder!" Cryptic Boy Wonder's soft voice says into my ear. "This festive season, I will chronologically discuss each murder, since the early twentieth century to the present. I've invited special guests, who have their own theories as to when the original killer might have been first replaced by a copycat, but to me it's clear that the frequency of murders changed within the past decade, going from them occurring every now and then in December to a pattern of at least one victim every year."

I step back to admire the tree, which is a focal point of the store. Thanks to the tall ceiling, it can dwarf every other decoration, reaching all the way to the second floor, and I love it that way. I'm a traditionalist at heart. Maybe it's because I was brought up by my granddad, or because whimsy gives my heart the warm fuzzies, but even my more avant-garde craft projects have a touch of nostalgia.

I inherited my shop from my grandfather (along with the Christmas Killer persona, but that's another story). I sense his spirit with me in the warm, twinkling lights, the glass counter he made himself, the words we both carved in the wooden wall behind the counter. The original fireplace had to be replaced with a fake one that is a projection for safety reasons, but I installed a heater inside so that the interior is as toasty as a marshmallow between two crackers.

My shop is an all-year-round Christmas paradise. Sometimes, I sit in the armchair by the bookshelves after closing time, drinking spiced hot chocolate and knitting by the fireplace, because the store feels like home. Perhaps even more so than my small apartment upstairs.

I'm about to lock the doors for the night when a girl of around ten runs in ahead of her mother. I bow toward her, matching my movements to the jolly music streaming from speakers hidden in wreaths of artificial holly. I pause my podcast just as Cryptic Boy Wonder rasps the phrase "*Bloody murder*" straight into my ear.

Rawr.

"Merry Christmas! Are you out helping your mom with shopping?" I ask the girl, who grins at me so sweetly I wish I could pinch her frost-flushed cheeks. Her red hat and coat are covered with fresh snow as she crosses the threshold, but it starts melting in the warm shop. Maybe someday, I can pass the mantle of the Christmas Killer to a kid of my own. For now though, my role is to brighten the faces of all children and adults alike, so I offer her a small candy-cane.

"Good evening, Nico," Mrs. Pratchett says before reminding her daughter to say thank you. "Sorry, I meant to come in earlier, but you know how it is in December."

I offer her a friendly smile. "Don't worry, the store's still open. What are you looking for?"

"Oh, I'll be back before Christmas, but I wanted some of that gingerbread loaf. It's Roger's favorite."

I smile at her and rush to the counter. "Good thing I kept one just in case." In all honesty, I was intending to eat it myself for dinner, but I'm getting more delivered tomorrow, and I know she'll appreciate it. If I had a husband, I'd also treat him to the finest artisan baked goods.

"Is that Rudolf?" the daughter asks, pointing to my sweater.

I'm very tall, so I squat to meet her eyes. "I'm not sure, but maybe if you boop his nose, we'll find out." I glance at the mother to make sure it's okay, and she grins at me.

When the girl pushes the pompom my sweater has in place of the reindeer's nose, the tiny mechanism built in there plays the melody of 'Rudolf the Red-nosed Reindeer', and both my customers laugh.

"Nico! That's the most ridiculous sweater I've seen you wear yet," Mrs. Pratchett says as I move on to wrapping her loaf in decorative paper. That extra touch of Christmas magic is what keeps my little shop afloat all year round.

That and the Christmas Killer merch.

"And December is just getting started." I wink at her.

"Will you be spending the holidays with someone special this year?" she asks, and yes, it's nosey, but everyone in Blue Grove is a little bit nosey. That's the small-town charm. It does make my side gig tricky at times, but I've got enough experience to manage.

I shake my head with a smile. "This is the busiest time of the year, I hardly have the time for that." Even though I might be stuck with an unexpected guest for much longer than either of us anticipated. Should I bring him a candy cane to sweeten his new reality?

She sighs as she pays for the gingerbread loaf. "You're so handsome, Nico, it's a shame."

The girl stands on her toes to see me over the counter, her expression serious. "Maybe you should wear an elegant shirt, like my daddy."

Mrs. Pratchett shushes her. "That's enough, Caroline, we took too much of Nico's time already."

I'm blushing at the compliment. "Don't worry about it."

"I'm not wishing you a Merry Christmas just yet, because we will be back before the twenty-fifth!" she says on her way out of the door, and the bells above it jingle when they leave.

I wave at them and lock my store before facing the warm interior full of colorful treats and decorations arranged on wooden shelves. My gaze is drawn to my little Pride at Christmas corner, where a set of hot guy-themed baubles hangs from a rainbow tree. One of them is a Santa's elf, and I can't help but think back to my reluctant guest, who's wearing the exact same outfit as the boy depicted on the trinket—tight green shorts, a shirt that reveals his chest, and candy cane stripe stockings. Could this be a sign that I might just have someone to kiss under the mistletoe this year?

We'll have to find out, but at least it's clear we both love Christmas.

I switch off the lights and head to my apartment first, to prepare enough hot chocolate to fill a large thermos. I then make a sandwich with turkey and all the trimmings and put both into a basket along with some other treats. My guest must be starving after a whole day on his own. The poor thing had a terrible night, and while I can't let him go, since he saw my face, we did get off on the wrong foot. I'm not his enemy, even though it might seem like that to him right now.

And a part of me wants to earn his smile, despite the unfortunate way we met. What can I say? He's exactly my type with that boyish face dusted with more freckles than there are stars in the sky, and the lean body of a runner. His dark locks are cut into short layers, giving him a youthful appearance, and while I was tempted to touch his pouty lips and lean closer to smell his minty cologne, I didn't touch him in any way that wasn't strictly necessary in order to move him from Tooley's murder basement. I've been the perfect gentleman.

I might be a serial killer, but I have standards.

On the topic of standards, I am frustrated by what he must have woken up to by now, as it's in no way the kind of space I would like him to experience. I grab a fresh blanket on the way down to Santa's little secret, as my granddad liked to call it. The sprawling hidden lair under the regular basement of the shop is where the *real* Christmas magic happens.

I stop in my tracks in the stock room and leave everything I've been carrying to go back and change. While I might enjoy Blake's sexy elf costume, I want to make the best impression possible after last night's fiasco, so a dark burgundy shirt it is.

As I open the secret passage behind the old wardrobe at the back of the stockroom, I remember how he looked yesterday when he pointed that gun at me. Terrified, yes, but also determined, beautifully flushed. I bet that deep down, he realized I was his savior and appreciated my presence. He was just too frightened to understand the situation.

I descend the stairs with my heart beating faster.

It's been quite a while since I've had a date.

CHAPTER 3

BLAKE

I'M IN HELL.

Cold walls of raw brick surround me from all sides, and I can't help the shivers running down my spine from the overwhelming cold. Despite it not being freezing, the chill seems to be reaching all the way to my bones. Is this place damp, or are the sensations I'm feeling caused by all the souls who've perished here over the years?

I've never believed in ghosts, but now that I'm in the hands of the Christmas Killer, all the crazy paranormal documentaries I've watched as a teen are coming back to shatter my composure.

This place appears *ancient*. The floor looks like it's been carved out of stone, there are no windows, and the bars making up my cell are iron, like this is a historical sheriff's department, not the second murder-basement I've woken up in within the past twenty-four hours.

At least this time, there's no torture equipment in sight, so maybe he intends to get rid of me fast, without making me suffer for his enjoyment? But if that was the case, I'd already be dead.

I pull the red-and-green blanket I've been covered with more tightly around me and sit cross-legged on the narrow cot taking up a third of my prison.

How on Earth has it come to this? I've always seen myself as careful, I read so many books about serial killers, I even feature the Christmas Killer each year on my podcast. What are the odds of my head ending up wrapped with his signature vintage bow?

I chuckle, but it soon turns into a dry sob as I slide off the bed and once again attempt to get the ancient lock of my cell to open, but to no avail.

Even if I did have mad lockpicking skills, which I don't, I would need some kind of tool to get myself out of this mess, but the only things I've been provided are the bedding, and a meal of milk and cookies. It's as though the murderer is fucking with me.

He probably wants to interrogate me, find out who I am, to work out how many people will be looking for me. Or, another grim option, he *does* know who I am, hates what I say about him on the podcast, and will carve a pound of flesh out of me for every perceived lie.

I've not touched the food, in case it contains drugs, or even poison. If he wants to stage my suicide, he'll need to try harder than that. On the other hand, I *am* starving. I was so nervous about my first outing to a gay club I didn't eat since breakfast, and now it's been who-knows-how-long since my last croissant.

Oh, what I'd give for Franklin's omelet with goat's cheese and a sprinkle of fried garlic... Right now, the sheltered life I've complained about in my mind so many times feels like a distant dream. A golden cage doesn't seem so bad when you're stuck in one made of iron.

I stiffen and back into the corner when I hear footsteps on creaky wood, but my blood goes cold when I hear the Christmas Killer's voice.

"Ho ho ho!" he says cheerfully like the deranged maniac that he is.

I stand straight, wrapped in the ugly Christmas blanket and try to keep calm as the door opens and the tall, handsome guy strolls in holding a neat little basket, and yet another blanket, even more garishly festive than the one I'm using. I would have dreamed about flirting with a man like him at the club. If I didn't know he has blood on his hands.

I open my eyes, but the stress eating me from the inside is so overwhelming I can't push out a single syllable, and stare at him, wordlessly begging, *Please, don't kill me.*

Yesterday (or is this still the same night?), he wore a soft long-sleeve that wouldn't restrict his movements, but now he's in a well-fitting burgundy shirt with one button open at the collar to reveal his neck tattoo. Several snowflakes. How appropriate.

His sleeves are rolled up to the elbow as if he were trying to distract me with his sexy forearms instead of cutting me up like he did my earlier abductor. Am I catnip for kidnappers? What the fuck?

He puts down the blanket, the basket, and cocks his head at me. "This is quite the pickle, isn't it?"

For a moment, I see myself marinating in a huge pickle jar, like one of those deformed fetuses preserved for prosperity, but I shake it off and clear my throat, because this is my chance to gain this man's sympathy, and even serial killers aren't immune to others stroking their ego. "T—thank you for saving me," I tell him just before my stomach makes a low gurgle that goes on and on, filling the silence between us.

He makes a concerned face. "Poor thing. Did you not see I left you cookies—" he pauses and his eyes widen when his blue gaze settles on the plate "—raisins. Of course. I didn't think you might be particular about that, I was in such a rush to prepare the space. Lots of people dislike raisins, I should have been more considerate about it. Any allergies?"

Does he want to... kill me via anaphylactic shock?

It would be an unorthodox but efficient and discreet way of disposing of someone who now knows this man's secret. And since I did go out to party last night, it would be plausible for me to accidentally ingest something I shouldn't.

But I shake my head. "Just dust mites."

He nods and his smile wanes as he looks around. "I know the space is not ideal, but I will spruce it up in no time, and it's well-insulated, so there's no damp here."

He's mad. In a world of his own, and I'm an unwilling participant in whatever unhinged fantasy of his this is. Then again, I should have already known this, since he is the Christmas Killer. No one sane rips people's teeth out then wraps their decapitated heads in ribbons.

But he isn't trying to scare me, and he didn't threaten me yet so... maybe I can make him like me? I've made podcasts about victims who managed to endear themselves to their captors and survived. Could this be my chance?

"I'm just so scared," I tell him, desperate to appear younger and more innocent than I am, so he pities me. That's right, Christmas Killer, I don't deserve to die. I'm a nice boy, who happened to be in the wrong place at the wrong time.

I think back to last night's party, and the thoughtless way I accepted a drink from a stranger, just because he was hot, makes me cringe. I know the methods criminals use to victimize people, and I should have known better. As it turns out, reading about crime is very different from actually dealing with manipulators trying to spike your drink. If my life experience wasn't so limited, I would have known that.

And now here I am, trying to make the most prolific killer in my state *like* me.

Fuck my life.

Trying to pressure him into releasing me would back-fire, so being 'nice' is the tactic I'll be sticking to for now.

"I understand. The situation is new to me as well. I've never had a witness before. Or survivors." He opens the basket to reveal a thermos, cups, plates, and food. Does he want to have a picnic with me, or something?

As much as I want to deny it, when he pours hot choco-late into the cups, my stomach demands to drink it *right now*.

But what if he's just being nice to fool me, like Sexy San-ta had? What could he gain from poisoning me, though? Unless it's his thing to watch someone die a slow and painful death.

"I imagine that must be extraordinarily awkward," I say with a nervous chuckle and stare at the marshmallows he tosses in from a cardboard packet. Could those be spiked as well? He didn't put any in his own mug.

My mind flashes back to the moment the saw ripped into my dead abductor's neck. I've seen so many photos of crime scenes, yet it can't compare to the real life experience. The sudden smell of blood in the air, the awful sound of the blade as it ripped through meat and cartilage...

Maybe I can go another hour without eating after all?

As he passes me the hot mug, I wonder if he chose a burgundy shirt so blood doesn't show on it as much.

"Let's consider it a Christmas miracle," he says with a smile and bumps his cup against mine. "My name is Nico, like, you know, Saint Nicholas. But no 'h'. It will be a while until I work out exactly what to do with you, so it would be nice to get to know each other."

I struggle to remain serious, because for all his prowess in remaining free over the years, this guy is utterly deranged. And unpredictable, and *that* means the next time I wake up, there might be a knife against my throat.

"Blake. And, uhm, my big brother must be worried sick about me," I add to check his reaction.

"I'll find out about that, but Blake... Sometimes life takes a turn, you know? A few years ago, I lost my grandfather, and he was the only family I had left. It wasn't an easy transition, but I adjusted over time."

Does he mean... I'll be adjusting to living in a cell with no windows?

"You want to just keep me here on my own?" I ask in the most sullen voice I can muster.

"It's all so fresh it's hard to tell. I don't believe in gifting pets for Christmas, but I could consider getting a puppy for you, if you think you won't deal well with solitude."

Is that even a question? I hate him so much already for restricting my freedom, for the abduction, for the farcical 'treats' meant to subdue me, but I'm still fighting back tears at the thought that this might be my life now. Stuck in some freak's cellar.

"What kind of life is that?" Rips out of my chest as I step closer to the bars, pinning him with my gaze. "There's no sugarcoating murder. Even if it's just murder of the soul, and *my soul* is going to die in these conditions!"

But it's as if he's not hearing me at all. He cocks his head and stares into my eyes so intently my heart rises to my throat. I overdid it. I couldn't stay nice, and he's gonna kill me. Or leave me here alone for a week to 'teach me a lesson'.

"'There's no sugarcoating murder'..." he repeats. "I could swear I knew your voice from somewhere! You're Cryptic Boy Wonder."

My blood might have just frozen over, and I want to deny it, to hide my interest in his work of blood and gore, but he's already decided what to believe. And I've never been a good liar. He's certainly going to kill me now, and make it his grandest spectacle to date, sending a message to every single person who ever spoke ill of him.

"I..."

Nico puts down his mug and reaches into my cell through the bars, extending his hand. I step back, afraid that he's trying to grab me, but his smile widens.

"I am *such* a fan. I love that you cover the local cases. I know I'm the December highlight for a lot of true-crime aficionados, but it feels more genuine from you. And your voice? Ah." Still keeping his hand in front of me like he wants me to... squeeze it (?), he pats his cheek as it darkens a little. Is he blushing? "I might have a bit of a crush on you. I hope that doesn't make you uncomfortable? I just figured that—I mean, your outfit..."

I couldn't have been any more scared, because not only does this maniac know my voice enough to recognize it, but he's also gay and has me in his clutches. Does that mean I'll have to navigate his sexual interest in me on top of everything else I'm already dealing with? How could my life take such a rapid turn, and on a night meant to be my step into adult life and toward freedom?

"I... don't know you yet," I say, because it's painfully obvious I'll get nowhere without pandering to him. Even my ears feel hot when I think I might have to get close to him to get out of here. How close? Shaking his hand? Kissing him? More?

I should definitely *not* be thinking about that.

He pulls his hand back, flustered. "Right. Of course. Too forward. After all, you, like me, hide under a pseudonym for a reason. I might have gotten a bit too enthusiastic. You don't like hot chocolate?"

Seriously? How is the reason for my wariness not obvious?

"I... that guy spiked my drink."

Nico tut-tuts and he looks at me with compassion, as if he's not holding me prisoner. "Oh no... that's how he got you? Look, I'm drinking it," he says and takes a sip. "I've also brought sandwiches and a fluffier blanket."

My stomach rumbles at the very idea of having a sandwich, and I bring the mug to my lips, tasting the creamiest, milkiest chocolate I've ever had. Or maybe it's just my hunger talking. "I don't know if I can trust you either. After all, you're not letting me go."

He passes me the blanket, and I once more glance at his muscular forearm dusted with dark blond hair. Am I admiring it or wondering how easy it would be for him to strangle me? I'm not sure, but I do know that without a weapon I won't stand a chance against him.

"Nothing is out of the realm of possibility." He's dangling freedom in front of me, which makes me wonder if his perky persona is just a manipulation tactic. "But while I have you here, I'd love to clear up some misconceptions about me."

Nico takes a big sip of hot chocolate and drags a small table close to the metal bars. He presses it against them, then sits on a small stool, which previously stood in the corner, as if he and I were sharing a meal. It's... bizarre, but when he places a sandwich overflowing with meat, cranberry, and other goodness on a plate, I can't resist and dig in.

It's so heavenly I end up grunting with pleasure, only to freeze when a grin appears on the killer's handsome face. "Uhm... yes?"

"Nothing, nothing," he dismisses it and looks down at all the paper crafts he has set up on the table along with scissors. But the way he's blushing suggests my moan might have been way too enthusiastic. I'm not used to being around a man who's attracted to me, and now I'll have to deal with that on top of the fact that he's a damn serial killer.

"Do you like it? I just love Christmas foods. I can have them all year round."

I might hate Christmas, but the seasonal food is all right. Or, in the case of this particular sandwich, damn tasty. I only hope the meat is in fact turkey, not human thigh. "It's very nice. Did you make this yourself?" I try to once again crawl into his good graces.

He lights up as if he's a star on a Christmas tree, and my heart skips a beat, even though I know he's *evil*. Is this Stockholm Syndrome kicking in already?

"I did! I make a whole turkey every few weeks, carve it all up then freeze it, but I'm sure you're more interested to find out the facts about me and my legacy. Who knows what will happen. If I die or go to prison, you'd be allowed to reveal everything I tell you."

Now it's him trying to reel *me* in. Whether he just wants me docile or to get into my pants, I don't know, since I have no experience in flirting.

Once again, I'm a fish swallowing the bait. "You're a copycat, right? You're clearly not over a hundred years old."

He looks genuinely offended as he bites into the sandwich. "Me? I might be twenty-seven, but I am a *legacy*, trained and allowed to carry the Christmas Killer name by my grandfather. There was a copycat though, I'll tell you that. Three years ago, that murder of the innocent bauble-maker. But that wasn't me. I found the bastard who did that under my name and disposed of him quietly. I didn't want his death to muddle the waters of *my* story, and I only found him in January. I don't kill willy-nilly. I check who's naughty and who's nice. And that guy was most definitely on the naughty list."

I have no words for this shit. And still, despite the fear that makes me shiver and the horrible things that have already happened to me, I can't help my curiosity. I've been following this guy's story since I first heard about him, years ago. To have him at arm's length and eager to answer my questions is an opportunity I can't pass. To be fair, it might be the last opportunity I might get, so I chew my food and ask.

"The Christmas Killer's victims appear to be chosen at random. Most were men, but investigators could never establish a preferred victim. I see how the copycat might have been a problem if they never figured it out. But you're saying there *is* a pattern?"

Nico grabs the scissors and starts meticulously cutting the green paper in front of him. "I watch over many local towns in the area. It's not perfect, I only have so much time in the day, but I have a system in place. I also leave gifts for those in need, but is that reported on? No. No one ever associates me with those acts of kindness. Ah, now it just sounds like I'm trying to boast. I'll tell you more tomorrow. Otherwise I won't be able to focus on this, and I promised a friend of mine to get it done. Have you ever made paper chain decorations? You could be a real life Santa's helper, make yourself useful. You're already dressed like one." He winks at me as if any of this was funny.

I adjust the blanket so my bare chest is no longer on show, and continue eating my sandwich, trying to process what I've just heard. "So you see yourself as a... Robin Hood-type of character? A folk hero?" I ask incredulously.

He gets up and brings me a pair of rounded kids' scissors. Is this a labor camp now? Still, I better comply, so when he explains what kind of paper strips he wants, I get on with it.

I have never done this before, actually. The house would always be decorated by our staff, Christmas tree included. Maybe it would have been nice to have a say in the colors of trinkets or something, but I've always just accepted reality for what it is.

"Well, yes, I do weed out the danger, so that people can have a lovely, peaceful Christmas time. And if I enjoy it a little? No one said you have to hate your job." His little smirk tells me how much he liked sawing a man's head off.

The ghost of the nausea that overcame me when it happened appears back in my throat, but then I think about the new microphone I was planning to buy, and it subsides. "This might be presumptuous," I say and clear my throat, glancing at my captor, who whistles as he continues making the paper cutouts. "But people never have a peaceful time when they worry there's a killer on the loose."

Nico hums. "No, that's thoughtful of you. Maybe I should make it clearer that there is a pattern. You're so smart. And your voice? Just like the podcast."

The dreamy look he gives me is as enticing as it is disconcerting.

"Don't you think all this would be comfier if I wasn't behind bars?" I ask in the most innocent tone I can muster, because while it is obviously a ploy to run, maybe someone as deranged as this guy might believe I'm on his side.

"It would, it would, but I don't have time to set things up tonight. I'm sorry, but you'll have to wait until to-morrow. Things will get better here, I promise. I have so many questions for you as well." He gets up, picks up the stack of papers he was cutting, then reveals it to be a long decorative chain. The links are shaped like hearts. "Ta-dah!"

Taken aback, I hide behind the mug of cocoa and use its sweetness to calm myself down. "It's not Valentine's…."

When Nico's face falls, I realize these hearts were made for me, and I don't know if I'm flattered or unsettled. "I just thought it would be nice," he mumbles. "Spruce things up a little."

To my disbelief, he gets up and hangs it from one prison bar to another with bits of string.

"I mean… it is, but it's Christmas season, and the paper is green," I mumble, too confused to think clearly. But then I remember what he said about Christmas, and clear my throat. "I appreciate the effort, really."

He pins me with his gaze, and it feels as though he's sawing right through me. "Are you single?"

The mug almost slips out of my hands, but I catch it at the cost of spilling some of the chocolate over my fingers. What the hell should I tell him? This freak is interested in me, and while that's terrifying, he seems willing to be nice about... however he's planning to handle this situation, so I nod, knowing that might be the way to make him more pliable to my suggestions. "What about you?"

"Same. I work a lot. Not just at the... you know, the killing. I have a lot to do. Even tonight. I can't spare much more time. But I'll get better about it. Promise."

"Maybe you could stay a bit longer?" I ask when he gets up. Because the longer we talk, the more likely I am to convince him I don't need to be under lock and key.

Do I even believe his vigilante fantasies? I don't know what connection he really had to the guy who tried to abduct me first.

"I'm so sorry, Blake, I have a lot of loose ends to wrap up after last night, but I'll come back as soon as I can. We will have the best Christmas *ever*."

Thoughts scatter and jingle all over my skull. Has he planned this? Was he working with Sexy Santa before betraying him?

"No! Wait, you can't just leave me here," I beg, grabbing the bars. I cannot be alone again between those hard, cold walls and with no access to natural light. I just can't!

But Nico shakes his head and a strand of hair slips out of his short ponytail. "I'm sorry, sweetie, but I have a long night ahead. I need to work out if Tooley had accomplices and who ordered your kidnapping in the first place."

I stare at him as my heart attempts to win a short-distance run in the Olympics. "'Ordered'? What do you mean *ordered*?" I choke out, staring at him pleadingly. "You can't just leave me with this!"

He waves me off but takes the big scissors with him. "Don't worry about it, I've got you. You can't be any safer than here. No one knows this place exists." He winks at

me and walks off with such an infuriatingly sexy swagger
I'm left raging in my cage.

How? How am I in this situation?

And did he just call me sweetie?

CHAPTER 4

NICO

FROM WHAT I'VE RESEARCHED about Blake, he's ridiculously rich, his only surviving relative is his brother, and he's been homeschooled. No wonder I wasn't able to find out that it's him who is Cryptic Boy Wonder, since there is no tie to his real identity.

It's still very early, before the midday and afternoon rush hour, and there's just a single pair of customers at the store. They're torn between two Christmas Village collections, and since gathering all the elements is going to take them several years, it's not a decision to be rushed. I remind them that I'm here to help and walk off to replenish the impulse buys on shelves closest to the counter. But as I stack small, imported gingerbread men encased in colorful foil, my gaze wanders to the collection of fancy gifts that so often gets emptied just before Christmas day, when forgetful people remember to buy presents for more or less distant relatives.

One of the snow globes showcased in the cabinet depicts Santa's elves frolicking in the snow, and one of them, young, handsome, and rosy-cheeked, brings to mind my new acquaintance. He's as trapped under the glass as Blake is in my basement.

"You've been staring at that snow globe for half an hour. Everything okay?" Owen, my employee, asks.

It pulls me out of my thoughts about Blake and his tight green shorts.

"What can I say? I'm partial to a cute elf twink," I joke, even though I've got serious matters on my mind. A part of me would love to keep Blake forever, create a nice little apartment for him down there, so that we can live in our own bubble where Christmas lasts all year long. We could make toys and decorations together, watch holiday movies, and have special 'Christmas' days once a month, then restart the countdown and do it all over again.

I know it's a little Groundhog's Day, but who wouldn't enjoy some seasonal magic?

"You seem awfully interested in this elf today. Does he remind you of someone?" Owen flashes me a bright smile. He's been like this since he started seeing a boy from his community college last year, and while I appreciate his concern, at times I almost miss the disaster gay he used to be before Adam tamed him.

But hey, I've seen this guy go through the highs and lows of his life, and he's like family to me. As entertaining as his past self was, he seems much happier now. Could that be me by next Christmas?

"There is this guy..." I sigh, because deep down, I know my situationship with Blake is fucked up. I'm losing my mind a little already, but it's partially because he's seen the real me, and I've never had that with a guy. Even Owen, who used to live in my spare room, and who used to spend every holiday with me before Adam's family pretty much adopted him, doesn't know the true me. As long as I don't let Blake go, I can imagine that he wouldn't go to the cops, and that he *likes* me.

But my reasons not to release him aren't entirely selfish. I found out from his abductor's phone that someone wants Blake gone, but when I tried calling the bastard's number, the line was dead. Danger is still somewhere out there, and freeing Blake would be like letting a prized turkey roam freely in a forest filled with foxes.

Owen's brown eyes dart toward the couple who can't decide between the 1950s Christmas Village and the 1890s Christmas Village, but he then rests his elbows on the counter and leans on it so hard I can swear his feet left the floor. He's grinning at me as if he's Krampus's little helper. "Do I know him?"

I pick up the snow globe and shake it, thinking back to the one I'm currently working on in my underground workshop. Maybe I should add an elf inside there?

"Nah, he's new in town. I don't even know how long he'll be staying, but... I just really like him, you know? Sometimes you just meet a person, and the two of you click." I smile at the memory of how Blake's gun had 'clicked' and then didn't fire. Wasn't that destiny at work? He could have killed me in that moment, but the universe had other plans for us.

Owen takes a deep, exaggerated breath. "Tell me more. What does he look like? Is he visiting family? Did you two hook up?"

I cover my face for a second, embarrassed that I'm even having this problem. But despite being twenty-seven, I've been either living and breathing all the work at the Winter Emporium, or spending endless hours researching my future victims. I'm one of those people who can sleep four hours a day and be fine, but I still barely have any time left to date. The last time I hooked up was months ago, and the guy didn't seem impressed by my attic apartment. And what's so strange about festive bedding? It was a classy set too, with pine trees.

"Oh, Owen... he's so hot. Green eyes, short dark curls, lashes for days. Freckles, long legs, toned arms, and a mouth you just wanna kiss for hours. He's on the young side, and I think I might intimidate him a little. I don't know how much time we'll have, it's all up in the air."

"But he's legal and gay? You think he likes you?" Owen asks, lowering his voice.

I've seen his ID, so I know he's twenty-one. Clearly not too young to almost fall victim to a violent murderer. He's so lucky I happened to be there.

I groan. "I'm not a cradle-snatcher. And I swear the spark is there. I wore a shirt to see him yesterday, and he was staring at my forearms much longer than necessary. If he just let me, I'd keep him in my bed for a week." Though I'd have to settle for the one in the basement for now.

Owen's teeth dig into his lower lip. "Maybe that's what you should do? When's the last time you took any time off? You know I'm only leaving to visit Adam's family on the day before Christmas Eve. I could cover the shop until then."

I look at the shelves stacked with all types of trinkets, the table set up by the window to showcase our selection of dinnerware, and the glass cabinet filled with festive jewelry. How could I possibly leave him to deal with it all? We do have two more members of staff throughout December, but they work part-time.

"I took some time last year," I say hesitantly.

"You took one day, Nico."

And that was enough to deal with the man I killed for Christmas last year. I had to travel across the state lines for that one. Risky, but when I found out he robbed houses of those who left for the holidays, I was enraged. Imagine coming back from a lovely time with friends and family only to find your home ruined. At one of the places he broke into, Edgar murdered a housekeeper, and that sealed his fate.

I shake my head. "Maybe I should just let this pipe dream go. Do I really have the time to date? In *December*?"

Owen cocks his head and clicks his tongue before adjusting the collar of the shirt I'm wearing under the sweater. "That is literally your favorite time of the year. When, if not in December, when everyone's mushy from the magic of Christmas, hm? Do you really want to be alone this festive season?"

Ah, it's so typical that once slutty people couple up and settle down, they think that's what everyone needs to achieve perfect happiness.

But then again, I have been lonely in my bed for so long.

"What if he thinks it's weird how into Christmas I am?" I grumble, putting away the globe.

"Come on, Nico, you've got your looks to fall back on. I know! You could take him to the Christmas market!" Owen gets so excited he grabs one of the red bells off the counter and jingles it. "Mulled wine to get in the mood, and fa la la la la, la la la *la!*"

I have to smile at that, because the vision is oh so blissful. Me and Blake, at the market, snow falling, lights twinkling, cups filled with hot chocolate, and our mitten-clad hands entwined as we shop for handmade gifts.

"I guess I won't know if I don't try, right...?"

Owen makes a fist-pump, and then lightly punches my chest. "That's the Christmas spirit! Set up a nice date, show him what you're good at. I know you have enough charm to make magic happen."

"Excuse me," the elderly woman calls out, waving at us. "Could you explain the materials used once again?"

At this rate, they're gonna be here until lunchtime.

Owen winks at me before heading off toward the pair, smile number five in place, and I exhale, glancing back at the snow globe and the young elf that reminds me of Hot Blake, who waits for me in the cellar.

Ah, if only things were as easy as Owen paints them.

'Show him what you're good at' bounces around in my mind, because, yeah, I'm already planning our date. I want him to get to know me, to see I'm more than just the Christmas Killer. And since he's so keen on true-crime stories, I'm sure he'd appreciate a glimpse behind the curtain. Wouldn't he like to know what I do with my murder souvenirs?

One step at a time, Nico.

First a nice dinner, *then* the snow globe filled with teeth shavings.

CHAPTER 5

Nico

I SHOULDN'T BE THIS nervous.

I'm a man of twenty-seven, with my own business and several notches on my bedpost, but somehow this young man, whose life I'm holding in my hands makes me jittery as if I'm about to embark on my first-ever date.

There's something about him. Something special, and it's not just his pretty face and hot body. And while I do feel responsible for his life now, that's not it either. I suppose after listening to every single episode of his podcast, being an active fan for three years now, pre-ordering his merch twice, and jerking off to his hot voice while imagining what he might look like spread out naked on the same desk he records at, I am a bit starstruck.

I don't want to give him that impression though and make things weird. He's stayed anonymous for a reason, and I don't want to cause him discomfort by using the knowledge I've already gained from the podcast. I prepare a nice hot dinner for us. Turkey, mashed potatoes, veggies, an indulgent gravy, and red wine to go with it, plus hot chocolate, in case he doesn't like alcohol. I put on a dark green shirt this time, and after half an hour of testing the look, I settle on two buttons open, showcasing my snowflake tattoos. I get a new one for every kill, and I kind of want him to ask about the ink. I put on a nice watch and use my favorite cologne with notes of pine, cedar, and pomegranate. A gift from Owen, who claimed it's gonna get me laid. Let's hope he's right.

And yeah, I discreetly pack some lube and condoms in case I do get lucky. I will be the perfect gentleman, but Blake has been through lots of stress in the past twenty-four hours, and adrenaline makes people horny. It's science.

I glance at the reindeer-shaped clock on my wall. The turkey's just come out of the oven, so it will be fine resting under aluminum foil, which should give me more than enough time to get my date ready. I grab the clothes I prepared for Blake earlier, my best, softest towel, and walk downstairs, all the way to the basement that serves as the main stockroom. There are three rooms down here, all overflowing with Christmas decorations and gadgets, and at the very end of the one that at first glance appears to be of least interest, as it contains many of my personal belongings, is the narrow staircase leading to the lowest level of the property, which is cleverly hidden inside an old wardrobe.

My stomach tightens as I prepare myself to see Blake again after a whole day of longing and questioning whether Owen's idea can pan out in my favor. I reach between the coats inside the wardrobe and pull on the lever disguised as an empty clothing hook. The mechanism installed by my grandfather many years ago is still functional due to regular maintenance, and it clicks as the back of the wardrobe opens like a door and reveals steep stairs.

Last night, after I hit the wall in my quest to find out who might have hired Blake's abductor, I came down again, but Blake was already sleeping. I took some time with impromptu decorating, so he could wake up to a more cheerful space. I even brought down a pink Christmas tree and hung some lights in the room containing the cell.

Blake slept right through it all, and it made me feel like a Christmas elf, just working through the night to provide a surprise. Every now and then I'd glance at Blake's serene features. He was adorable. I wish I'd been there to see his reaction when he woke up to all the magic around him.

I could have set up a camera to capture it, of course, but it would be impolite to violate his privacy like that.

"Good evening," I call out on my way downstairs. The rooms here are very old, and my grandpa theorized the original owners of the house must have used them to store illegal cargo, maybe even booze during the prohibition era. The walls are whitewashed with something that looks like lime rather than modern paint, but I never cared whether it was aesthetically pleasing before.

It's quite exciting to share this family secret with Blake.

I hear no answer, so I speed up, walking past the secret craft room where I create festive mementos of my kills. There's two more chambers down here, but I head straight for Blake's and knock on the open door as I stare at the Christmas tree I left for him last night.

My worries ease when I hear him shift. "Hello?"

"Hey there, Cookie Monster," I say with a smile when I notice he went through all ten cookies I left him. My heart beats faster as soon as our eyes meet. "Oh look at this! You've been busy." I point out the long paper chain wrapped around a few of the bars like a snake. "I can't wait to hang it."

He offers me a smile and gestures at the tree. "Thank you for the decorations. They're very nice. They make this place feel... less lonely. Were you at work?"

"Yes, I'm sorry I couldn't keep you company. But I made us dinner, and I have more time for you tonight."

Blake stands between the cot and the bars, tightly wrapped in the blanket. His hair is messy, as if he spent all day resting, but the number of links in the paper chain and the scraps creating a pile in the corner of the cell tell me he's been busy. The book I left for him, an illustrated edition of Charles Dickens's A *Christmas Carol* is resting by the pillow, indicating Blake spent some of his day reading.

"What are we having? More cookies and milk?" my guest asks, licking his lips as his elegant fingers curl around the bars. I lean forward and, in a moment of daring, slide my own over his. He has such soft, beautiful hands!

"No, a whole feast. Turkey, potatoes, veggies, home-made gravy. Do you like wine? I got some red." I'm aware that he might intend to hurt me. We're not out of the woods yet, but I'm hoping we can come to an understanding once I convince him that my basement is the safest place for him to be.

He swallows, watching our interlocked hands. "Thank you. That sounds amazing! But I think I might need to freshen up before dinner. You know, shower, use a normal bathroom," he says, nodding toward the camping toilet I provided for him.

"Yes, of course." I reluctantly let go of him. Kissing every one of his knuckles has to wait until he's ready for it. "I don't usually keep anyone here. That's why I'm so unprepared. But I brought you some clothes that will hopefully be your size, some toiletries, and I can take you to the shower. You do have to promise to be nice though. Naughty boys don't get gifts." I wink at him.

Half a second passes before he lets out a chuckle. "I promise I'm nice. Most of the time," he adds and winks right back at me.

"Oh, I recall the story of you hiding your brother's favorite fountain pen and then launching a search, as if you had no idea where it was," I say, remembering that story from one of his old podcasts.

I watch him as I open the padlock to his cell, but I also doubt he'd attack me with the kid scissors. Those, of course, could do some damage if wielded with enough force, but we can consider this a test.

I step back to make room for him, and I already know he will look cute as a button in the festive pajamas I've gotten him. He watches me like a cat entering a new home and appears overall serious, so maybe I should have gone with a more elegant set. On the other hand, he did wear the elf costume when Tooley abducted him, so he must have a sense of fun.

Blake removes the blanket from his shoulders, folds it, and then throws it onto the cot, which leaves him in the sexy costume, exposing his long legs and chest. He's wary but keeps his head low and his hands to himself, which is a good sign. At this rate, our date might actually work out as planned!

He clears his throat and pulls on the folds of the thin shirt, struggling to cover one of his nipples. "Sorry, I think this size is a bit too small for me," he says and adjusts his hair with a swipe of fingers.

"Don't worry about it," I assure him, but steal a glance at his dark pink nipple anyway.

Fuck. I could eat him up. His parted lips are so inviting, his long legs in stockings tease my dick, and the green shorts are indeed too small, so they dig into his crack the way I want my fingers to.

I distract myself by handing him the towel, and he hugs it.

"I've got a sweater for you that will definitely not be too small." I smile and show off my own creation with nerves eating me up. The oversized knitted top is red, and adorned with all the Christmas goodness one could want. Gift boxes with ribbons, reindeer, turkey, funny Santa faces and candy canes, all surrounding the words *Oh what fun!* I made it with thick wool, and then sewed on some of the other elements I'd crocheted.

Maybe I did have a bit too much time on my hands last Christmas.

Blake smiles and takes the garment from my hands. "Wow! That's... really something. Very festive. And looks warm. Thank you," he adds, meeting my gaze. The green hue of his eyes might be cool, but I can sense warmth when they settle on me. "I wish my brother was here to see this."

I reach out to him, and when he doesn't shy away, I gently stroke his arm. We leave the sweater behind, and I lead him toward the bathroom.

"Do you usually spend Christmases with him?" I ask, eager to know more about him.

Blake clears his throat. "Um... not really. He likes to visit his friends in Aspen during Christmas time. But it would be nice, right? You could meet him."

My heart melts. He's already envisioning me meeting his family? I don't want to get ahead of myself, but I think the near-death experience must have bonded him to me in ways matching on Grindr never could.

"It would. And there's still quite some time left until Christmas. Maybe the dust will settle and we'll be able to plan something special? I'm sorry it's so basic here," I say as soon as we walk into the bathroom, which is covered with white tiles from floor to ceiling. It has an open shower and features a toilet behind a wall farther down.

"No, no, I'm very grateful for everything. I don't even want to think what that other guy wanted to do to me. But you came. You saved me," Blake says, and as he swallows, I greedily follow the movement of his Adam's apple, already imagining my dick in his soft mouth.

He toes off his shoes and as he enters the wet room, I can't help but focus on his pert ass flexing as he moves. He points to the sink. "May I brush my teeth first? I must have had a million cookies."

"Sure, yes, of course." I pass him a new toothbrush and toothpaste.

Blake doesn't waste any more time, but as he leans over the sink, he gives me the most perfect view of his ass. It's impossible not to look.

"I wish we could have met under better circumstances," I say, leaning against the door frame as he glances over his shoulder, seeking *something*.

Once he's done, Blake turns around to face me. "Me too."

I swallow as he takes another step back, and then lifts the tight shirt. Stretchy fabric rolls up his perfect skin and leaves his nipples pebbled. He stills with his arms tangled up in the top behind his head and glances straight at me.

"D-do you need help?" I choke out, already stepping forward.

He has the perfect body. Lean but with defined muscles, his shoulders are wide, and the shorts hang low enough on his hips to show off the V-shape I wish to follow south.

His bare chest sinks as he exhales before offering me not one but three nods. He's nervous, I can see, but it warms my heart to see him reach out.

I step closer, and he spins on his heel again, showing me his naked back. I should focus on the fabric tangled around his arms, but how can I resist the lure of his spine when it directs my gaze into his shorts?

He smells faintly of spice and wood, the mint of the toothpaste and hot chocolate. Maybe it's just been too long since I've been this intimately close to another man, but the hesitant yet sensual way he's moving draws me in, as if he wants to tell me something without words. When our eyes meet once again, I feel myself leaning in.

The fabric stretched between his forearms presses against my throat, but then he's touching his minty lips to mine.

CHAPTER 6

BLAKE

I'M TERRIFIED AND ABOUT fifty percent sure this whole thing will end with my death, but when Nico opens the seam of my mouth with his tongue, my knees go so soft I grab him to steady myself. I'm giving my first-ever kiss to a homicidal maniac, and it should not feel this good.

Warm, thick arms wrap around me as I utter a brief yet embarrassing noise, and then he's pushing me at the wall, and I'm sandwiched between his chest and the hard, cold tiles. I exaggerated my problem with the thin green top to appear even more defenseless than I am, but now something about it turns me on too, and I get to my toes as he rips the fabric off.

My heart is pounding like mad. I'm playing with fire, but I'll only get to make my move if he doesn't see me as a threat. Too bad it's hard to focus on attacking him when his tongue teases my palate. I've not been *hugged* in years, let alone touched this way by anyone. And he isn't just a random guy at the nightclub either. Nico's painfully handsome, I have to give him that. When his large hands slide up and down my sides, I don't have to fake a reaction. I shiver.

I've fantasized countless times about what it would be like to be stroked and petted by another man, but this is so much more than I could have imagined. He's confident, he smells so good I want to press my face against him, and even the touch of his shirt is pleasant against my skin. If only he was *anyone* else. Or at least not the literal serial killer I've been following for years. That's not really so much to ask for, is it?

I've been psyching myself up to seduce him all day. I came up with lines I could say and whole scenarios I was ready to follow in order to get his guard down, but none of that could have prepared me for the sensation of being cradled, for his insistent yet gentle lips, and the way my body would fill with heat in his presence.

How ironic that in the process of distracting him, I have done it to myself.

"I... I mean..."

Nico steps back, and I hate myself a little for already missing his touch. I thought I was smarter than that, but my body didn't get the memo from my brain, and it's horny.

When he looks at me with piercing blue eyes and licks his lips like he's about to eat me, my dick twitches in excitement. I should be worried whether he's a cannibal, not getting turned on.

"Sorry, I might have gotten ahead of myself." His voice is like a purr, all softness and promise. How fucked up is it that *this* is my first experience? What if it imprints on me, and I'll only get hard in high-adrenaline situations?

That's what therapy's for, I suppose. All I care about is getting out of here, because even if he doesn't plan to murder me like that other guy, what if I end up being his prisoner for years, locked up in this terrible basement of always-Christmas, away from the sunshine, my wings clipped on the cusp of leaving the family nest?

With new determination, I grab the front of his shirt and pull him right back to me. While having his weight press me to the wall again is sending electricity to my balls, this time I'm ready for it.

This is a distraction. This is a distraction, Blake. For survival, I tell myself as my entire body shivers with delight when he cups my ass.

"I guess we can have dinner later," Nico whispers in my ear, then *licks* it. "You're so beautiful. I've been dreaming about this ass all day." He squeezes my butt, making me get to my tiptoes so Nico can grab more of me.

I'm a mess with a rattling heart, because what if I miscalculated? What if I'm unable to escape yet put too many promises in his head? I can't become some psycho's basement fuck toy. That can't be my life.

I shouldn't want his touch as much as I do.

When his fingers tease my crack through fabric as he lazily kisses my ear, then my neck, I get lost in my own game. How can something so wrong feel this good? And while we're at it, how can someone so violent be this hot? It's not fair.

Excitement rushes along my limbs, and I cup his face as we kiss. I knew I was drawn to muscular, dominant guys, but as he kneads my buttocks and cages me against the wall, it's all but confirmed, because my pleasure centers are on fire.

"Yes. Later," I agree, but there's enough brains left in my overcooking skull to stay alert. I open one eye and, once

Nico's lips descend my throat, I look around for potential weapons.

But as I consider if the ceramic cup on the sink will be hard enough, he slides one hand between our bodies and pets my dick through fabric. I mewl and arch into him instinctively as if he's pressed a sex button in my brain.

I'm realizing I might have shot myself in the foot with this whole seduction idea. If he was an ogre with warts on his face, I'd have no trouble separating myself from what we're doing. But he's not. He's young, handsome, smells so fresh, and after what I've been through, his warm body is soothing rather than repulsive. I want the hug. I *need* the comfort of his arms.

I, Blake, wouldn't have given in to his deluded idea of romance in his basement, but because it was 'just acting', I let myself touch him. Let *him* touch me. And now I'm in over my head.

Nico murmurs against my neck and gives my cock a squeeze. "I can't wait to see it."

In a moment of absolute abandon, I pull on his shoulders, signaling for him to kneel, and while I'm mortified as soon as that happens, he offers me a wide grin and... scoots down.

I'm embarrassed when it occurs to me that I haven't yet showered, but then my gaze returns to the ceramic cup, and I'm reminded of my real goal. Nico isn't yet fully down when I grab the mug and slam it down on his head as hard as I can.

It feels like trying to hammer a thick nail into a stone wall.

The handle stays in my hand while the rest of the mug falls off and collapses alongside Nico, who rolls to the floor at my feet, clutching at his head. A part of me is already regretful and wants to help, but that would be suicide, so I leap over him as if I were training for the Olympic long jump.

His groans resonate in my ears as I flee the bathroom and dart for the narrow stairs.

I'm not a cryer, but my eyes sting from the nerves of it all. The world is a blur as I dash up the steps, and an unholy mix of images rattles in my head.

Nico sawing into a man's neck. Nico on his knees about to press his handsome face against my cock. Nico in the creepy balaclava with cute round ears. Nico presenting me with the ugliest Christmas sweater I've ever seen.

A part of me expects a locked door, and for my plan to be easily thwarted. I knew I needed to try *something* to free myself, but deep down, I didn't believe I'd manage. But I find the door easy to open, and I'm faced with... coats. I'm at the back of a wardrobe, as if the cellar is his personal fucking Narnia.

The muscles of my throat are so tight I can barely breathe, but I won't have another chance to flee, so I dash between a collection of old bicycles, boxes, and furniture. I hit the light switch I vaguely see in the dark.

Colors gleam ahead as strings of Christmas lights come to life on the ceiling and walls of the next room. They flash in different rhythms, giving life to a crowd of figures gathered all too close for my liking. There's the popular image of the Christmas Killer, based on a witness testimony that was clearly inaccurate, as the figure has a pot belly and a white beard. Next to it stands Krampus, an ancient witch, a monster with a horse skull head, and even some zombie elves. I stumble when the red and green flickering tricks me into thinking one of the life-sized statues moved, reaching its bony hand for me.

Where am I even? The room is stacked floor to ceiling with rows of shelving units filled with boxes and Christmas decor. Everywhere I look it's red, green, and gold.

A sob rises in my throat, but I manage to hold it in as I make my way through the winding maze of festive crap. He's mad. He's absolutely mad, and I don't even want to know why he might need so many different types of nutcrackers in the form of painted soldiers. Their eyes follow me as the colorful glow reflects on their faces, constantly altering their expressions.

The warehouse is massive and seems to contain everything from fake Victorian street lamps to large rolls of gift wrap. There's a door on its other end, so I dash down the lane left empty in the middle, only pausing when I remember that it's December. There could be a snow storm outside, and I'm wearing stockings and shorts. One of the massive steel shelving units arranged in neat rows to my left is filled with clothes, so I grab the first coat I can find and unfold it, revealing itself as a red bath robe with a fur trim.

Good enough.

Somewhere behind me, feet stomp over a hard floor, and I freeze, only to dash across the warehouse, already putting on the robe. I'm not dying here, not at eighteen, before I even got to start living!

The exit is so close I can almost taste the fresh air awaiting me outside, but as I reach for the handle, something yanks me back, and I fall over, banging my knees against the floor as plush gingerbread men rain over me, followed by a cardboard box.

I try to get up, but my robe catches on the shelf, and when I pull, the unit tips forward. I scream when it falls, and I cover my head to protect it from more plushies, which are now like quicksand around me.

My only saving grace is that the top of the shelf had gotten stuck against the opposite wall, so it can't crush me. I wade through the toys, shrugging the robe off to leave it behind. This might be what getting a heart attack feels like. I'm dizzy from stress, my heart is pounding like mad, and I know Nico—no, the Christmas Killer is somewhere behind me. Just because he was nice to me to get into my pants doesn't make him any less of a monster.

He saws off people's heads and takes their teeth, for fuck's sake!

I'm about to get up when a hand wraps around my ankle and yanks me back with so much strength I shiver in terror.

"No, please!" I shriek and kick back with my free foot. The pulsating glow of the Christmas lights seeps through the shelves above me, transforming the trap I've found myself in into a hallway straight from a horror movie, but that doesn't mean I'll go down without a fight.

"You will wait down there as long as I say!" Nico grunts and drags me from under the shelf despite my kicking. He's no longer the nice guy he tried to present himself as.

I grab the edge of the shelf to keep him from pulling me back, since it seems my weight is nothing for him. When one of my hands slips, I grab the plushies and start throwing them at him with helpless fury. "Let go! I just want to go home!"

But it's all for nothing. With a forceful tug, he drags me over the floor until I'm under him, terrified and defenseless. I try to kick, to push my thumbs into his eyes, but he rolls me to my stomach as if I weigh nothing, which, I suppose, I do when compared to his muscular form.

It's only then that I give up on the fight and sob, wondering whether he'll grab my hair and slam my head against the floor until my skull cracks, or if he'll rape me beforehand.

I hear a click, and metal cuffs pull my wrists together.

He picks me up, not even bothering to gag me, which tells me screaming would be useless.

He wants to *keep* me, and I don't know if an eternity in his Christmas lair isn't worse than death.

CHAPTER 7

BLAKE

I FALL ONTO THE cot as Nico shoves me inside the cell uncuffed. Despite bruises I can already feel forming on my body, I'm still breathing. But for how long?

My breath hisses as I stand back up and throw myself at the iron doors that just locked behind me. "How can you do this to me? I did nothing wrong. I just wanted to have fun, and now you imprisoned me here, like I'm a circus animal!"

"If you'd have made yourself known before I took off the mask, we wouldn't have this problem!" He rubs his head with a scowl.

Good. At least I hurt him. Too bad my self-defense classes turned out to be useless in the moment of absolute panic.

"Oh, sure, it's all *my* fault. It has *nothing* to do with you liking me," I rasp, tapping my chest to drive that point home. "You're no hero. I bet you're just lying to me about that other guy being hired to kill me, so that I'm too scared to leave!"

Nico screams with so much fury I take a few steps back from the bars, afraid of what he'll do next. He doesn't reach in for me though and instead turns to an old chair in the corner and kicks it so hard the leg breaks.

"Any other fucking complaints?" He turns to me with madness in his eyes.

I'm aware that I'm poking a rabid bull, but I'm too angry, and the bars give me a false sense of security.

"Yes, that sweater you gave me? The ugliest fucking thing I've ever seen, and that counts for something!" I roar, staring straight into his fiery eyes.

They dim, and for the longest time, he's just breathing hard, his nostrils flaring, but his shoulders sag. He kicks the fallen chair without the same energy as before. Seems like I hit a nerve there.

I don't get a curse-filled answer. Nico walks off, and even though I want him gone, now my stomach clenches in fear. He could leave me here and I'd starve to death. He could torture me by giving me spoiled food, or blocking my access to a shower. He could do anything, and I'm neither strong enough, nor good enough at fighting, to stop him.

I shouldn't have run. I should have bided my time and gained his trust before risking it, because there's no way he'll ever let me go after what I've done.

Hope seeps out of me, and I slide to the floor, grabbing the bars and pressing my face to them as I scan the room in vain hope that maybe there's something he didn't account for.

But there's nothing. The keys hang on the farthest wall, and I don't have anything that could help me bring them any closer. Unless I befriend the rats and get them to do my bidding, I'm fucked.

Nico is gone for a long time. Or it just feels like forever because I'm scared. I do hear some rummaging in a room farther down, but I don't know if Nico's sulking, punching walls, or preparing a Christmas-themed torture room to end me in style.

The last thing I should be thinking about is how he kissed me, but it's weirdly soothing, so I don't ban myself from it. My first kiss. With a serial killer. How appropriate for Cryptic Boy Wonder.

"Nico?" I try eventually, tortured by the wait.

"I'm coming!" he grumbles from another room.

"Your head.... d-does it hurt?" I try, because he would have murdered me if he wanted to. Maybe I can work on him until he gives me another chance at an escape?

"Yes it fucking hurts!" he yells back, and I cringe. Will I now have to soothe this sulking monster?

I hear him stomping, and then he comes back into my view with a stack of folders. He grabs the first one on top and opens it in front of my cell.

"This is your abductor. I mean... the previous one." Nico won't look into my eyes. "He raped and tortured his victims, often as made-to-measure blackmail he'd record for whoever paid him for it."

He passes me the folder, sending a whole avalanche of mixed feelings through me. Fear, confused gratitude, but also morbid curiosity of someone who researched far too many crime scenes. They all buzz in my skull, locked in a continuous fight.

The first thing I see is a woman with most of her skin stripped off her back, and it doesn't get any better. I could have been one of those poor souls with haunted eyes, and just thinking about it makes me lean harder against the bars.

"You weren't supposed to be there," Nico mumbles.

"How do you have all this?" I ask, and Nico sighs with exasperation, pressing a small bag of frozen peas to the side of his head.

"I found incriminating footage on one of my previous victims. I followed the trail, but most of what you see here is actually straight from the collection of snuff he kept for his own use."

I flinch, and nausea once again crawls up my throat. "And... someone hired him to do this to me? Are you certain?"

"Yes," he says without hesitation and grabs another folder with printouts of a message exchange. "This was on his phone. When asked about what he's allowed to do to you, the person ordering the hit responded that they don't care, as long as at some point in the future a 'hand or foot' of yours surfaces so the death can be confirmed. I know I look like the bad guy here, but *these* are the naughty ones." He taps the stack of folders, no doubt containing evidence on the other people he killed.

I have no words, and as scary as it is that someone paid a sadist to hunt me down, the fact that they didn't care to even give me a quick death makes my heart too heavy, and I clutch at my chest.

"What did I do?" I whimper, meeting Nico's gaze through the bars.

He shrugs. "I... have no idea. Do you have any enemies? People can hate others for really small things."

I wade through my mind but have to conclude the search with a shake of my head. "No... I don't even know that many people. There's the staff at my family home, but it's my brother who deals with their pay, benefits, and the like. And I don't remember ever being mean to any of them, other than, *maybe*, in childhood."

"And your brother? You said he'll be worried about you, but at this point I'm assuming you could have lied." Nico flicks through the folder with the messages, but I think he's only doing that to avoid my gaze.

"My brother what?" I ask, utterly confused. It's only when Nico looks up, offering me a dead glare when I realize what he's suggesting. "What the hell? Normal people don't order kills on family members! He literally raised me since our parents died and always took great care of me." I stall, swallowing. "Maybe it's someone who hates *him* and wants to hurt him through me?"

Nico nods. "That's an option. Until I find out, it's not safe for you out there, and... I can't give you the choice, Blake. I don't kidnap people, I don't murder innocents, even if you don't believe me. But I'm not going to prison either. You were an unfortunate witness. We will figure something out eventually."

I swallow, pumped out. "How is this happening to me?" I mutter. "I did nothing."

Nico scowls and spreads his arms. "And me? I only do good deeds! This guy was my perfect target, an early Christmas treat, and instead, I'm stuck with you!"

I glare at him, too tired to be afraid of someone who clearly doesn't plan to kill me. "'Christmas treat'? All this time, I thought you were killing people around Christmas to mock the whole fake cheer atmosphere."

His eyes meet mine, filling with the frustration of a declawed cat. "No! It's my Christmas gift! To the community! Why don't people understand?"

"Because in all but four cases since the 1910s murder, the victim was just a regular innocent person."

"They were not," Nico insists and pokes his pile of folders again.

I sigh. "Well, you say that, but neither the media, nor the police have the same information as you. How come?"

I tell myself that I'm willing to keep up the conversation to endear myself to him, so he doesn't just leave me alone for another day, but in truth, I'm itching to find out more. I want to get my hands on those folders filled with crimes even the police databases don't have.

"A lot of my intel isn't obtained legally. I..." Nico glances at the broken chair, then sits on the small craft table with his arms crossed. "I install Christmas lights and decorations in many big houses. And while I do that, I'll often plant a camera here and there. Like Santa, I watch over the community, and sometimes, I find a very, very naughty person. If I have a confirmed kill, they're fair game to me."

A shiver runs down my spine when I imagine him watching me from afar, checking the hidden camera once in a while. Would he watch me get undressed or pleasure myself?

Something I *definitely* shouldn't imagine.

I clear my throat. "You said your grandfather was the Christmas Killer before you. Was he also killing... *naughty* people?"

Nico runs his fingers through his hair, and I wince when I notice blood in it even though I shouldn't feel sorry for him at all. "He showed me the ropes but didn't let me kill anyone until I was twenty. Kinda arbitrary, if you ask me, but I followed his rules, and I still do. He killed very rarely, only a few times, really. His first was a guy who kept beating his wife. In those times, it was very hard to prove or prosecute that kind of crime. In the end, Grandpa lost his patience and killed the fucker, then decided to stage it as a Christmas Killer thing, since it was in late December, and the memory of the serial killer from the beginning of the past century was still fresh. We don't know who that original murderer was, though."

"He's long dead anyway," I fill in and nod, regarding Nico in a new light. "So... your grandfather was a vigilante, and you... like killing but only kill bad people?"

He hesitates with the answer. Maybe he knows how fucked up it is.

"It... sates my appetite. Judge me if you want. I don't care."

I don't like how defensive he is. The wall between us is high despite us sharing secrets.

I rub my face and hug the bars, watching him in pensive silence. "Look, I'm sorry I hurt you, okay? But imagine yourself in my shoes. What would you have done?"

Nico groans. "I wouldn't have ran. I would have used your moment of confusion to cut your throat with a piece of the broken cup."

He's either trying to provoke me or show his claws, and I don't like either. Talking to him reminds me of the many interviews with psychopaths I've seen.

I blink, touching my neck as if it were already bleeding. He's so intense, and I don't know if it scares or arouses me, which is bad in itself. "I don't want you dead."

Nico squints. "I think you do. I think you're lying. Are you even gay?"

No. *I'm just really into psychos who keep me in a dungeon,* my mind offers. But if I am to ever leave this basement, I need to use any advantage I have.

I press my cheek to the cold bar. "I'm not like you. I don't want *anyone* dead. And yes, I am most definitely gay." When he doesn't stop his accusatory glances, I exhale and continue despite my throat borderline closing.

"And yes, I planned to distract you in the shower, but that doesn't mean I disliked touching you. It's just... complicated."

He lights up a little, no longer a lizard man with dead eyes, but a scolded puppy. He pulls on his fingers, slouching. "I guess I'm a bit of a dreamer. I *wanted* to believe you could like me. You're so pretty, funny, you've got a hot voice, *and* you're into crime."

Incredible.

But I go with it and sigh. "That was actually my first kiss."

"*Now* you're definitely lying." Nico snorts and shakes his head, but his eyes are glued to me.

I no longer want to just find a way to escape. I don't believe he could have fabricated those messages about someone ordering a hit on me, and that means I'll be in danger even when I leave this psycho's basement. I wouldn't even dream of calling Nico naive, but the delusional crush he has on me could prove a useful tool.

As long as I don't lose my head in the meanwhile, because I never met a man so openly enamored with me, and it's giving me butterflies when it shouldn't.

I shake my head and slide my hand between the bars, reaching for him. "I'm not. I've never been naked with anyone either," I admit, hoping it will wipe away any fantasies he might have about a quick fuck before the day ends.

He's reluctant but ends up hooking one finger with mine. It's weirdly sweet.

"Is it because of homeschooling?"

I shrug and slide my thumb across his palm, hoping to coax him closer. "I suppose so. My brother worried I might end up in bad company, or start doing drugs.

But now I'm old enough to make my own choices," I say, shivering as his blue gaze licks my chest.

"Your ID card said you're twenty-one. But you're *not*, are you?" He puts down the frozen peas and gets up, watching me intently. It's obvious he has a weakness for me, but I have to admit I like his attention too. Especially now that I know how well he kisses, how confidently his hands can glide up and down my body.

I... should stop thinking about all that.

"I'm eighteen," I tell him, sliding my fingers up his wrist, under the fabric of his shirt cuff.

I could have lied, said I'm still a minor. If he's as *decent* as he claims, maybe he'd back off sexually. But also... he might *back off sexually*. And as much as his closeness frightens me, deep down I'm not sure if I want him to stop flirting with me.

"And now that you can make your own choices, are they bad company and drugs?" he asks with a smirk emerging on his lips.

It shouldn't make my chest stir with excitement.

"Define 'bad company,'" I say and pull on his hand.

He takes a step back and slides out of my grasp. He's wary. Like a golden retriever that's been hit on the snout, but which is still interested in a treat. "A notorious serial killer who might want to see you naked a bit too much."

I whimper and cover my face as soon as the sound comes out, because it's a scenario I would very much enjoy in fiction. "I might want to see him naked too. One day."

"Now you're just being cruel. But I'm not. I will let you shower, and I won't be peeking. But if you try something again, we'll have a different kind of talk."

Sugar-coated threats. Yay!

I make myself smile. "Will I get to sleep in a normal bed after that? This one's going to ruin my spine," I say and uncover the mattress, revealing its uneven surface, with clear marks of where its previous occupant usually lay down to sleep.

Nico shakes his head. "Is this the Prince and the Pea now? I'll look into getting you a better mattress. Maybe dinner will make the night more bearable for you? I made fresh turkey…"

Will I now be eating turkey and cranberry every day until I die?

"Are you really going to keep me like a fish in a tank, just because you can? I have so much potential. I could help you so much, even with finding the person who's after me," I say and reach through the bars, grabbing his finger. A flash of heat travels from his hand to mine but I ignore it, because, unlike him, I am not deranged enough to see this situation as a romantic opportunity.

But if worse comes to worst, I will use any means at my disposal. At least he's hot.

Nico cocks his head, and the way he plays with my hand gives me goosebumps. "You? Help *me*? You'll go to the police at your first opportunity, so we're in a bit of a bind."

My stomach cramps from the stress of it all, and I'm proud of myself for keeping a clear head as I meet his gaze. "I also have skeletons in my closet, okay? I hired a hacker to break into the FBI database to steal some information. More than once. I couldn't reveal it on my podcast, but it gave me an edge. What if I gave you the evidence? We would both have dirt on one another."

Nico trails his fingers from my chest to my stomach. "You actually want to go hunting with me?"

I *have* him. The Christmas Killer has taken the bait.

I wipe my face with my forearm and nod. It will be scary out there with a hit ordered on me, but I won't be on my own. And once I'm out of this prison, access to a phone will only be a question of time. My brother and his lawyers will surely be able to weasel me out of trouble with the law if Nico reveals my wrongdoings.

"I've been into true-crime all my life, and this is my chance to see it from the inside. Please," I add, because he seems genuinely excited that I share his murder *hobby*, even if in a very different capacity.

He stands taller and smiles. "If your hacker story checks out and I let you out, you'll go on a date with me. A *real* one."

I stall, my mouth falling open as I try to process his words to make sure he's asking for what I think he's asking. Romance of any kind has never been high on my agenda. I planned a life of travel, fun, and friends with benefits, and this guy, this ruthless killer with a hard-on for Christmas wants to take me out on a *date*?

"As in, you want us to hook up?" I ask to make sure I understand him correctly. As terrifying as it would be to be naked and vulnerable with someone like him, I could do it. He's good-looking, and the kiss proved that we have sexual chemistry. If I'm to lose my V-card soon, might as well do so in style and use it to buy my freedom.

Nico raises his hands as if he's an innocent. "Whatever happens, happens, but I mean a *date*. I'll plan everything, you just have to bring an open mind and a joyful spirit. I promise there won't be any dismemberment," he adds quickly.

I laugh even as dread coils in my guts. "That would be preferable, I'm rather fond of all my limbs, digits, and appendages."

Jesus. Will he now think of my cock as an *appendage*? Why couldn't I just keep my mouth shut?

"And I'm fond of them too," Nico's eyes glide to the front of my tiny shorts and I suddenly feel so naked even the festive pajamas don't seem so bad. "It would be a shame if you had to lose any as punishment for screaming when we go up."

As terrifying as the not-veiled threat is, my heart pounds faster because he did say when not if.

"I'll give you the passcode for my email. You can find the proof there and send it to yourself. We'll have a mutual destruction pact to ensure we both behave. Does that sound fair?" I ask and stroke his palm to stimulate his dirty thoughts, because if I get stuck down here, he might never choose to let me go.

"My apartment is a bit messy..." he warns, but unless he's sleeping on a bed of corpses, it will be preferable to the cot two storeys underground.

"That's fine, I'm messy too," I lie, though to be fair, I never needed to keep my place tidy, as the staff would do that for me. "I'm curious how you decorated it, since you put so much effort and thought into this," I tell him, indicating the tacky trinkets around the cell.

He lights up, and while for all the wrong reasons, I have to admit his smile is pretty swoony. I wouldn't be surprised if he spent his free time volunteering at a soup kitchen.

"Just a warning. I do only have one bed."

What a fucking surprise.

CHAPTER 8

BLAKE

I AM NOW REASONABLY sure that my kidnapper doesn't want to outright kill me, which is a huge relief. Though if he does end up taking my life, I hope my head is found wrapped with the Christmas Killer's vintage ribbon, so that I stay in the public consciousness as the next victim.

I can imagine my fellow podcasters expressing their not-so-genuine grief as they report on the serial killer's revenge, while all that sweet ad money pours into their accounts. What would be the appropriate thing to advertise during a podcast or video discussing my death? A VPN service, so a dangerous individual cannot track you? A point-and-click murder mystery game? An online therapy service, to help deal with the trauma of listening to details about gruesome murders and whatever other mental health issues fans might be dealing with?

I know a few people who'd just say *fuck it* and have a segment promoting microwavable meals before discussing violent crime. To each their own, and I won't care once I'm dead anyway.

Nico did keep his word, and once he was satisfied with the contents of my phone, he gave me some privacy in the shower, which was a huge relief. A part of me suspects he might have been watching me through the keyhole, but I'm clean, I smell of Caribbean storm (at least that's what it said on the bottle of shower gel I used) rather than sweat, and I'm no longer wearing the tight shorts/stockings combo. I detest the cheerful reindeer pattern on the cozy one-piece pajamas Nico left for me, but the garment is soft, warm, and not too tight around the hips, which is a giant improvement. I hope it means he does actually want to do more than perv on me at every opportunity.

I need to understand him better to play my part right. If he's practically begging me for a date, then he does want to please me. Which means he won't be throwing tantrums about not getting to fuck me yet. I can be his Scheherazade and draw out our *courting* if that's what he's been fantasizing about. It's hard to imagine him as a romantic, but okay I guess.

My heart is in my throat as Nico leads me up the same stairs which almost took me to freedom before.

"I prepared some of the food while you showered, even though it's much later than I expected. You don't mind eating late, do you?"

"I haven't seen the sun since you brought me here. I have no idea how much time passed," I say before I can stop myself, but he's walking behind me through the warehouse full of boxes and decorative statues and doesn't immediately grab me by the throat, which is... a positive. I wouldn't go as far as thinking he wants the real me, but maybe he likes a challenge, since the date idea is his attempt at wooing me.

"Three days. You'll see the sun tomorrow. In fact, you will have the *best* day tomorrow. Like Christmas come early." Nico smiles at me as we pass the flood of plushies and he pulls out a set of keys.

It's happening. I've really managed to get out.

I will *not* be a basement-dwelling prisoner who loses his sight from the lack of vitamin A.

When I realize I'm feeling grateful to him for letting me out, I have to shake my head to force away the ridiculous thoughts. He trapped me there in the first place, and he's no kind soul, but a psycho murderer.

I'm so antsy about leaving the underground that I can't stay still and keep shifting my weight as Nico unlocks the exit before stepping into a short corridor. He switches on the light, grabs both my shoulders and leads me out of the hallway into...

Holy hell.

Golden lamps arranged in several spots around the cozy yet spacious interior finished with dark wood cast a warm glow on rows, piles, and racks of Christmas-related merchandise. It's as if I've stepped into one of those tooth-decay-sweet holiday movies and entered Santa's own workshop while the elves are all on break. It takes me a moment to realize that we are inside a... shop. Freedom is just outside the frost covered windows. I can see the street lamps, but as much as I want to seek help, I cannot afford another false start. Nico won't give me a third chance, so I need to focus on milking his crush on me and seize the opportunity to escape when it presents itself.

The silence stretches between us, and as I notice that Nico's watching me, I realize he craves a reaction.

"Wow," is all I can give him. "This is... quite something."

Never have I hated Christmas more.

My mind is racing. I can't imagine him being a night security guard for a shop this small. He wouldn't be able to hide his murder basement so easily. I remember what he said about his grandfather handing him the mantle of Christmas Killer, and while I can't be sure, it seems plausible that he also inherited this place.

Talk about hiding in plain sight.

"Welcome to the Winter Emporium," Nico says and strides in. "We have several themed sections, and oh!" He grabs my hand and pulls me away from the windows, deeper into the store that smells of cinnamon, orange, and pine. I clock a phone by the counter, which could be useful in the future.

We arrive at a large table hosting a miniature snow-covered wonderland. It has a little town, a train station, tiny shops, and a herd of reindeer in the forest.

Nico ducks under the table, and the whole scene lights up. "I made a lot of this with my grandpa," he says with a smile, as if his hobby isn't cutting people into pieces.

I clear my throat, trying to grasp at the remainders of my sanity as a miniature train emerges from within the artificial mountain with a whistle. "After New Year, does this place become the Love Emporium, and then the Spring Emporium?"

Nico looks bewildered. "Fuck no. Christmas all day every day, baby. This is an all-year-round Christmas shop. Don't you just love it?"

I don't want to completely gross him out with my attitude, but I also have my limits. "I kinda wish Christmas wasn't a thing. All that fake cheer and the pressure to buy things..."

His eyes grow wider. "Oh no... You can't be one of *those* people. Don't you feel all warm and gooey inside in reindeer pajamas?"

I glance down my body. "It is warm, I'll give it that. I don't like how loud and garish everything is at Christmas. How does your shop survive selling only Christmas products all year?" I ask, gesturing at the interior.

Nico turns off the lights on the table, which also stops the train from moving, but he doesn't seem angry with me for speaking my mind, so that has to count for something.

"It can get tough, but the town is known for impressive Christmas displays, so we get a lot of tourists in the winter, which helps get us through the summer. The shop's been in my family for almost a century. It started out as a toy shop, and I don't want to let the tradition die. I used to help out here when I was just a kid. We would lock the shop on Christmas day, pull the curtains shut, and have our dinner right there," he points to a table set with festive plates and napkins.

When I imagine two serial killers, a master and his apprentice, carving the turkey here, among all this gaudily cozy finery, I get a sense of almost overwhelming distaste. God, how I hate Christmas. "I'm already tired of the festive season. Are you really trying to tell me you just eat Christmas ham and gravy all year and pretend it's snowing outside in the summer?"

Nico wags his finger at me with a smile. "I'll make a believer out of you yet. I'm all about the Christmas magic."

And murder.

I won't lie, I do have a morbid curiosity about what makes him tick, what made him this way. He is the Christmas Killer after all, and this is his origin story. Is he a born psychopath, or did he see his grandfather do some messed up shit, and that scarred him for life?

He leads me up wooden stairs decorated with garlands and baubles, and when he leans past me to dim the lights downstairs, I take a discreet sniff of his cologne. It's spicy, deep, with a hint of something fruity. I wonder if I'm too horny for my own good, or just touch-starved, because deep down I toy with scenarios of what I'd do if he tried to kiss me under the mistletoe we pass beneath.

As we reach the upper level of the store, I'm confronted with a large assortment of clothing and accessories, as well as some less orthodox items, like pet toys or perfume. I'm somewhat overwhelmed by the selection as my host leads me to a table with men's underwear, where every single item is Christmas-themed too.

What is this madhouse?

"Go on, pick up a few things," Nico offers with a wide smile as I stare at a legless mannequin presenting a pair of tight red boxer briefs made of velveteen and featuring a fur trim.

"Is this your idea of sexy underwear for our date? Do you want me to dress up as an elf again?"

Nico smirks and though he avoids my eyes. "You did make a pretty picture as an elf, but I want you to feel comfortable. I know it was a costume, I'm not unreasonable. Maybe this?"

He shows me a green velvet jock strap with *Ho Ho Ho* on the waist band. He's ridiculous, but the idea of wearing something that leaves my whole ass on show still makes me blush.

"You just want easy access," I say, chuckling, because if I don't laugh, I might just go mad. "There's a reason why we wrap gifts, you know."

"I like a bit of mystery..." Nico steps much closer and alarm bells ring in my head. I need to put a lid on this.

"But, as I said, I don't like garish colors," I say, moving away from the themed underwear with two pairs of the simplest red and green briefs. "And my skin is very sensitive, so I only really wear natural fabrics. Do you have any?"

"Yes, over here. What made you dress up as an elf then if you're not a fan of Christmas? Or artificial fabrics," he asks, leading me away from the briefs, to a long rack of ugly sweaters, which surely are all made of polyester rather than wool.

I clear my throat, ignoring the garment featuring a tyrannosaurus dressed as Santa and handing out gifts to other dinos. I've already told him what happened, but he clearly wants to build some kind of connection, so I shrug and give him what he wants.

"It was a themed party. Everyone's all crazy for Christmas, and I wanted to be noticed. It got me what I wanted, but instead of a kiss, I got abducted by a psycho. I thought you have to go to a club at least a few times before you get targeted by some maniac," I mumble unhappily.

"Did you underestimate what your face and body can do to people?" He turns to a corner filled with much darker colors and I spot the Christmas Killer merch right next to a whole array of Grinch-themed products.

My mouth dries as I follow the harmonious lines of Nico's back, identifiable even under the shirt. He has a beautiful shoulder-to-hip ratio, and for a moment I'm almost tempted to step closer and smell his top where the fabric dips between the shoulder blades. If I'd met him anywhere else, I could have been persuaded to give him my first-ever blowjob. Hell, I might have been the one doing the persuading.

But while I need him to like me enough to spare my life, I don't want him to become possessive. This game is already far too dangerous without him on top of me.

"Don't you think that's a bit on-the-nose?" I ask, following him to the Christmas Killer's corner, which features everything from T-shirts to mugs. "If you ended up tied to the murders somehow, the merch might be a giveaway."

"Nah, people like you, Cryptic Boy, come here all year round. In the summer, these are actually some of our bestsellers. If I were able to reveal my identity, I could have been married to one of my fans by now."

He's just showing off to make me jealous. *Am* I jealous?

"And," Nico goes on, picking up a black T-shirt with a grin. "One hundred percent cotton."

I take the T-shirt, scrambling in the heat of his gaze. What is he trying to say? That he wants me to become his husband in the future and support his bloody endeavors? I'm not the marrying kind even if I could get on board with vigilante justice.

My heart beats faster, and I curl my toes as a wave of his scent reaches my nose. All this would be infinitely easier if I wasn't a horny virgin. I need to redirect my thoughts. Now.

"So, you profit from your kills?"

The black top is stylized to look like a band T-shirt with a cartoon head wrapped in ribbon and a list of murder dates on the back alongside locations.

Is it better than a festive onesie? I'm not sure.

"No, I profit from T-shirts," he says with a sneaky grin I'm finding weirdly endearing. Maybe it's the edge of danger hanging over me like a guillotine, or just the contrast between my current situation and the one I was in two days ago that's making me such a sucker for him.

"Or this one?" he suggests, showing a top that says *I met the Christmas Killer and all I got was this lousy T-shirt.*

"Can I get them both for free?" I ask, meeting his gaze. He is a dangerous animal, and it would be unwise to make myself appear too weak.

It's as though he's been waiting to shower me with gifts. Not only do I get those two, but three more, a pair of Grinch pajama pants, a big green hoodie from the eco section, and cozy socks.

In the end, we leave the store with a whole pile in my arms. I suppose it makes sense for him to offer me something from his own store rather than paying way more someplace else, but I still want to roll my eyes at the hoodie featuring a very angry Krampus. Ah well, at least it's not an elf.

As it turns out, Nico lives in the attic above his shop. I take note of the easy-to-open lock on the door and follow my host into his apartment, which is surprisingly pleasant after half an hour of the Christmas cacophony in the shop.

A massive skylight reveals a clear sky covered in stars, and Nico turns on fairy lights, which decorate the whole living room with a warm orange glow. The sloped wooden ceiling makes the place seem small, but the rustic kitchen area has enough room for a sofa. A Christmas tree adorned with green and red baubles is the main feature next to a table with two chairs, already set for dinner just as beautifully as the fake one in the shop. I only now realize how hungry I am, and the smell of potatoes with gravy makes me salivate.

When I spot the wrapped boxes piled up under the tree, I forget for a moment that I'm a prisoner here. And while, it seems, I can't escape the most lonely of holidays for the duration of my stay, I intend to be a gracious guest. I wonder if there's a phone inside the apartment, or if I'll need to sneak out into the store once Nico falls asleep. For now though, all I want is to fill my stomach with savory food, because I can't live on milk and cookies.

"And you live on your own?" I ask, trying to gauge what I'm dealing with.

He pulls out a chair for me like the perfect gentleman and rushes off to the kitchen counter, locking the door on the way. Of course.

"Yes, but I'd love to share it with someone special one day." Nico winks at me as he puts on a green apron with his name on it in a whimsical font. For half a second I toy with the idea of being his boyfriend. How would such a life even look like? Would this love-bombing eventually stop, replaced by encroaching violence, as it often happens? Or would he always stay like he appears now, a maniac with a knife on December nights, and a perfect partner at any other time?

"How about you? Do you live with your brother?"

I'm surprised that he'd care, but I pour myself some water from the bottle in the middle of the table and take a sip. "Technically. He divides most of his time between New York, Austin, and LA. But he visits me almost every month," I say, stumbling over the last word when Nico folds his sleeves, once again revealing the thick forearms. They look as strong as they felt.

He carves the turkey for us with the proficiency I'd expect from someone who claims to cook it once a month. I'm reminded of the saw cutting through my abductor's neck and strangely enough, now that I'm removed from the situation, the memory doesn't even make me lose my appetite. What if something's wrong with me too? I've always kept the extent of my interest in true-crime from my brother, because I know it's a bit morbid, and I don't want him to worry for no good reason, but I think my tolerance for seeing violence is higher than most people's.

"Oh, so you're not close?" Nico asks and puts a generous pile of mashed potatoes on both plates. "Are you out to him? Or did he not know what club you went to?"

I stick my finger in the hot potatoes and bring some to my mouth. They're creamy, soft, and so heavenly I find myself grunting. "Um... no no, we are close! We often send each other memes and stuff. And he knows I'm gay. Other people aren't lucky to have such accepting families, but he was actually the one to help me get the fake ID. Said it would be better if I got to meet other gay men in real life rather than online."

Nico places a feast-on-a-plate in front of us both, takes off the apron and lights a few candles on the table.

I think my hormones are messing with me after the ordeal I've been through so far, because my chest gets all warm and fuzzy. Who would have thought the Christmas Killer could treat me to a better dinner than my own family?

"So first he won't let you go to a regular high school, and then he sets you loose at a gay nightclub?" Nico raises his eyebrows but clinks his own glass of water with mine.

I stall. "I mean, I'm eighteen now. I know better. He thinks I'm ready," I say and dig in, humming in pleasure as I try the juicy meat. Nico is an excellent cook, I'll give him that.

"Do you know better?" he asks with a devilish glint in his eyes, reminding me that he's a predator. And yet the atmosphere around us is so cozy I'm relaxed. Maybe too relaxed.

Maybe this is a trap, and he's trying to fatten me up a bit for next year's Christmas?

Still, when I see the spark in his eye, heat flashes down my body, and I shrug. "Probably not, considering I accepted a drink from a perfect stranger. What do *you* think?"

"I think we need to find out who is trying to kill you so you can enjoy the life you deserve, and I hope I'll be a part of that life."

Uh-oh. *That's crazy*, passes through my head, but I force my features to remain unchanged as I listen. He focuses on the plate in front of him and flushes as if he were getting to spend time with his favorite celebrity.

With no input from me, Nico goes on, "You... you've been with me for a while now. As in, your podcast. I really love how much attention you pay to detail and how much you dig into a killer's psyche. I might have discovered a few things about myself that way. When you recounted some of my kills, the ones of known criminals, I got a bit of a thrill from how much you seemed to enjoy the righteous justice."

A shiver runs down my spine, because he's right. I never say it openly, because I don't want to deal with haters claiming I'm a bad person like a certain colleague of mine, but I'm not entirely against someone taking out people who are evil to the bone.

Many would say it's not up to me to decide who deserves death and who does not, but the way I see it, someone who tortures, kills, or hurts others for some kind of self-gratification should not be treated as *a person*. They're beasts that deserve being put down. So yes, I might not outright say that, but Nico must have read that between the lines and understood, because it's an opinion he shares.

Knowing that every single person he killed was an evil creature without a shred of humanity deep in their heart offers me a new perspective on the Christmas Killer, and I almost want to reveal it to the world. "Why don't you make it clear why they died? Your victims, I mean."

He sighs over his last piece of turkey. "I worry the evidence might be tracked to my cameras. Speaking of which…" he goes on to tell me about something he accidentally witnessed.

A man was notoriously cheating on his wife, but one day, she came home early so the husband hid the other guy in the garage before accidentally locking himself out in the cold. As he circled the house to return inside, he ran into a bear busy eating from trash cans. As Nico later learned from a newspaper, the husband survived but lost a leg. And his wife.

He promised to show me the footage, as he's never gotten to share it with anyone, and maybe it's messed up, but it made me feel kinda special.

"Nobody likes cheaters, right?" I quipped, and we shared a little laugh at the man's deserved misfortune.

I spent the rest of dinner entertained by my charming (if deadly) host, and I did end up eating pumpkin pie for dessert because why the fuck not? I'm an adult, and nobody can stop me!

We brush our teeth together, and by the time we're done, my eyelids feel heavy. The clock on the wall tells me it's almost three in the morning, but as I enter Nico's bedroom and face its cozy interior, with a sloped roof on either side of me, I'm reminded that he warned me about there being only one bed. I'd ignored that fact, too focused on trying to get out of the basement prison, but seeing the large wooden frame with piles of snowflake-patterned pillows makes my situation all too real.

"Cozy," I say as strings of fairy lights illuminate the ceiling, providing mood lighting. "And not messy at all."

"I just want it to be perfect for you." He bites his lip, but things get serious when he starts unbuttoning his shirt.

Oh, fuck.

Was the dinner date a trap, and he never intended to wait for my invitation after all?

A shiver makes its way up my back, because when I imagine him forcing himself on me, my heart beats faster for all the wrong reasons. I have a few messed-up fantasies he doesn't need to know about. I don't want any of them to really come to life, of course, but I'm the one controlling what goes on in the scenarios I imagine, and the vision of him on top, pushing me down hard, does... things to my body. I steady myself and watch him, because if he really wants me to, he's going to make it happen anyway. Better not to prod the bear.

Or at least that's what I'm telling myself as I watch his fingers descend down his chest, popping button after button. I can already see some of his chest hair and find myself wondering how it would feel against my back while a body just like this moves on top of me in a hypnotic rhythm.

"Thank you, that's very considerate."

"I'm so stuffed!" Nico pats his rock-hard stomach, and I've got no doubt this is his way to tease me and humblebrag, because he's ridiculously fit. He pulls the band out of his hair, letting it loose. With the skylight behind him, the gentle lights caressing his skin, his attractiveness seems unreal.

And he *wants* me. I know it. If I said the word, I could be getting my dick sucked tonight.

But then, I'd entangle myself more with a killer. Which is not only morally wrong (debatable), but also dangerous (certainly).

"You're staring, sweetie." Nico winks at me with his fingers on his belt. "If you're feeling shy, you can change in the bathroom." He points to the door behind me.

I definitely should not be getting a boner, but he is tall, and built, and has such pretty blue eyes.

"What if I am staring?" I ask and face the window, looking out into the small town street to calm down. It is in my best interest to slide under the covers, because if I do go into the bathroom now, I might be tempted to get relief from my right hand.

"You're invited to. I'm just giving your modesty a warning." He chuckles and the *clank* of his belt follows. The sound goes straight to my dick.

I will be in bed with an insanely hot guy. Also, the Christmas Killer. My growing erection is extremely inappropriate, so I step toward the bed and lift the covers on one side. I hide under the comforter as soon as the slippers he gave me are off.

"I'll just stay in the onesie tonight," I say.

The mattress is made of memory foam, which I register as playing in my favor, because I'll be far less likely to wake Nico up when I sneak out to call my brother. Or the police. For now though, I give in to temptation and rest against the pillows as my host pulls his belt out, watching me like a hawk assessing if he's ready for another meal.

There's something wrong with me, because despite being here against my will, despite knowing who this man is, I cannot help the arousal making my balls tighten and my cock fill as I feast my eyes on his handsome features and broad chest.

"And by the way, I'm inexperienced, not modest," I tell him, determined to stand my ground.

My face flames when he pulls down his jeans, revealing muscular thighs and black briefs that tent a little over his package.

When he climbs onto the bed in his underwear, my breath quickens. I've never been more aroused in my life. My survival brain has been overridden by sex drive and all I can think about when I stare at him is how badly I want my head between his legs.

He kneels by me, and I didn't think it was possible for the air between us to become denser with lust, but here we are.

Nico leans over me, one hand by my head, and just as I think he's going to kiss me, it turns out he's reaching for the drawer in the night stand on my side.

It's happening. He's getting a condom. Or lube. Both?

But... no. Something rattles and he straightens up with a pair of handcuffs.

"Now, let's get you ready for bed."

A soft whine leaves my lips. "You're into that kind of thing?" I ask as my cock sucks blood out of my brain at a rapid pace.

Nico's eyebrows rise. "What...? No. I mean, yes, but also, no, that's not what they're for tonight." He strokes my cheek and grabs my wrist. "I trust the incriminating evidence you gave me, but there's only so much risk I can take if I'm to sleep next to you."

I'm such an embarrassment, but how can I be expected to think straight in a situation like this one? This is the first time I'm in bed with another man, who, by the way, looks like my wet dream, and the adrenaline of knowing his secret identity seems to fuel my fantasies rather than extinguish them. In an alternative world, where Nico is just a fit guy, I'd want him to kiss me. First on the lips, then down my neck as his hand slides into my pajama and holds my painfully stiff prick—

So why does the fantasy morph to him wearing a fucking balaclava and watching me with intense eyes?

Nothing like that is going to happen, nor will I get to make a quick phone call, because when the first cuff closes around my wrist, it's obvious I won't be able to slide my hand out.

Fuck.

"Sweet dreams," Nico says and gives me a kiss... on the fucking forehead?

He then lies down under the thick comforter, and closes his eyes, peaceful as a baby while I stew in my horny juices, dick as hard as a damn candy cane.

With the lights off and my arms cuffed to the headboard, I have no choice but to try willing my erection down, because my host wouldn't have built a pillow wall between us if he wanted to unleash his lust on my restrained and defenseless body.

Typical, just typical. First, he teases me, then doesn't even follow up on his unspoken threats. The part of me that wanted him to itched for an excuse to go with it, but he gave me blue balls instead.

His breathing evens out, until I'm certain he's asleep, but dreams refuse to claim me too, so I stare at the ceiling, bathed in the warm scent clinging to the sheets. I'm about to drift off when Nico moves on the other side of the partition between us, and I consider if I really want him to molest me after all, but when his arm slams my ribs, and a soft snore comes from his direction, I know the night is lost.

CHAPTER 9

NICO

WHEN I WAKE UP after my four hours sleep, I get so excited to find myself hugging Blake I have to remove myself from the bed before I can do something I'll regret. Fortunately, my precious captive sleeps through me untangling myself, as if he's a hibernating bear.

Even though I need to deal with my hard-on in the shower, I still start the day on a positive note simply because he's here, in my bed, after a lovely dinner date and some sizzling flirting. He can play hard to get all he wants, but I noticed his excitement, his flush, and even though he hit me and tried to run away, before that, our kiss was *real*.

I'm an understanding guy, I can see that he's under a lot of pressure. He's found out that someone is after him, which has to be extremely stressful, and he doesn't know me that well yet. I'll need to reassure him, prove to him how worth his time I am and that he doesn't need to be afraid of me. All the other inconveniences will be sorted out.

As I prepare a morning feast for us and run some errands so everything's ready when he wakes up, I can't get over what a good fit we are. Not only do sparks fly whenever we flirt, but we share a morbid sense of humor, and we both need to be loved. Between the lines, I read his relationship with his brother isn't as rosy as he tries to portray it.

They *text* often? Blake sees him every few *weeks*? Blake is eighteen, so it means he's been neglected, left to his own devices, and without much access to people his own age. And then after all that, his brother just pushes him out of the nest and into the sharp-toothed wolf jaws of men who would gladly leave the imprints of their teeth all over his pale body? It's such a good thing I found him and can take care of him from now on.

I'm arranging our food on the wooden tray when a soft grunt reaches my ears from the room next door, followed by a rustle of sheets. Ha. My guest is up and running. Well, he will be once I take the cuffs off, but that's a minor detail.

I use my phone to start playing instrumental Christmas music in the bedroom, and then place a single poinsettia flower into the miniature vase in the middle of the breakfast spread. Happy with my work, I stroll next door, already excited to see Blake's pretty face again.

"Good morning," I say, popping my head through the open door. He lies prone with his head tucked deep into the soft pillow and the covers tangled around his legs, as if he's spent the past few minutes of sleep tossing and turning. With his hands up and cuffed to the headboard, he's like a gift wrapped especially for me, but I don't want to distress him and remove the shackles as soon as I place the tray over his lap.

His thick, dark brows lower over green eyes, which watch me intently as Blake swallows. "Hello, Nico."

"Good morning. You look so sleepy. It's adorable. I hope you're hungry? I got us coffee from the place next door too." I sit on the bed right next to him as he rubs his wrists.

He's still in the festive onesie I got him as pajamas and I imagine we could wear matching ones on Christmas day. Today, I settled for simple jeans and a T-shirt. It's white, with a print stating 'Nice until proven Naughty'.

There's fresh pastries, a selection of sandwiches on the tray, and even some fruit, if he's up for it first thing in the morning. I'm rather proud of myself.

He goes straight for the coffee I poured into my best mug and watches me from behind it. His eyes are puffy, his curly hair in disarray, and if I could have my way, I'd be kissing his neck already. But I'm not about cheap hookups with the person whose voice I've fantasized about for a long time, the person who got to know the real me, so I remain patient and help myself to a croissant with pistachio cream.

"I didn't even notice you leaving," Blake says and puts down the coffee to follow my example.

"You sleep like a baby. I'm usually well-rested after just a few hours. Which is very convenient when I need to run a shop, stay ripped, *and* plan my kills." I slurp some coffee and then bite into the pastry. It's flaky, but soft inside, with homemade cream. I move it to Blake's mouth and urge him to take a bite now that I know it's perfect.

He's about to sink his teeth into a bear claw, but when I move my own pastry close to his face, his gaze drifts to it before meeting mine. A jolt of pleasure spears through my body, but I remain still and only bite the inside of my cheek when he leans in and tries what I'm offering. His lashes flutter, and he hums, nodding. "Those are very good!"

I'm so happy that he's pleased I fist-pump. "And I have so much planned for us today. I got you new clothes, hopefully your size, because you seemed not as eager to show off your Christmas spirit all the time. My employee's been encouraging me to take a day off for a long time, and I always worry that I need to be at the shop, but you know what? He's right. Fuck it. I need to live a little, and with you here, it just makes sense."

"So we're going out to find the guy who's after me?" Blake asks and hurriedly takes a sip of coffee, as if he's ready to stuff the rest of the pastry in his mouth and bolt out of bed.

I stall, chewing my treat, then rub his knee through the blanket. "Hmm... you did promise me a date first."

Blake's pouty mouth opens farther, and he stares back. "Oh... I did, didn't I? The weather looks pretty decent," he says, pointing at the window, which show-cases a blue sky smudged by wispy clouds. "What do you want to do?"

I straighten up, almost bouncing with excitement. "We will go ice skating, I'll show you my town, we'll go on a very special tour. I picked a restaurant for us that does local venison and desserts made of foraged ingredients, and the crown jewel at the end..." I lower my voice for effect, "it's a surprise!"

Blake drinks more of the coffee, and while his silence is almost unsettling, I get the sense that his green eyes are blades slicing into my soul to uncover hidden layers. "I saw you cut into that guy, and there's a prison cell in your basement, but I'm still having a hard time accepting that *you* are the Christmas Killer. You murder people. How are you so positive all the time?"

"Oh. I guess I'm just quite excitable, and my... *needs* are met by what I do." I get so thoughtful I calm down and sit next to him again. I extend my hand to him, and while he hesitates, he does take it. "I wasn't always like this. My dad drank too much, and while he wasn't violent, it was destroying him. He argued a lot with my mom, and I had all this pent-up rage inside of me, mixing with morbid interests I didn't understand well. As a kid, I overheard my parents arguing about me. My mother said something was wrong with me after I didn't want to give up my teeth to the tooth fairy, and in hindsight, I guess she was right. She didn't like to spend time with me, and I only became more sullen. I spent more and more time with my granddad because my father ended up in rehab several times. All around, not a great situation, Blake, but throughout all that, the Christmas shop, the crafts I did with my grandpa, they were an escape into something stable and happy." I squeeze his hand. I had no idea how much I needed to be listened to like this. I have all of Blake's attention, and he hardly even blinks. "I was eleven when my father died, and my mother ended up leaving me to my grandpa shortly after. It's the best thing she could do really, because I was out of control. Always angry, picking fights with other kids, filled with a darkness I couldn't contain."

Blake frowns. "A murderer? Out of control? Who would have thought?" I'm not sure if he's trying to offend me or make a joke, but then he strokes my hand with his thumb and frowns. "Did you go after small animals? Or set stuff on fire?"

My mouth quirks when I realize he wants to know more about my childhood. He wants to find out how well I fit the typical serial killer profile.

"I'm not proud to admit I did set my dad's car on fire after he died. Hope it doesn't make me a stereotype. My grandpa caught me, and I thought he'd beat me, but instead, he talked to me about my anger and listened when I admitted how I want to see some people suffer, how it builds up in me like an impending avalanche.

"That night, he took me to a faraway cabin. I think he wanted to either test me, spook me, or teach me a lesson, but he showed me the body of a man he killed. And I wasn't scared, I was fucking fascinated. That night is a blur, but as we talked, and it all poured out of me, I wasn't afraid. He could see that. He ended up letting me take the man's teeth, and then we set the house on fire. I got to throw the match. I never had a more peaceful sleep, and yes, I never wet the bed after that." I chuckle and roll my eyes.

Blake's face blooms a bright red, and he averts his gaze. "Seemed too personal to ask. But.... yes, I wanted to know that too. And above all else... I suppose I'm almost envious of how at peace you seem to be with everything. I'm not even close to that."

I stroke his hand with my thumb. "I have two big things in my life that make me happy. Christmas and murder. And thanks to my grandfather's forethought, even if I'm caught one day, I'll be able to show evidence of my crimes being vigilante justice, which makes me sleep peacefully at night. I always have something to look forward to, and now... I have you as well," I say more carefully, because I don't want to spook him with my intensity. "If you let me, of course. But you don't need to make any decisions just yet." Even though I wish I could unzip his outfit and pump him full of my cum.

"It must be nice to have such peace of mind. I always feel like I'm not quite where I belong," Blake says and as he bites into his pastry, a crumb stays on the skin close to his lips like the palest of beauty spots. I lick my lips, tempted to kiss him when I remember our mouths pressing together in the shower. But I'm older, more experienced, and need to keep a lid on things until he's ready, so I swipe the flake away with my thumb.

He'll be where he belongs when he knows he's mine, but I have to be patient.

Green eyes meet mine, deep and soulful. "Now that your grandfather is gone, do you have any family left?"

"No. My mother moved to Florida after leaving me and we don't keep in touch. But I have friends, a lot of people know me from my shop, they just... they don't know all of me. Not like you." I lift his hand to my lips and kiss his knuckles. "And I *want* to be known. I've never told anyone any of this. Maybe this is what I've been missing when I tried to date."

Blake snorts but doesn't pull away, and I don't miss the color rising to his cheeks again when I keep my lips against his soft hand. "T-this isn't a romcom. We'd need to hate each other first, and you're acting like you're already all-in."

"Isn't *you* hating me enough for our love to bloom?" I tease, but my shoulders fall. I struggle to keep a lid on my excitement when it comes to romance.

Blake licks his lips, startled by my question. Tiny spiders crawl up my arms as we watch one another in silence, assessing the strength of the energy sparking between us.

"I don't *hate* you," he says in the end. "I'm just confused, because you're not what I expected."

"In a good way?"

Blake laughs and rubs his face in a careless way I find adorable. "Yes. But I also know you're a killer, so I keep expecting you to turn me into your new project."

I let go of him, because I don't want to smother Blake. "You're safe with me, Cryptic Boy. After all, I need new podcast episodes."

He laughs once more, and I freeze when his hand touches my thigh, only to immediately pull away, as if he remembered he's not supposed to be this touchy-feely. "I don't doubt you'll give me plenty of material to work on. Now that I know you only kill bad people, I'm almost sorry I can't do a countdown to the next victim each December." He drinks the coffee, finishes his pastry, but then starts wiggling closer to the edge of the bed.

"We'll have to wait with any podcasting until I'm sure the person who ordered the hit is dead. For now, let's enjoy the day. I left you a selection of clothes here," I point to a chair, "and I'll wait for you in the living room." The very idea that someone who wants my precious sweet potato dead is out there makes me want to rage, so I take a deep breath.

"Thank you. I won't be long," Blake says and stretches on the way to the bathroom as if to show off the shape of his shoulders.

I in turn, can't wait to show him off to Owen.

CHAPTER 10

BLAKE

It's a bit overwhelming to have the kind of morning I considered relegated to romantic movies. Sure, I *was* in chains when Nico first entered, but he brought me coffee, pastries, and even new clothes, which he must have bought for me, since there's no way he owns anything my size.

Unless the garments belong to one of his past victims.

I grab the burgundy sweater with a Scandi pattern on the arms and chest, and sigh in relief when I find an intact label. It also says the piece is made of hundred percent wool, which starts a little fire inside me. It's nice to know Nico remembered what I told him last night.

I'm tempted to have another pastry, but it would be a bit too indulgent on a normal day like this one, so I rush into the bathroom for a quick shower, and then pair the sweater with dark blue jeans that fit me perfectly.

Despite Nico clearly having a taste for loud patterns and bright colors, he took care to pick out something I'd feel comfortable in, which is a rather new development in my life. I've been choosing my own clothes since I was thirteen.

Carl does sometimes offer me wearable gifts, but he never understood my taste. I didn't have the heart to tell him, but I don't think he notices that I never put on the belts with big, flashy buckles, or wear the uncomfortably large wristwatch he gave me for my last birthday. He doesn't wear such things either, but I suppose he considers it a more youthful style, suitable for someone my age.

I stand in front of the tall, wall-mounted mirror to adjust my unruly curls and wonder if my host/jailor is starting to feel annoyed by how much time I'm taking. I'm ready, and I look good in the outfit Nico picked for me, but I'm almost afraid to see him again. The tension of last night is like a splinter under my nail, and I worry what might happen if things get out of hand. He seems nice enough as a person, and I can't help being physically drawn to him, but he is a killer, who might just be playing nice to manipulate me. And this whole date thing is like an obstacle course full of quicksand traps.

I've never had a boyfriend.

I've never been on a date.

I only had my first kiss last night, with the Christmas Killer. Things seem to be moving way too fast.

When I finally emerge, I'm met with Nico's sharp gaze and languid smile. He eyes me from head to toe, and I feel naked despite the layer of clothes on my back. He wants me. I've never been so sure of anything in my life. And he could have had me whether I wanted it or not, yet he's giving me space and showering me with gifts.

He holds a coat for me like the perfect gentleman, and we put on hats and gloves as we head down the stairs. Nico looks so perfectly normal in a plaid red jacket worthy of a sexy lumberjack. Only the snowflakes on his neck, which I now know extend down his chest give him a bit of edge, but lots of people have tattoos. Not in a thousand years would I pick him out of a lineup as a killer. Heartbreaker? Definitely.

As he lets me through the door after tying a soft scarf around my neck, I let my thoughts drift to an alternative world where he and I met in the town closest to my home, where I would sometimes go to look at strangers and pick out books.

If he knocked my shopping out of my hands by bumping into me, would I let him invite me for a coffee? Could we maybe have great rapport, good enough that I would consider anything resembling a relationship? That would make my life unnecessarily complicated, and I always dreamed about a free and uninhibited life once I was of age, but *he* could have charmed me.

Problem is, Nico is not the guy from my simple fantasy. He is the serial killer who's been fascinating me for years, and that's a whole other can of worms.

I can't unsee him sawing a man's head off, or the way he looked in a balaclava, dragging a body down a flight of stairs. I can't unhear him talking about the darkness inside him, or how he's at peace with killing because of a code.

But the worst thing is, I'm drawn to that side of him too. Morbid curiosity of the same kind that made me spend countless hours watching murder scene footage. He's a car crash, and I can't look away.

"Hey, Owen!" Nico says as soon as we're downstairs, and one glance at the counter reminds me of my failure to alert my brother to my peril. The phone's still there, so close and yet so far.

A young guy with dusky skin and short black hair looks up from a large container full of balls of ribbon and string. He's dressed in a brown loungewear set meant to imitate a reindeer, but the smile he's wearing for Nico briefly dies at the sight of me.

I stall, unsure what to expect, but the stranger's face brightens up like sun in the spring, and he leans against the counter separating the back of the shop from the space meant for customers.

"You didn't say you had a guest, Boss!"

"Owen, meet Blake, my new boyfriend." Nico puts an arm over my shoulders, but there's nothing casual about the fire I'm instantly engulfed by. He's showing me off, which is flattering, yet I'm also put on the spot, because we've not talked about me being his *boyfriend* at all. He said we'd go on a date. But the weight of his arm is so pleasant I'm finding it hard to think altogether.

I know I'm good-looking, so maybe he just wants to boast, but he still should have informed me about his plans instead of unleashing them without a warning. It's a reminder that I need to keep him at arm's length.

Owen grins. "Oh, the guy you mentioned? Damn, he is a catch!"

I give a soft chuckle, embarrassed by the attention. "Um... it's all quite fresh."

"He might be insufferable sometimes, but trust me, you've got a good one," Owen tells me with a wink. "This guy here took me in and gave me a job when my family threw me out the moment I turned eighteen. Don't know where I'd be if it wasn't for him."

Ah, so Owen fancies himself Nico's wingman.

"Come on," Nico laughs, "you were a good fit for the job."

Owen snorts. "Half the time I was late or crying on your sofa, but if you say so..."

"I get it, you're such a good, caring guy," I tell Nico and shake my head to make sure he understands I see this exchange for what it is. Yet I don't want to slide out from under his arm yet. Even after three days in his murder basement. I'm so messed up.

"I said no single lie," Owen says and returns to his box of packaging materials while Nico leads me past the counter toward the door opening into the street. "Leave it open, I was about to unlock the door anyway. Have fun you two!"

"But if there's a sudden onslaught of crowds, do call me!" Nico says with a worried expression.

Owen rolls his eyes. "No, I'll call the temps first."

Nico sighs and waves at him. "Thanks!"

I'm in disbelief when my foot hits the pavement. After the few days I've had, the outside world almost feels like a simulation. Nico has allowed me outside. If I screamed my head off for help right now, he'd be unable to stop me without someone noticing, because while the picture-perfect town is still waking up to life, there's already some tourists admiring the Christmas decorations contrasting with snow that must have fallen last night, locals running errands, and a postal truck stops in front of a butcher's shop just as we leave the Winter Emporium.

A part of me wants to do it, to break the trust he's placed in me, but it's a bright, sunny day, and I have so much to still find out about the Christmas Killer. I don't want to waste the chance I'm given because of fear. I'll be smart about this, so I can have my cake and eat it too.

"Why did you tell him we're a couple?" I whisper as we step into the frosty air.

Nico clears his throat, but when he tries to hold my hand, I put it in my pocket. This is all too much, too fast. I'm guessing he knows the town isn't too homophobic for such a display of affection, but I'm overwhelmed.

"Is that really a problem? We are dating..."

Whatever positive things I've been thinking about him need to be retracted, because he is insane. "This is only our first date. What if it doesn't work out?"

He groans and puts his hands into his pockets too. "Then I'll tell him we broke up. What's the big deal? Are you ashamed of me or something?"

"What? No! I just don't know if I'm ready for relationships. You're moving really fast, and I'm only about to start my own life," I say, walking toward a picturesque church at the end of the road, and a Christmas tree almost as tall as the red brick buildings on either side. I don't drive, and even though I can ask my brother to pay someone to take me places, I rarely end up going anywhere. It's both exciting and overwhelming to be here. I don't even know the name of this town.

"Fast? I barely kissed your forehead last night." Nico is disgruntled like a big baby who didn't get to lick the lollipop they stole. I look back, glad the sidewalk has been dusted with salt already, because the piles of snow under the building facades are pretty substantial.

"Yes, fast. I don't know you well yet, and I don't like that you're pushing. I'm too young to seriously consider commitment. We just share a common goal."

For a while we walk in silence, his face no longer the sunshine I got in the morning. I worry if maybe I should pander to him more, but why does he get to be real with me and I don't?

"I spilled my guts to you about my deepest, darkest secrets. How can you say you don't know me well?" Nico mumbles without looking at me.

This feels like trying to teach a rottweiler how to be human. "That's not how it works. You can't expect me to move at the same speed as you, just because you want me to. And what happened to friendship?" I say, wanting to offer a meaningful alternative to his fantasies.

"I don't want friendship. I want to kiss you and fuck you," he growls, spearing me with eyes like two icicles.

Wow. Okay then.

I look around, worried someone might have overheard him, but the street is empty. My insides pulse in response to the harsh way he pronounces the word *fuck*, and I need to redirect my thoughts, because they now contain as much fear as they do excitement. "If you don't accept 'no' for an answer, how come you're taking me out? And, by the way, people don't need to be in relationships in order to have sex," I add, speeding up to rush past a lady walking her dog.

I sense the intensity of his gaze on my back, so I try to focus on seeming like I'm just looking at a shop window in passing when in fact, I don't even know where we're going. On top of that, I can't stop thinking of the intense and straightforward way in which he proclaimed his intentions. I imagine Nico taking me into some alleyway, pushing down my jeans and going for it. Which is hot, as a concept, but also frightening if I consider it seriously. I don't know how much I'll even like sex.

When Nico catches up to me, my heart skips a beat, because he walks even closer than before. "We don't need to be, but we could. I don't get why you're so opposed to it. I would be the best boyfriend."

"Until I do something to piss you off and you cut off my legs so I can't run," I tell him, trying to calm myself as pressure rises in my chest.

Nico's frown deepens, and his lack of answer is more terrifying than I could have imagined.

"Oh my God!" my voice rises in panic. "You're actually considering it!"

"I wasn't!"

The frosty air stabs my throat as I suck it in and cross the street, wondering if I shouldn't ask someone for help after all. He wouldn't dare make a scene in the town where everyone knows him.

This has been a terrible idea. I should have acted immediately, and now all I want is to return to the side of the street with more people.

My breath turns into vapor. My mind is scattered, and I couldn't have been more aware of the tall presence behind me as I step onto the sidewalk.

I back out toward a shop behind me while watching his every step.

"Blake. This is completely unreasonable. Be careful on the ice—" he says, but then glances up and before I know it, he dashes at me like a mountain lion hungry for flesh.

I scream out when he grabs me, ready to fight tooth and nail for my life as I land in his tight hold. Only several loud thuds right behind me make me realize what's happening as I look over my shoulder and see snow collapsing to the ground alongside long claws of ice that might have speared my head, had Nico not held me back. Focused on the danger, he pulls me farther away as I go limp in his arms, clutching onto his jacket for dear life.

"Oh, dear God," someone calls out before people around us erupt with expressions of shock.

Nico points to the rooftops. "Watch out for the thawing icicles!" he yells to the public, hugging me. "I've got you," he whispers to me and kisses the side of my head. "You're safe."

I'm melting.

Heat streams in my limbs and pools in my chest as Nico holds me up, proving just how strong his arms are. With the world spinning around me, I have a hard time rejecting his embrace, and when he stands straight and pulls me against his chest, I stay there, my eyes closed as I inhale his scent to calm down.

As scary as this man is, stepping away is the last thing I want.

"What the hell? Someone should have removed the snow long ago," I mumble.

"It happens," Nico says, stroking my back.

When a few people start clapping, I get so embarrassed I finally pull away, but my wobbly feet are like marshmallows.

"Thank you. So, um... where are we going?"

Nico beams at me and points to a cafe not far from where we're standing. "Our date begins there."

The sandwich board outside states: *Cookie decorating workshop today!*

"Will it be all Christmas trees and gingerbread men, or will I get to also do zombies and severed heads?" I mumble, but my heart skips a beat, because this is one of those things I've always wanted to do but never got to. I often watch my private chef cook, so maybe that counts for experience?

I don't have friends, not in real life, and the idea that Nico came up with this on his own warms something deep inside my frosty heart.

"I'd love to do a severed head with you," he says sheepishly as we start walking again, away from the argument erupting around the broken snow and ice, and I find myself gravitating closer, until I can sense his warmth on my hand. I'm not ignorant of how crazy my actions are, but I'm scared, and he saved me, and we're going to decorate cookies together, as if he's known me for years, not three days.

I press my fingers to his hand, which twitches before grabbing them as we pass beautiful Christmas displays in shop windows.

I probably shouldn't encourage him, but I did promise him a date.

CHAPTER 11

BLAKE

THE COOKIE DECORATING CLASS was even more fun than I expected. We created a whole herd of zombies, one of which I even based on my brother. And while I still remembered accusing Nico of wanting to take my legs, the longer the date lasted, the sillier I felt about jumping to such outlandish conclusions.

Once the event ended, he took me to the ice skating rink, where I got to demonstrate my quite formidable skills and show off a little, and for lunch we went to a fancy little restaurant priding itself on modern cuisine based on products obtained through hunting and foraging.

Nico was shocked to find out I have never shot a gun and promised to teach me, which actually sounds like a fun day together, unless it turns into him hunting me down with a rifle. Though as I spend time in his presence, I worry less and less about being hurt. How odd, that being around him feels almost as if I'm living in a movie about happy people going on adventures together.

We laughed at some unfortunate people slipping on the ice outside, had the most amazing cinnamon mochas, and by the time the sun started descending the sky, he surprised me with a group tour focused on the mystery of the Christmas Killer.

Mrs. Pratchett, like most of the business owners I've met today, knows and likes Nico. She delivered a colorful experience as she leads us through the snow-covered streets and points out sites associated with Vermont's most famous serial murderer.

We stay at the back of the tour so Nico can fill me in on details or correct some assumptions. The focus is mostly on the historical murders, to not spook the tourists, but the guide does mention two kills from the last few years, strongly suggesting that there's a pattern to the beheadings. When she talks about the bauble maker, Nico is once again eager to whisper to me that it was the copycat's doing. He even promises to share details of his investigation once we're back home, and I can't help being giddy.

I've never been on a date before, but I have to admit this couldn't have been a better day. Maybe aside from Nico being a dangerous man who abducted me. Then again, am I not free now? Sure, he has his eye on me, but I don't have a self-destructing chip in my brain. I've been in the proximity of people and phones all day yet keep delaying my plan to alert someone. It doesn't feel urgent when I'm having fun with the person whom I've found fascinating all my life, not in spaces that promised me safety.

So as we near the end of the tour and walk into the town's famous Christmas market, bustling with joyful people and full of stalls offering everything from traditional crafts to snacks, I can't believe how fast time has passed.

"And remember, *Be nice or the Christmas Killer gets you,*" Mrs. Pratchett says, accompanied by the whole group, which at this point knows the slogan by heart. This is where the tour is to conclude, so we all applaud our guide, who in turn recommends a visit to the Winter Emporium, before winking at Nico.

"Look at you, so excited you're all flushed," Nico teases and pinches my cheek.

If this day wasn't magical enough already, I notice snow falling, the flakes glistening in the lights all around us and above the market stalls.

I grin, meeting his gaze as the small crowd of tour-goers disperses, leaving us alone by the big Christmas tree that looks straight out of a cheesy movie. For once, I don't quite hate that.

"Well, I just had the most exclusive serial killer tour. Crime Mind and Dead Pumpkin would have cut their arms off for a chance like this," I tell him, beaming with joy.

It's so incredibly exciting to get firsthand knowledge correcting popular misconceptions about the murders, and each time Nico whispers in my ear, my skin heats up, until I no longer know what cold is. He puts his hand on my back as he leans in, and every time he does that, my insides flutter like a shaken snow globe. I have to admit I have a bit of a crush on him, but even now, I scan our surroundings for an opportunity for alone time so that I can get my hands on a phone and call my brother. That's not what someone does on a normal date, which reminds me that my situation is anything *but* normal.

"Are they your podcast nemeses'? How did you get so into true-crime anyway?" he asks as we stroll past stalls filled to the brim with handmade soaps, candles, and crocheted angels.

I snort. "They tried to create unnecessary drama earlier this year. I don't *hate*-hate them, but feel free to leave negative comments and downvote their content," I tell him, bumping my shoulder into his arm. It feels good to talk to someone with such ease, someone who's close enough to touch, not somewhere in the virtual space, and I breathe in the sugary aroma of donuts as we pass a stall making them fresh. "This is a bit dumb, but I got into true-crime, because I was afraid of crime."

"How so? Did something happen to cause it? Is this about your parents?" Nico asks in a softer voice and strokes my shoulder. His gaze penetrates me like a sharp needle, making my heart beat faster. He's a handsome man, I've seen how people look at him, yet his attention is on me only.

I clear my throat. "No, my parents died in a boat accident. But when I was younger, Carl would often talk about home invasions, and people who might want to take advantage of me if I wasn't careful, so I started researching to prepare myself and know what to look out for. To have some peace of mind."

Nico's hand slides across my back, awakening my skin, and I don't want it gone, not when it's so cold our breath creates beautiful swirls of vapor. "Did it help?"

I snort. "No. I mean, yes, in the long run. I decided to take precautions and even hired a self-defense teacher. Look how useful *that* was when that fucker spiked my drink," I add, shaking my head.

Nico nods. "Don't blame yourself, unless you're always alert, someone can sneak up on you. So the crimes don't unnerve you anymore? You often sound excited on the podcast when you can share new tidbits."

I smirk as we come near the Winter Emporium and see it full of customers. It is the weekend after all. "I would ask if you think it's weird, but I already know the answer. I guess it's fascinating to know what motivates people, especially serial killers, who really don't seem to think like the average person. It's... so interesting," I say, meeting Nico's gaze. "And yet, there are commonalities. Does the Christmas Killer collect the teeth as trophies, or is there some meaning to pulling all of his victims' teeth?" I ask in a low voice.

Nico's smile widens, and my heart skips a beat. Could I ever feel this way about a normal person? Maybe his true identity is part of the thrill and I'm just ashamed to admit it to myself?

A normal person in my situation would have long sought help. Maybe I'm not as normal as I always thought?

That, or Stockholm Syndrome is already taking root.

"I have to keep some secrets to keep you interested," he says playfully as if we weren't talking about murder trinkets but his shoe collection.

"Well okay, do you take photographs then?" I ask, biting my lip.

"If I do, would you like to see them?" Nico repositions my hat, but it's surely just an excuse to touch me and I don't mind. Wearing clothes he got for me, all the way down to underwear gives me a buzz. It's as if he's marked me with them. The question stirs something deep in my chest, a hunger for information no one but me would be privy to.

I would be disturbed if I found a dead body, but it's different to see pictures. On top of that, if they're all of terrible people who deserved what came for themn

"Yes," I whisper as we stand still, intimately close, our eyes locked as if we were telling each other personal secrets. And while my plan for today included getting the hell out of his grasp, here I am, considering a reason to once again follow him down to his basement.

Maybe I'm one of those idiots who believe themselves to be way smarter than they are?

The tension between us thickens, and I wonder if he's about to kiss me. We are standing so close, and Nico is openly gay in this town. He might do it. Would I be okay with that? A chaste little smooch at a wholesome Christmas market?

What's happened to my brain? Am I really melting at the very idea?

"Eggnog, Nico?" a man yells from a nearby stall, and the moment is broken, yet I still ache down to my bones for a kiss. Before my fateful nightclub outing, I had no idea how starved my body is for touch, yet being in Nico's presence makes that painfully clear.

Nico turns to the guy and pulls me along. "I can't say no to that."

I glance at a mobile coffee shop closing for the evening. It's in the form of a small old-fashioned truck in shades of brown and navy, but as the owner gets in the driver's seat, I join Nico on a bench under a wooden roofing. The burner in front of us has real flames inside, and the heat they produce feels delightful on my icy hands. Within moments, we're holding a paper cup of eggnog each, and I dive in, showing the stall owner a thumbs up. The beverage is rich, and creamy, with notes of nutmeg and vanilla, and it's either the best I've ever had, or just tastes exquisite at a Christmas market, with a handsome man at my side.

It feels so normal to do this, but then I spot a sheriff's deputy marching across the square, and my mouth dries. If I'm wrong about Nico's intentions, I will think back to this moment when he squeezes my neck, but my mouth remains closed, and the officer enters her vehicle, out of reach.

A choir starts singing a jolly song and as I admire Nico's beautiful profile illuminated by twinkling lights, the festive spirit gets to me. It's not even Christmas yet, but I'm already feeling all gooey inside. Is it just because I'm not alone for once?

Nico takes another sip of eggnog and turns to me with a smile. "What?"

I swallow, torn about what I should say, but as I'm about to open my mouth, a strange creak tears through the air, followed by several shrieks. One glance toward the noise has me rooted to the ground, because the coffee truck has somehow backed into the main tree in the square, and while there are ropes meant to hold it vertical, the decorated fir is already starting to tip.

"Help! Let's pull it up," shouts someone.

Nico rises to his feet. "Wait here," he says and darts toward the tree, which is on the brink of collapsing. Adrenaline sends me up as well, but as the deputy dashes out of the car alongside a colleague, I'm reminded that my situation is as unstable as that damn Christmas tree, and I can't take any chances if I'm to survive.

"Your phone. Can I borrow it for a second?" I ask the gentleman who sold us the eggnog. He blinks, frowns, surprised that this is the moment I've chosen for my request. But he mumbles out a sure and unblocks his cell phone before handing it to me.

The device feels like a brick in my hand, but I need to call my brother before Nico remembers that I am in fact his prisoner.

CHAPTER 12

NICO

I'm huffing and puffing by the time the tree is stable, but I know we're done when someone pats my shoulder, laughing.

"Way to go, Nico! Saving Christmas as usual."

I glance back to spot an ex of mine. Though it's hard to even call him that since we barely lasted two weeks. I'm pretty sure he just wanted to show me off to his family for Christmas last year. Still, we had a few nights of fun.

I smile, but my mind is already on Blake, and I secretly hope he was watching my feat. "You know me, anything to help," I say.

"You wanna hang out tonight?" Miles smiles at me, but his dimples leave me cold, because I can only think of green eyes and dark curls.

"Sorry, I've got a boyfriend," I say as my insides flutter with excitement. I hope Miles is jealous.

"Free grog on me to all who helped," Denise says from her stall, prompting all the people who just won a tug of war against a massive tree to cheer.

I would gladly stay, but my feet are already heading back to my forgotten eggnog and the boy who—I stall, noticing that across the square, the bench in front of the burner, where we sat together moments ago, is vacant.

I swallow as I approach in nervous steps and a cold, slimy feeling spreads in my stomach. What if Blake was biding his time for an opportunity to run? Sure, I've got details about him paying a hacker and being up to no good, but if he's scared of me, jail might still be preferable to my company. And deep down, I know my crimes and his are not equivalent. I've got much more on the line. If he reports me, I'll spend the rest of my life behind bars.

I get to the bench and rise to my toes, looking around the crowds for a black hat with a red pom-pom, but it's gone. Gone along with the prettiest, most interesting boy I've ever met and my trust in humanity.

Because of course he'd run.

What have I been thinking? That he actually found my jokes funny? That a great kiss can make him forget I'm a serial killer? I'm a joke. I deserve prison for being a dumb fuck, and as the sheriff's deputy starts walking my way, rubbing her hands on her jacket, I'm frozen, because there's nowhere to flee. If Blake used my moment of distraction to his advantage and told the cops about me, I cannot run, not when I'm not even armed.

I steady myself and try to calm down. Maybe there is a way I can play dumb for long enough to disappear, but as my heart is about to stop, deputy Harris shakes my hand. "Thank you, Nico. I think the whole town deserves to pat itself on the back tonight."

A heavy weight drops off my chest and a hand rests on my back. I glance to the side to spot Blake's pretty smile and shining green eyes.

"That was amazing! I wish I could have filmed it," he says with a wide grin.

I relax and meet the deputy's eyes as I put my arm over Blake's shoulders. "Will I get to light the illuminations next year?"

Harris chuckles and taps my chest. "Might take it up with the mayor. Have a good night," she says, tips her hat, and walks off, leaving me stunned. So many highs and lows in a single day!

"For a second there, I was convinced it would collapse," Blake tells me with a soft exhale and hands me my eggnog, watching the square, as if he hadn't even considered running from me.

"But the hero was there," I boast, greedy for praise.

I'm so desperate for him to love me I'd lift the damn tree myself to impress him or die trying. But maybe I won't have to. Maybe there are other ways I can impress him...

The cool air sparks with heat between us, but just as I am about to hide him in my shadow and kiss those soft lips again, he speaks.

"It was a great day. But long. Maybe let's go back home?"

My pulse quickens. Does this mean he wants to be alone with me? The shop is about to close anyway, so we wouldn't have to worry about me being called in to help with the customers. Or making too much noise for that matter.

I can already imagine him moaning and squirming under me, and maybe it's wrong, but I'm so excited to be his first.

First and *only*, because I would never let him slip through my fingers.

"Sure. Would you... like to see what I do with the teeth?" I whisper as we head to the Winter Emporium.

His eyes go wide, and he steps closer, about to touch my chest when a group of teenagers walks past us, and he quickly hides his hands in his pockets, blushing the prettiest shade of pink. "Yes..."

I chuckle to myself. He'll love it.

I lead him to the shop and promise I won't be long as I help Owen with stragglers. Blake hangs out by the Christmas Pride display featuring our artisan rainbow baubles, and he looks so thoughtful as he picks up a small statue of Santa in a *Love is Nice* T-shirt and a rainbow flag in his hand.

"Isn't he just stunning?" I whisper to Owen, not even caring about today's sales numbers. I love Blake's serious expression. It goes with his dark humor, which I absolutely adore.

"He's definitely your type," Owen tells me with a smirk, and I have to roll my eyes, because he likes nerdy boys with hearts of gold, who are so very different from my skittish deer.

"I'll remind myself what I like about him the moment you step outside."

"Aaand this is my cue to go," Owen says with a snort and steps out from behind the counter. "I'm watching the *Star Wars Christmas Special* with Adam."

I shake my head at him, but he waves at both me and Blake before disappearing outside.

I notice Blake glancing into the street as I lock up, but when I approach him, he offers me a smile.

"I thought you'd never be done."

I grin at him and lead him through the shop, holding his hand. "Is that how much you can't wait?"

He clears his throat. "Well, you did tell me you'll show me what you do with the teeth. I'll be the only one to know!"

I'm nervous he won't like it, or that he'll find me too weird, but I want him to know all of me. And he actually asked about it, wasn't creeped out. That has to count for something.

"What if you get a taste for it and you'll want to create your own crafts?" I tease as we walk into the storage room. His hand tightens at the back of my sweater, and he clears his throat. "I have a bear tooth pendant at home. Teeth don't scare me," he declares, but as I lead the way toward the hidden entrance into the lowest level of the basement, I can feel him stall.

I open the hidden door in the back of the wardrobe and extend my hand to him, but I'm getting tense. Does he still not trust me? After what I showed him? What I told him? After I let him out and all but offered him freedom on a platter by focusing on the falling tree?

The muscles at the sides of his jaw twitch as his dark brows lower further, but he keeps his distance from the door. "I... it's so cold down there."

"Blake? Sweetie? I didn't let you out just to put you back down there. You're safe with me. But that's where my craft room is." I clear my throat, deflated. "We can see it another time if you don't want to go."

Though it's clear to me why he might be hesitating and I don't like it one bit.

He licks his lips, staring down the narrow flight of stairs leading to the bowels of my home. I can see the exact moment he makes his decision when he swallows and takes a deep breath before grabbing my hand with his warm fingers. "I need to see it."

His hand is slender, but his grip is strong, as if he's seeking reassurance, and I'm more than happy to give it.

I lead the way down feeling like a winner. He trusts me. I showed him who I am today on our date. My creative side when decorating cookies, how playful I can be at the ice rink, and that I'm willing to try new things when we sampled boar pâté. Now, he'll get to know all of me.

He's silent and tense when we pass the cell in which I held him, but past it is my workshop, and as I switch on the light, revealing my kingdom, he squeezes my hand more firmly.

The space is extensive, as I gathered many tools here over the years. A large table of raw wood occupies one side while my finished trophies stand on a shelf opposite the work space.

"It's a bit messy, sorry, I wasn't expecting a guest," I say, leading him inside. I'm feeling a bit vulnerable, as though I'm letting him touch my beating heart without gloves, but a part of me knows he'll be gentle. I can see it in his eyes that deep down he's very sensitive.

Blake steps toward the shelf full of large snow globes with wooden bottoms just as I switch on the lights illuminating my work. His jaw goes slack with recognition, and he looks back at me, pointing to the lone car standing in the middle of a clearing, surrounded by naked trees and snow, a human head displayed on the hood and wrapped with a red ribbon.

"The George Howe murder," Blake says in a breathy voice before examining the other pieces in my collection. "Iris Shakti. And Donald Robson. You *made* these?" he asks excitedly and rubs his chin, shifting his weight. "What is it? Wood? Resin? 3D print?"

"Yes, I make them. They're cast in resin for pieces that are unique and some elements, like the car, I bought. They're the kind of miniatures I can't exactly put in the tiny town in the shop." My heart beats faster at the fascination in his eyes. "Each one represents an official Christmas Killer murder. So the copycat isn't included and the like. And I even have one for the killing in 1912, but there's no snow in it because—let me show you."

I pick up the Howe one and hand it to Blake. When he looks at it with adoration, I know I've found my person. He's just slower to acknowledge how well we fit together. But that's okay. I'll give him time.

"Shake it," I encourage Blake with a smile, and when he does, a flurry of white whirls in the liquid.

Blake frowns and sends me a curious glance, as if asking what he's supposed to notice.

"That's the teeth. I shave them into the tiniest flakes. I like to think that it's poetic justice to take a predator's teeth. Each of the globes contains the shavings from the specific kill." I point to the shelf as his eyes widen.

"Oh. My. God," he utters and shakes the globe again, marvelling at the spiralling motion of the shavings. "That's so—"

Cool? Creative? Morbid?

Air leaves Blake's lungs as he puts the globe down with the care it deserves as a one-of-a-kind artefact. "Those are the best trophies in the history of serial killings."

I stand taller, filled with pride. "Thank you! They take a lot of time and effort to make. But I get to relive all the details whenever I handle them. Come, I'll show you the other trinkets," I say excitedly and pull on his hand, leading him to my table, where teeth are carefully arranged on a steel tray. "They're the copycat's, I've been experimenting with making them into a tiny ornament."

I hand him a magnifying glass so he can see the details of my carvings. "They're supposed to be snowman heads, but I'll add the carrot noses when I'm done linking them all with a chain."

"Oh, wow," Blake utters, resting his elbows on the table as he manoeuvres the magnifying glass to see every little detail. He's so focused he doesn't know how tempting his ass looks when he pushes back his hips, and I don't plan on making it known. But eventually, he rises to face me, and I place my unfinished project on a cabinet by the wall, where it can't be as easily pushed off.

"You are an artist! You should take commissions. I mean, not with teeth, obviously, but maybe custom snow globes?"

I laugh, overjoyed with his approval. The way he looks at me makes me want to eat him alive. "You have no idea how much it means to me that you like them. Even my grandpa, he... I think he liked that it kept me busy and away from mischief, but he didn't get it. I never fully fit in. People think I do only because they don't know all of me." I grab his hand, because I feel he might actually understand, and his fingers entwine with mine, bringing my heart to palpitations.

"I never really belonged with any group either. You have friends in town at least. And Owen," Blake tells me and rubs his nape, as if he were embarrassed about being lonely.

And he's not wrong. Being a part of the world around me brings me peace, makes me feel less alone, but it's not the same as being truly seen. I meet his eyes and pull him closer. He's not afraid to be here with me. He's come down here despite the danger I pose.

"It's like other people are stars, but I'm a black hole. We're in the same universe, but we are not alike."

Blake nods, and his lips quiver so beautifully I lean closer, my hands resting on the table on either side of him. In the glow of the lamp above, his skin looks so alive, so flushed and ripe, and when he doesn't try to push me away, my mouth finds his, and we both gasp.

The kiss is an answer to insistent needs that have been gnawing at me all day, and when I push him harder against the table, he sits on it, opening his thighs like a good boy.

Desire pools in my balls, but I take my time and slide my arms around him, exploring his mouth with my tongue. He's so sweet, still smelling of eggnog and the outside world.

If I'm a black hole, I will pull in this starshine boy until he's all mine.

His hands sliding up my back tell me all I need to know about his curiosity in me. Blake is eager, his legs open, like his mouth, and I indulge with my eyes closed. If he's about to use the scalpel I use for carving to slit my throat, then so be it, I'll die happy.

But no, both his arms settle around me, and he crosses his ankles on the small of my back, moaning when I slide my tongue along his, deeper inside his mouth. He's rocking his hips now, already steaming up with desire, his lusty body ripe for plucking, but just as I squeeze his thigh and am about to open his pants, he frantically twists his face away.

"I'm... sleepy," he utters.

I place my hand on the table by his thighs and take a deep breath against his cheek. Maybe it's this space. While he might appreciate my art, it's possible he doesn't want to fuck here. Fair.

"What are you doing to me, Blake?" I mutter and shamelessly press my erection between his legs, just so he knows.

A shivery breath escapes his lips, but he's already closing his legs, not wanting to let this go any further. "The same thing I've been doing every time you listened to my podcast and enjoyed the sound of my voice," he says with a small smile before sliding off the table.

It turns me on so much that he knows what to say yet keeps me at arm's length. He might be a virgin, but he's no innocent. I can't wait to make his composure fall apart.

"I jerked off to it once," I offer to tease him. "Still wearing my balaclava, I imagined surprising you while you record an episode."

The shiver going through his body is so obvious I notice it without touching him. His eyes glaze over. His lips part, as if he wants to taste my cock, and he squeezes his pec as he stares at me, visibly aroused by what I've just told him. Oh, does he like the idea of me jerking off to his voice? Me in a balaclava? Both? I so wish to find out.

We stew in tense silence, but eventually he snaps out of it and clears his throat.

"Sleep," he tells me with a tense smile.

I smirk and make a gentlemanly gesture toward the door.

CHAPTER 13

BLAKE

I avoided staying in the cellar, because the cops could have arrived at any moment, but as Nico and I prepared for bed in complete peace, anticipation turned into worry. When I reached Carl, he was surprised to hear from me, but when I told him that I was being kept against my will, he wrote down the name of the town, and Nico's shop, and told me help was on the way.

I assumed he'd alert the sheriff's department, but if he worries about causing some scandal that might affect both our futures, maybe he called a private investigator, or something of that nature, to deal with Nico instead?

I assumed he'd be arrested and put on trial, but what if whoever Carl hired ended up hurting Nico? I never wanted *that*, but it's not like it's in my power to call off the hounds.

Why am I regretful at all when he is a murder. A kidnapper. A damn serial killer who makes snow globes with people's teeth.

Though I have to admit those are pretty impressive.

My heart clenches when I think of him describing himself as a black hole. I sense the depth of loneliness in that, and I empathize more than I'd like to admit. Nico will surely feel betrayed once he finds out I've reported him. I can hardly bear it, and it hasn't even happened yet!

I'm in knots over asking to be rescued only to then go downstairs to admire his art and suck his face. Fuck. He's so unbearably attractive I'm losing my mind. Or was it the all-day date that's short-circuited my common sense?

I can't be falling for him, can I? *That* would be insane.

I had so much fun earlier. He was interesting but also listened to me as if he really cared about what I had to say.

Am I so unused to people having conversations with me I find that impressive? Or is it the way he's set on me that turns me into goo? There is no wishy-washy I-maybe-like-you-a-bit. He's made it clear what he wants. And it's *me.*

In the dark, the stars I see through the window on the sloped ceiling seem almost as bright as the electronic clock showing that it's almost three at night. And still, nobody has called or knocked on the door.

This can't be right. What is Carl waiting for? I can't keep being torn like this.

Especially not with Nico hugging me from behind as if I'm his personal body pillow. He only has a pair of pajama pants on, and it's melting my brain how hot he is. Not just because he's tall, muscular and ripped. He's literally overheating me. Or am I so excited by his presence and touch that I'm turning into a human radiator?

Whenever his dick presses to my ass, I remember our little make out session in his murder memorabilia room and how hard he got back then.

I'm impressed by my own self-control, because I was on the verge of giving in, but still remembered I couldn't stay down in Nico's hidden lair too long.

But I wanted to.

I want to kiss him more and have him touch me before he's taken. I want to feel him on top of me and smell his arousal. How come I'm such a messed-up pervert at only eighteen? Will I be the kind of creep who ends up writing filthy letters to him when he's in prison?

I barely keep in a whine when his nose rubs my nape before releasing hot air that has my toes curling. He's holding me firmly, as if he were ready to part my buttocks with his cock. Which is hard and poking at me.

I'm sweating.

I can't think.

But tonight, he didn't even cuff me. I could...

My balls throb when he moves again and I remember him teasing me about his fantasy of accosting me in my studio. Would he wear the balaclava? Would every single one of my live viewers hear us having sex? Would they comment in the chat?

I bite my lip to hold in a moan, and I'm not even touching myself. Yet. I press my ass against the cock straining in his pants. With my luck, the cops will burst in here when Nico's balls-deep inside me.

I have to take a deep breath, but I wiggle against his cock nevertheless, just... feeling it.

He's asleep and likely having erotic dreams, but I imagine him to be awake and testing me, waiting for me to give him the green light. For me to tell him I can't wait any longer, or just slide my hand into his pajama pants.

I place my warm palm on my throat, and then slide it down my chest, reimagining it as Nico's as I squeeze my pec and open my thighs enough to relieve the pressure of fabric on my growing cock.

His arm embraces my waist, and I ever-so-gently run my fingers over it. He's like steel, and I love that he's a bit older, more experienced, and confident. A dampness on my thigh tells me I'm leaking pre-cum already. What would it feel like to have his strong big hand on my dick?

My pulse speeds up when his breath tickles me again. I'm in bed with a man. Tightly hugged. I'm both at peace and erratic from a mix of fear and arousal. He's so handsome I'm sure he'll get serial killer groupies offering him marriage on day one of his trial.

But for now, he's with *me*, and I'm the only one who knows the truth about him.

Nico lets out a little groan, and when he shifts, I have to bite my lip, because the jab he makes with his hips sends me up the wall with lust. His dick is only two layers of fabric away from being buried in me.

Reckless fantasies take hold, showing me his cock plowing my hole on the floor of my bedroom. He's still wearing that balaclava, his bare chest and arms are sprayed red, and the metallic aroma of blood emphasizes the earthiness of his arousal.

In my imagination, he makes me feel whole each time he plunges in, and I find myself grabbing my cock as he rubs against me in his sleep. I instinctively clench my ass when I feel that thick length against it.

'*I want to kiss you and fuck you.*' I remember his stern voice, and as it echoes in my mind, the heat inside me becomes more and more difficult to bear.

I've never been the object of anyone's desire, but I indulge in it now, under the soft light of the moon and stars. His arm is solid, and I have to brush over it to reach my dick, which makes this all the more illicit. He could wake up at any moment and catch me in the act.

And yep, I've leaked pre-cum in my pants just thinking about him. I don't even care if I'll be sticky, because this could be my last chance for such closeness with him. Or… is this wrong of me to do this when he's sleeping? His dick didn't ask for *my* consent when it got rock hard and pressed to my crack like it's his God-given right.

And why do I even care for the consent of a serial killer who *abducted* me?

My nipple gets hard when he brushes his arm against it, and I squeeze my aching cock, imagining all the filthy things he'd do to me given half the chance.

And I'd let him. Not just because he's attractive or a good listener, but also because he's a maniac. And he wants me so, so much.

I bite back a moan and rub the head of my cock with my thumb before sliding my hand up and down the shaft, sinking ever deeper into a realm of fantasy where he's awake and touching me.

Nico's arm shifts, his hand going up, and I wonder what he's dreaming about when his fingers reach my lips. Fuck it. I taste them. Just a little lick of his salty skin because I'm messed up. Though I'm not making Christmas trinkets out of people's teeth, so maybe I'm not *that* bad.

I sigh when his other hand snakes under my waist, but then it's on my dick, and it's too late to deny what I'm doing.

Nico presses his flattened tongue to my nape, then licks all the way up to my hair. The touch is hot, wet, and makes me shiver.

"Naughty," he whispers, brushing his teeth over my skin as if to warn me he could bite.

I freeze, my hand tight around my cock, and I don't dare move it away even when he cups my balls, prompting me to tremble.

"No, I—" I still when he rolls his hips, rubbing his shaft against my ass.

"Hm? You what? I can feel you clenching that ass. You want to be filled, don't you?" Nico murmurs, then bites my nape without much force. His fingers are still at my mouth, while his other hand sneaks into my pajama pants and covers mine. It's so fucking big, and as he brushes his thumb over my cockhead, my back arches, and I lean into him, presenting my neck without thinking. When he bites in, I can't stop myself from moaning, my cock straining against his palm, my hips working back and forth, seeking touch while I imagine how he would feel inside me.

"I—I've never done this," I mumble, because I don't think I'm ready to be *filled*, no matter how often penetration features in my secret fantasies.

"Nothing to be scared of. Just let me enjoy you a little first," he says and even his voice, so low and raspy, is making me horny.

Nico peels my hand off my cock and replaces it with his. I might just come on the spot from that alone. Instead, my dick twitches in his grasp, spilling pre-cum over his knuckles.

"So responsive," he purrs and kisses my neck while the hand he had at my lips now dips under my T-shirt and goes straight for my nipple.

And while I'm a bit scared, that only fuels my fire because I feel his adoration in every touch. I press against his hard dick again, and I moan when even with the fabric between us, it manages to push between my buttocks. My whole body is on fire.

"Oh my God. Oh, God," I whimper and reach back, grabbing at his bicep as his dick hardens even more. My flesh can't cope with the onslaught of sensation that's so different, so much more intense, than anything I've ever felt. His hand feels so deliciously rough against my nipple, and each rub darts straight to my balls, making them throb.

"Nico," I rasp when my lover, the Christmas Killer, jerks my cock faster, caressing the side of my neck with his tongue. Each stroke, each lick tugging me closer to a sense of hot perfection.

"You taste delicious," he murmurs between one lick and another. He might not be biting, but I'm being devoured. How would I ever explain this to my brother if he found out? Self-preservation? That he *made me*?

Lies. I'm moaning like a bitch in heat as he jerks me off.

"Feel my dick? So hard for your tight little hole," Nico whispers, and that's it. I come harder than ever, my cock twitching in his grip, and I cry out while he chuckles and licks my cheek.

"Yes, it's so hard," I mumble, shaking as Nico lets go of my dick. In the dark, I expect the sweet oblivion of sleep to finally take me, but he's flipping me to my stomach, and then tugs my pants halfway down my thighs.

I have no words when he climbs on top.

Fear trickles into my muscles, but desire overpowers my will, and I keep still, spreading my thighs as wide as I can as he lowers his hips, and his cock dives between my buttocks.

Burying my face in the pillow, I bend my knees until my heels dig into the sides of Nico's ass, and wait, in no position to protest anymore. I'm too tired, and too horny to resist a man who feels so fucking good on top. He's so heavy, and I love every pound of his muscles.

There's no barriers between us, and I tremble from the nerves of it all, but at the same time, my mind is scrambled. I barely finished coming, I can't catch my breath, and Nico's slick length slides over my crack again and again. I sense his cockhead stopping at my oversensitive opening, and I don't know if I want this to happen, but if he does push in, I know I'd go with it.

"I'm too horny to stretch you tonight, sweetie," he rasps against my nape, just rubbing himself against my crack. "But it's gonna happen. Sooner or later, I'll come in your tight, hot body as you moan my name. Feel how it's throbbing for you?" He squeezes my ass cheeks on his cock and I'm about to lose my mind at how much lust floods my body. He must have used my cum to lubricate himself.

I scream into the pillow as he speeds up, trapping me under him and frantically rocking his shaft in the warm valley between my buttocks. With one hand, he squeezes my thigh, the other is buried in the hair at the back of my head, and as he pumps over me, plowing the sensitive cleft, shivers overcome my body, even though I've just come. It's not another orgasm, but ecstasy still rises, setting me on fire, and unless he doesn't stop soon, I shall burn down.

"Don't stop," I whimper, rocking against him as overwhelming need takes root in my skull. When he's like this, so hot it feels he might brand himself into my skin, I don't feel alone anymore.

It seems my words are all he needs to hear, because his grip on my hair tightens and he fucks my crack with abandon. Every time his cock slides over my hole, I wonder if he'll decide to change his angle and push in after all. A filthy side of me wants that.

But then he stills, trembling, groaning, and he's like a magnificent beast on top of me when he comes. I sense his spunk splash my skin, drip down the small of my back, and he even positions his throbbing cockhead at my oversensitive anus so I feel it when another spurt of cum drips straight on it.

I'm shocked, aroused, and brainless.

For once, I get to *feel* things instead of overthinking, and I'm a sweaty but happy mess with my pants pulled down and a man on top of me.

I don't care what anyone thinks about me, because that was the single greatest experience of my under-sexed life.

I whimper when he drags two fingers between my ass cheeks, spreading his cum as if to mark me.

Under the cover of darkness, it's somehow easier to ignore the nagging bite of shame.

"You've got pretty little dimples," Nico murmurs and it takes my overheated brain a moment to realize he's not talking about my face.

I shiver and roll against him, savoring the sticky sensation between my buttocks. I know the police, or someone sent by my brother, might arrive at any moment, but right now I'm only a guy who's just had his first sexual experience, and I want to abandon myself to my lover's arms, forgetting that he's a serial killer and that I've sold him out.

Knowing my luck, he'll turn on me *before* he finds out.

"Thank you," I tell him awkwardly, because years of watching romance in movies and reading about it in books did not prepare me for *this* kind of compliment.

Nico chuckles and kisses the back of my head as we lay there in a sweaty mess. "I wasn't expecting to be on top of you so soon," he says, still lazily stroking my ass.

I created a monster. I got too horny, I let him touch me, and now here we are. No matter how hard I try, I can't hate the tender way he pets me. As though I'm worth all this attention, as if he doesn't see my neediness as a turnoff.

But what now? I shouldn't have let this happen. I should have told him off for touching me, and I sure as hell should not have started jerking off with him next to me. What the hell is wrong with me?

"I—maybe being sleepy got to both our heads," I respond with a weak laugh, but I can't deny that I enjoy his touch all over me and knowing that he's now marked me with his scent. And yes, I'm still slightly turned on by lying under him with my pants down.

"Oh, I've never been more awake, sweetie. But let me know what you need. Snacks? Shower? Back to sleep?"

I don't know how to feel when he calls me that. Like I'm already his, like he knows my hard outer shell is just that. Because yeah, it is nice to be someone's *sweetie*. No one's ever called me by a pet name, and I didn't know how much my body needed it until now.

The soft tone of his voice is like a caress, and I arch closer, only satisfied when my nape is tucked against his warm flesh. I should say shower, because I am sticky, and tidy people wash up after having sex, but that is the *last* thing I want, closely followed by a conversation I'm not ready to have. So it's a *no* to snacks as well.

"I... I think we should just try to sleep."

Nico turns to his side, but pulls me with him, wrapping his arms around me as if I'm his personal teddy bear. My pants are down, and he's not bothering to pull up his underwear, so I have a sneaky suspicion that if no one comes to save me tonight, I'll be getting sticky with more cum first thing in the morning.

...Which is not a bad prospect?

"Are you my boyfriend yet?" Nico asks, nuzzling the back of my head and leaving me speechless.

My breath comes out as a whine, which is a level of embarrassment I can't take, but before I need to declare my intentions, something stomps on the roof above us, and we both still.

"Santa?" Nico utters, and I imagine the stars in his eyes despite knowing that it's definitely *not* Santa.

Chapter 14

Nico

A SHADOW OBSCURES THE sky, briefly watching us through the window in the sloped ceiling above, but then glass breaks, and the mysterious figure descends on us in a hail of transparent shards. I pull Blake close, to protect him from the glass, but when a serrated dagger flashes in the faint glow of my electronic clock, my lizard brain takes over.

Big, green eyes stare at me in panic. Blake stumbles off the mattress on wobbly legs, like a lamb that's never seen a wolf before. The heavy man in black, smelling of leather and oranges, reaches for him instead of focusing on me like I expected him to.

I don't have time to consider why he's here. But I know knives, and the blade in his hand is sharp enough to cut halfway through a man's neck in one go. I jump off the bed, standing between the attacker and Blake, and turn my back on the bastard to avoid getting stabbed in the guts.

Pain rips through my back as my flesh opens up, spilling blood, but I slam my elbow into his arm, already turning, and the fucker drops the knife, stumbling back.

He's not getting Blake unless he pries him out of my death-stiffened hands.

A split-second decision makes me reach for the knife, but I realize how wrong that is when a garotte tightens around my neck and yanks me back.

The thin metal thread sinks into my flesh, so deep I can't loosen it with my fingers, and when I find myself unable to breathe and my mind goes fuzzy, panic sets in. I sink my nails into the thick hand tightening the wire around my throat, but it doesn't budge. When the stocky form of my opponent lays its weight on me, I attempt to break his ribs with my elbow. The down jacket he's wearing softens my blows. As the garrotte tightens, darkening the edges of my vision, I struggle to come up with ways to free myself. I'm like a seal caught between a killer whale's teeth, and unless some miracle—

A loud *thud* is followed by the thug's grunt. The encroaching darkness retreats as the wire loosens. Blake emerges from the black spots dancing in my eyes. He pulls up his pants, panting, eyes wide with terror, and the large wooden Santa gnome I painted last year trembles in his hand.

I want to tell him he did good, but there's no time for praise yet.

The assassin is dazed but already tries getting up from the bed where he fell. I grab the comforter and pull, dragging him off with it. Blood drums in my head, pain in my back radiating all the way to my fingers, but I don't let go of the fabric and pull again. He rolls off the comforter and to the floor like a toy. I finally have the upper hand. I drop the cover on him and descend on top while he's blinded.

I don't know how he found out where Blake was, but this is clearly yet another assassin out to extinguish his life, and that is not going to happen on my watch. The bastard twists under me, and I lift my body in the last moment when a dagger pierces the comforter, emerging in an explosion of down. I go rigid as I attempt to block his arm with my knee without giving his lower body too much wiggle room. The dagger punches through the layers of fabric and duck feathers again. I'm in a daze and slam my fist into the bastard's head over and over, determined to protect Blake from this monster. I might have delivered more blows than was strictly necessary by the time it becomes clear my opponent has gone limp.

I'm breathing hard, but there's no time to lose in case he's not dead. I actually hope he's not, because this fucker might have the information I need.

Blake is still holding the wooden statue and stares at me with raw fear in those green eyes. "I have a box of fairy lights in the living room. Behind the sofa. Bring them."

"Wh-what?" he utters.

I grin when I sense movement under me. "They're cables. To tie him."

Blake gives me a frantic nod and makes a step toward the door, only to stop with a little whine. I don't know what this is about until he switches on the light, revealing the glass scattered everywhere. He twists his leg to pull a shard from the heel of his foot.

Our eyes meet, and he places the figure back on my nightstand. "I'll... get shoes too," he says as he takes a long stride and exits the room.

"Be careful," I add, but soon enough, he's back with both slippers and the cable.

I'm just glad the assassin is still dazed as fuck, because he's like a puppet in my grip when I tie his arms and legs, then attach the ties to the footboard of the bed for good measure.

I slap his face several times. "Wakey wakey, fucker." But then I look up at Blake as I grab one of the knives. "I need to find out who sent him. You... might want to wait in the living room for this."

He's pale, and his skin glistens with sweat, but despite glancing to the door, his feet remain firmly on the floor. I know he made up his mind when that green gaze hardens. "No. I need to know."

He doesn't specify what he wants to learn, but I don't question it. The assassin must have come for him, and he deserves to find out why.

I'm about to slap my prisoner awake when gentle fingers trace my back.

"He cut you," Blake utters. "Where's your—"

"It can wait," I tell him, because it's only a superficial injury.

The assassin opens his bloodshot eyes, his head still lolling from side to side, and I grab his jaw so he looks at me.

"Fuck you," is all he has for me to start with, so I punch him in the stomach, and that snaps him to attention.

"We're not calling the cops until you tell us who sent you." We're not calling the cops either way, but he doesn't need to know that just yet.

He frowns through the pain and spits some blood my way as he speaks. "Sent me? What the hell are you talking about?"

I punch him square in the face so hard the back of his head thuds against my footboard. I already detest the future clean-up, especially so late at night, and in my private, murder-free space at that!

I can sense Blake's presence behind me, but he remains quiet, letting me work. I kinda like him watching me when I'm in my element.

I cock my head at the man in front of me, then grab his hand with mock-concern. He looks average. Brown hair, crooked nose, flat, forgettable face. The perfect features for an assassin. "Oh, so you came here with all these knives and a garotte out of your own volition. Just a random little murder spree?"

"What else would it be?" the bastard asks, but his words turn into a choked scream when I snap his finger and twist it out of the socket at the knuckle.

"Tsk, tsk, tsk. It's very naughty to lie," I tell him as his brown gaze zeroes in on me. He doesn't know *me*, but he knows my type, and he's getting scared, because where he expected a regular civilian he found a worthy opponent.

"You ex-military, or something?" he asks, only to cry out as I snap the next finger.

"Answer me."

"Pay me," he says with a bloodstained grin, but he can't sustain the fake tough guy act when I break the next finger.

"I don't think you understand the position you're in. I'm not bargaining with you. If you give me the answer promptly, I might let you live. That's the only the deal you're getting."

"Fuck you, asshole! You're just collateral damage anyway."

I squint at him but extend my hand to Blake without even glancing his way. "Give me the knife, sweetie. The big one," I specify because I took two more off this bastard when I restrained him.

Blake hands me the dagger without a word, and our prisoner glances at him over my shoulder, shaking from the pain. "What is it to you?"

"He's my boyfriend, so if you came here to kill him, it is my fucking business! How did you know where he was?"

When he starts laughing, I'm done playing nice. I grab his nose and start sawing from the nostrils up. The chuckle dies on his lips and turns into a scream before I even get through half of it. Once I'm done, I throw the piece of flesh in his lap as he pants, bleeding all over the bottom of his face.

"You fucking psycho!" When he looks over my shoulder, straight at Blake, I consider taking his eyes next. He struggles to breathe, but his gaze is overflowing with wrath. "Your *boyfriend* called his brother to get out of here, so I don't think he loves you very much. Too bad his brother wants him dea—"

My stomach's plummeting by the time Blake appears right next to me. He yells something I can't decipher through the thudding in my ears, and then sinks another of the assassin's knives in his neck. When he rips it out, along with a flood of blood, it's over.

"Oh God... oh God..." Blake utters as the dagger drops from his hands. He covers his face, only to realize they're stained with blood, and promptly pulls off his top to clean himself.

Which makes me wonder if his goal is to show off his lovely body to manipulate me further. My blood is so cold I can't seem to move and all of a sudden the pain between my shoulder blades comes back in full force, like a physical manifestation of the ache in my heart.

I get up, feeling like fury personified. "You did *what*?" I roar at him and spread my arms.

Blake steps back and hits the wall, his big eyes filled with fake innocence. "I— this must be a lie. Carl would never—"

"That's why you were so desperate to silence the fucker, you actually stabbed him? What else are you not telling me, huh?" I make sure to stand between him and the door, in case he wants to run. The betrayal hurts more than any physical cut could. We had the *best* day. I opened up to him. I showed him my craft room! Was he just pretending to like it and biding his time to escape?

"He came here to kill us," Blake mumbles, hugging the bloodstained T-shirt.

"I told you I'd protect you, and you brought danger to my home! Look into my eyes and tell me you didn't call your brother."

Blake swallows and looks at the glass scattered over the floor as his chest sinks in defeat. He knows he's been caught, and there's no weaseling out of it now. Still, he tries.

"There were cops at the market. I could have gone to them, but I didn't, because I didn't want you to get in trouble. I just wanted to go home, so I called my brother. I thought he'd come and get me, or send someone, or... something."

I shake my head and stretch my back, because at this point, the pain is a welcome distraction from the turmoil in my head. "And here we are. He sure sent someone. I told you it wasn't safe, and you just wouldn't listen."

Blake takes in a shivery breath, and his eyes start glossing over. *Now* he's sad. Too bad he didn't feel that way before fucking me over.

"I didn't think Carl would—I couldn't have known... We're brothers. He practically raised me."

"And yet he *did*! At least now we know," I grumble, because seeing him so distraught brings me no pleasure. "He now knows where we are, so we need to leave, *and* I have a body to deal with."

Tears spill down Blake's cheeks, and his shoulders jitter as he hugs himself, lost in self-pity. Boo-fucking-hoo.

"What did you tell your brother, huh? Did you want me gone?"

Green eyes meet mine, and he shakes his head. "What? No! I was just scared, because just last night, you literally cuffed me to the bed. I don't know you well. What would you have done in my place?" he asks and rubs his skin as the temperature in the room drops further.

It's a bitter pill to swallow, but I just shake my head, because I can't bear watching him cry. "Will you listen to me now?" I grab a fluffy blanket off the bed and drape it over his shoulders.

Blake nods.

As the adrenaline dissipates, I get cold too, but I have to deal with my back first, so I send him for the first aid kit and sit on the bed, staring at all the mess I'll have to clean up. The assassin's blood has soaked into the comforter, and he's now a grayish-purple. I hate the fact that nothing about this can wait if I am to get the window replaced.

What a fucking nightmare. And during the Christmas season at that!

Now I wonder whether I should have kept Blake in the cage after all. He would have eventually come around.

But then we couldn't have had a lovely time ice skating. Relationships are hard.

Blake returns with the metal box containing bandages and all the other stuff I occasionally need to patch myself up, and he sits behind me. We're so quiet I can hear him breathing.

"So... how do I do this?" he asks.

I instruct him through the wound-cleaning process and treat the pain as my punishment for trying to steal myself a boyfriend. Only when the needle starts piercing my skin, and I do need a few stitches going by the photo he took for me, can I focus again on the situation we're in.

"What did you tell your brother about me? Should I expect a police raid soon?" I ask bitterly.

He sniffs, and I hate myself for being the cause of his tears, even though it's him who's betrayed *me*, not the other way around. I guess I just never was as sensitive as him, even as a child, so I might have to adjust to what a *normal* person would feel, especially when out of their depth.

"Um... just that you're obsessive, and that I went home with you, and you're not letting me go. And that if I'm not upstairs, I might be in a cage in the basement," I mumble. "But if he wants to get rid of me, he's not going to involve the police."

True. "I'm not 'obsessive'," I grumble even though he might have a point.

Silence, and then, "seriously? You barely know me and already act like we're a couple!" he says before adding another stitch.

I want to believe he's being as gentle as he can, but it's hard when I get such harsh words thrown in my face. "Because I know you're a good fit for me. You said my snow globes were amazing, and then you grinded against me in bed like I was your sex toy."

Blake inhales, and drops the needle, letting it hang against my skin. "I 'grinded against' you? I woke up with your boner pressed to my ass!"

I groan at that happy memory. "Can happen to anyone."

"Yes, so don't twist it like I was molesting you. You wouldn't let me go, so I wanted to deal with my problem and go back to sleep. But no, you just had to make a whole thing of it, and now you're telling me I started it?"

So he's backing out. After such a glorious romp. After he spread his legs for me and moaned. He's deep in denial if he believes he doesn't desire me back. But I have more pressing matters to deal with.

"Why did you stop stitching?"

"Because I'm angry with you and I don't want to make it worse just because I'm agitated." He sighs, and just as I'm about to look back, I sense his hair against my shoulder. "I was so scared."

"So... you *don't* want me hurt?" My question's a little needy, but my back is tender and so is my heart.

I feel him shake his head, and his warm hand squeezes my forearm. "No. I just... don't know what to believe anymore."

"Well, you sure can't believe your fucking brother." I have to take a deep breath, because I know I'm being too harsh on this boy who's never known violence. "Do you have any idea why he wants you dead?"

"No. He always took good care of me. I just don't understand. What did I ever do to him?" Blake asks, sending hot air against my flesh. "It makes no sense. But... if he did order the hit, then I need to know."

"Do you know where he is?" So I can stick a knife through his fucking eye, but I leave that bit out, because he's still confused and might not like to hear that his brother has it coming.

Blake rests his forehead against me, and his arms briefly tighten around me. But then they're gone, and he grabs the needle.

"I have an idea how to locate him."

CHAPTER 15

BLAKE

I SPENT TWO HOURS on my knees. And not in the way I'd want to.

By the time I managed to get the blood off any surfaces it needed to disappear from, the room was painfully cold and smelled of bleach. I was like Cinderella with the cramps in my freezing hands. Nico boarded the window up, and we stowed the assassin's body in a freezer in the secret basement. By the time the sun came up, I was dozing in Nico's car while we sped toward Toronto, to meet the hacker who earlier helped me break into the FBI database.

How the hell has my life devolved into this *Pulp Fiction* fuckery? Just a few days ago, I was a teenager living a comfortable, if boring, existence in a huge house surrounded by a park. I've since been abducted twice, and had not one but two men try to murder me. And, apparently, my own brother is behind all this.

How come a serial killer has become my only ally?

Nico's not dressed in any ugly Christmas sweater and looks more serious than ever. His dark blond hair is tied back, his eyes focused on the road, since it's snowing, and a black scarf covers his lower face.

We both had a thorough wash after the cleanup, so he also smells good, teasing me with his scent even though he was the one to propose we shower separately since he still had work to do at the time. I should appreciate that, yet all I feel is regret that I didn't get to see him naked. Maybe at this point he's become my emotional support serial killer, and that's why I don't feel safe unless I'm hugging him?

The moment I stabbed the assassin's neck keeps replaying in my mind, and each time, more gory detail is added. It was necessary, and if I hadn't, Nico would have killed him anyway. But the fact that he wouldn't have appeared if it wasn't for my actions weighs heavily on my heart. The scent of blood still clings to me even after thirty minutes in the shower, and as I watch the road, the plunging noise the knife made is a constant echo in my ears.

I don't think I'll ever be the same after this.

Nico packed some basics for both of us, including that repulsive knitted Christmas sweater. When I complained about it, he bristled up and said it was warm, so I gave up. It wasn't worth fighting over when I get to sit in the car in my warm woolen coat anyway.

There's a wall between us despite him being in the market for my brother's head. He seems unable to understand just how confusing the situation is for me.

For him, my decision to contact Carl was a betrayal, but it made sense to me at the time to seek help, because—*hello*—he's someone who's murdered many people. That's bound to cause trust issues.

So why do I feel so guilty about it all? Is it because Nico got injured while covering me with his own body? I told him I don't know him well, but *he* was willing to put his life on the line for me, something no one else would have done. I didn't ask for any of this. Not to be abducted, not to need saving, and not for his dick against my ass.

And yet here I am, in his car, sulking that he hasn't called me sweetie once since the whole assassin drama. But he does have all the niceties in the world for *Owen*, whose voice I'm beginning to despise through no fault of his own.

"Sure, no problem, I'll get it done. You know I'm fast. If push comes to shove, the temps are always happy to do some overtime," he says cheerfully as Nico chuckles.

"I promise this won't encroach on your holidays with Adam. I'll be back in a couple of days tops."

"A spontaneous winter getaway. How romantic," Owen says, happy for a relationship Nico and I don't actually have.

I find myself annoyed by the confusing emotions this whole situation is stirring in me. Sure, he blew my mind in bed, causing me to temporarily forget I wasn't supposed to mess around with him, but that doesn't mean I want him to be my *boyfriend*...or do I?

He's not even touched my thigh since we got into this car three hours ago. Do I want Nico, the Christmas Killer, or do I just crave to be desired, and he's simply the only one who's given me a taste of how that feels?

I don't have the answer, but I sure as hell ogle his muscular thighs, which are hugged by a pair of jeans.

Should I make a move? And if I do, then what? I can't blow him while he's driving. What if I'm bad at it? Or so *good* at it, that he loses control of the car? Or if there's a bump in the road, his cock accidentally lodges itself in my throat, and we have to go to the hospital, and then I'd forever be that guy on the news who had to have throat surgery because of sucking dick in a moving car?

"What can I say? He's making me lose my head a little," Nico chuckles, but won't even look my way. Which shouldn't feel hurtful but does.

"Well, have fun you two, I have a customer," Owen tells us and breaks off the connection, once again leaving us in a limbo of silence.

My stomach chooses this moment to grumble, and I cross my legs to do something, anything, with my limbs, because at this point I don't know what I want anymore.

"You and him... you ever—"

Nico frowns. "Any reason you're asking, or is this your idea of small talk?"

I look out at the snow-covered trees, air stuck in my windpipe as I sense his gaze on my body. I despise the fact that his attention makes me so content. "You're very friendly."

"We jerked each other off once. It made things awkward, so we agreed to be just friends after that."

It's as if he's set off several bombs in my head at once. Bomb one—jealousy over Owen. Ridiculous, I know, but it would be even dumber to deny that's what I'm feeling. Bomb two—his capacity to be *just friends* with a guy he was intimate with. Bomb three—awkwardness after a one-time fling leading to the friendship.

Bomb three is somehow most alarming, because... are *we* being awkward now? Are we on the trajectory of fuck-to-awkward-to-friends? And if I never wanted to be his boyfriend, why does this bother me like an itch I can't scratch? Wouldn't it be for the better if we decided to forgo any sexual tension between us?

Can I pretend I didn't come when he rutted against me? That I didn't moan and thrash when the Christmas Killer was on top of me? That I don't long for his touch every minute since that very first kiss?

I don't know if this is Stockholm Syndrome, or if there's something very wrong with me, but denying that I have these feelings seems as futile as sending a letter to Santa without a stamp.

Nico turns into a road headed for a strip mall with some shops and a supermarket. "I want to buy us provisions in case we need to stay put somewhere."

"We'll be in Toronto. I'm sure they have shops there," I say, even though my stomach's demanding food.

Nico sighs. "You can wait in the car if you want," he tells me. He knows I won't run from him anymore, not after what happened last night, and I hate what it's done to this strange thing blooming between us.

"No. I'll go with you."

He frowns as he drives into the parking lot. "I can leave the heating on."

Like this is about the fucking heating!

I grab his wrist and hold it, instantly calmer yet at the same time self-conscious about touching him. Why can't I be normal?

His eyebrows rise, but he has to look back to the road as he's parking, and now I'm jealous even of the damn asphalt. "You want to... choose your own produce?" he tries, and the way he keeps his distance from me is making me want to scream. It's too late. He should have kept his hands to himself when I wanted him to. Now, after we kissed, had sex, after yesterday's date and him protecting me with his own body, how dare he be so cold?

I want him to *see* me again. To care for me again, and what better way to do that than by showing some Christmas spirit? "I want to bake you a cake."

I've never baked in my life, but how hard can it be?

Nico stops the car and cocks his head at me. Whenever he does that, I'm always reminded of the first time I saw him. In the black balaclava with ears, dragging a body down a flight of stairs. I got his unwanted attention when I gagged, and he turned to me, cocking his head like a wolf smelling prey.

It shouldn't excite me, but it does.

"A cake? Okay," he says, but squints at me. I'm guessing my request is so out in left field he's doubting my good intentions. Still, he gets out of the car and waits for me.

"What do you like? Gingerbread? Fruitcake?" I ask, adjusting my coat as I join him in the cold, and we both walk toward the supermarket.

Nico puts on a big aviator hat lined with fur, and that, paired with the red plaid jacket makes him look so hot I'm tempted to slide my hand into his pocket. If only I wasn't so unsure about where we stand.

My heart skips a beat when he gives me a soft smile. "I do love a fruitcake. Infused with lots of rum."

"Okay, then we need flour, and eggs, and sugar, and some dried fruit," I recite before licking my lips. I do like his smile. "I'll check the ingredients online, so we don't forget anything." Then I realize I don't have my phone and I still, worried I've just made things *even more* awkward.

Nico hesitates, but after grabbing a shopping cart he unlocks his phone and hands it to me. It's either trust or a test.

"When we went to the cookie decorating workshop, you said you never baked anything," he says and I'm torn between being happy that he listened to me so carefully and annoyed about it.

I look up, glad to be in a more bearable temperature. "Well, yes, but it can't be that hard. People do it all the time."

We start making our way through the store and I'm glad there aren't many people around, because I'm paranoid that anyone could be an assassin and pull out a knife on me. For all I know, even the old lady with her dog paw print handbag reading *Stay Pawtastic* could be a killer in disguise, so I stick close to Nico as he picks up some essentials.

"Has anything... prompted this idea?" he asks with a smirk that melts me a little.

I swallow, walking the long aisle that has all kinds of baking and dessert products. I'm a bit confused by the look of this place, with its old tiles and pipes hanging over our heads. There's even a spot where one leaks, and a bucket is gathering the drips in the middle of the floor, surrounded by a barrier of plastic cones and tape. A fishy odor comes from one of the fridges, and my chef often told me to never eat at a restaurant that smells like this. But we're here to buy provisions, not raw meat, so we should be safe from the possibility of food poisoning.

"I feel bad about... tattling on you to my brother."

Nico stops with me and stretches, which only makes him appear taller. "I appreciate that and hope there's more trust between us now." He appears so wholesome with the hat, the strands of blond hair peeking out, his knock-off Timberland boots, but his blue eyes, while intoxicating, tell the true story of what a predator he is. I wouldn't have been able to tell if I didn't know that he's a killer, but I sense it now. A cold calculation combined with desire that makes me feel naked despite the layers of clothes.

A shiver makes its way down my spine, like a drop of hot oil about to make me sizzle. Now that his attention is back on me, I'm again torn between apprehension and pleasure. "I would like to think so…" I say before grabbing one of the many boxes. "White cake mix? Is that a type of flour?"

Nico hums. "Hm… no, it's mix. It has most of the ingredients in there and it tells you one or two that you need to buy. Have you ever done *any* cooking?"

I clear my throat, feeling exposed in ways I don't wish to be. "A little. Supervised. I do make my own sandwiches. I like the bread crispy. I just don't usually do the shopping, so I'm not sure…" I drift off, feeling like a spoiled idiot.

"So who did the shopping? Your brother?"

I'm not sure if I should be honest, but he's looked into me already and knows what kind of family I come from, so I settle on, "the housekeeper, or the chef."

"You'd never go with them? You weren't curious?" he asks, but there's no judgment in his voice.

"The housekeeper would usually order a delivery, and the chef would shop on the way. It just wouldn't be very practical," I admit, unsure what to do about the cake now that the extent of my ignorance is obvious. "I would sometimes ask someone to drive me into town, but I'd never really get groceries there. I… liked being around people, but I'm not good at befriending them, so I never got to bake for anyone before."

"Why do you think you're not good at making friends? You always sounded pretty charming on the podcast," Nico says and places a hand on my shoulder, causing a release of endorphins that makes me feel like I'm floating.

He's the only one I have now. My brother wants me dead, the staff at home might be in on it, and Nico was the one to put himself between me and an armed man who broke into our bedroom at night.

I suddenly want to kiss him so bad.

"It's easy to sound entertaining when you can switch off the mic or edit the recording. But I don't know how to talk to people. I've been homeschooled since I was twelve, and I didn't really have many playmates since then. Other than my dog, but he died last year," I add bitterly. "I've been so lonely. It's why I went to the nightclub. I was just trying... trying to..."

"Oh, Blake, I'm so sorry," Nico pulls me into a warm hug.

It's so sudden it feels like sensory overload, and I'm reminded just how under-hugged I am. He strokes my back, and I melt into him. In the baking aisle. Under the leaking pipe.

A lady passing us with her shopping clears her throat, but when I want to pull away, Nico keeps me close.

"His dog died! Have some compassion," he snarls at the woman.

"Oh, I'm sorry, I—"

"Do we look like we need the pity of a stranger?" Nico asks, and I snort against his fragrant sweater, pushing my nose between the folds of knitted fabric, so very at peace.

So very safe.

Now that I inherited half of my family fort—

My blood runs cold as reality slowly sinks in, and I stutter. "N-nico? I think I know why he did it."

"Hm?" Nico pulls away enough to look into my eyes, and I shake my head as the world around me crumbles.

"He's doing it for the money. He doesn't want me to inherit my half of the fortune now that I'm a legal adult.

He… wants it more than he wants me," I rasp, hypnotized by Nico's blue gaze.

"Oh no… Is it a lot?" Nico asks and I'm relieved we're alone in the aisle now as he strokes my back.

I nod, though I don't know how much money I'm supposed to receive exactly, since Carl has dealt with all our finances since I can remember. "But I'm his little brother. How could he… he's still gonna have his portion, and that's *millions*. He'll still be free to pursue whatever he wants."

Nico takes a deep breath, processing all of that. "I'm sorry, Blake. For some people there is no 'enough'. And… from what you were saying, he wasn't exactly brother of the year. Now it makes sense that he got you the ID. He encouraged you to go to the place where you were abducted."

I hide.

My hands rise, covering my face as tears fill my eyes and drizzle down my cheeks. Not only did he not care for me, but he's actively tried to get me killed.

I can't believe it.

"It was all a trap. I thought he wanted to help me get out of my shell…"

Nico pulls me close again and strokes the back of my head. What does it say about my life that I'm getting more affection from a serial killer than I ever did from my brother?

"Sweetie… He'll get what's coming. I promise. And I'll keep you safe through it. *And* we'll make the cake together." Nico kisses the side of my head, and it makes me a bawling mess, because he's here, protecting and helping me, even though I've betrayed his trust and caused him so many other problems. Any other killer would have disposed of a witness immediately, but not him. He chose to not only spare me but treat me as someone special. I don't deserve it. And he called me 'sweetie' again. I'm so relieved I could cry over that too.

"Thank you... I want to make the cake nice," I sob, utterly pathetic. It's almost too much to take.

But for once, I don't feel alone with my feelings.

"It will be. Come on, let's choose one," Nico says with a smile and encourages me to browse the shelves, but then his phone beeps, and he pulls it out of my pocket. His expression turns serious, and he shows me the screen. "It's the hacker. Your password."

My heart rattles, but at least my attention is diverted. As soon as I put in the agreed-upon code, the next message appears.

[He's in Aspen.]

Nico reads over my shoulder. "So I guess there's no point in meeting the hacker in person after all?"

I shake my head as anger rises in my throat. "But if he's in Aspen... he'll probably only visit me after Christmas," I mumble and meet his gaze, greedy for a solution. Because I don't know what to do.

Nico kisses the side of my head. "Okay. More time to make cake then. We'll prepare, and I know exactly where to go so you're safe in the meanwhile."

A flash of panic goes through me, and I grab his forearm. "Don't leave me!"

Nico stares at me. "Together, sweetie. We'll go together."

My worries disperse like snowflakes in a puddle. I squeeze his arm, then look to either side of the aisle, and when I see we're still alone, I lean into another hug.

Maybe things will be all right after all.

Chapter 16

Nico

I HAVE MANY FOND memories from my grandpa's cabin. Learning to hunt, knit, make simple meals over the fire. Even hard days of training when he put me through my paces ended up feeling rewarding when he praised me for my endurance. He knew that if I were to succeed at becoming the next Christmas Killer and remain anonymous, I needed to be disciplined, strong, smart, and decisive. And then, if all else failed, the survival skills he taught me were supposed to save me if I needed to go off-grid.

The cabin is where we brought the decapitated body of my first kill. It's hard to imagine only seven years have passed since that cold evening. Some days it feels as if it were yesterday, while at other times, I don't know where the years have gone. I was so excited that night I almost left behind a glove, but Grandpa was there to pick it up.

I miss him.

My grandpa's old cabin isn't all that far from my home-town, but we'd originally headed in a different direction, so between the snow and the narrow roads, it took an-other few hours to reach it. But once the atmosphere between Blake and me cleared, the drive passed with silly games, trying to find a Christmas song Blake likes (yet to be determined) and easy conversation. I'm still upset over his betrayal, but I've found it in my heart to forgive him. Now that we've learned about his brother's intentions, he seems more inclined to put his trust in me, the one man ready to be there for him.

He opened up about how he was raised, and how his brother resented him even before their parents died. Carl is fifteen years older than Blake, and in hindsight, Blake can see that his brother's jealousy has never extin-guished. He just learned to hide it better, and since kind words and gifts kept coming, Blake attached himself to his only remaining family member and was unable to view their relationship critically.

That's now over, and as he reminisced about his life, I could see his facade crack whenever we returned to his brother in one way or another. He even recalled a conversation from a few months ago which now seems so ominous.

His brother took him out to the movies, and treated him to dinner after, which was unusual in itself, but Blake was just happy to hear about Carl's escapades in the Maldives. At the restaurant, Carl nonchalantly mentioned Blake's inheritance, and suggested that maybe nothing would need to change once Blake came of age. In that scenario, Carl would remain in control of both their mon-ey and continue managing all of Blake's finances. When Blake pushed back against that idea, they had what felt like a minor disagreement at the time, and the topic never came up again. But in light of the facts we've dis-covered, Blake's wondering if that evening wasn't the trigger for Carl's plan.

If Blake had died before his eighteenth birthday, his inheritance would have gone to charity. But now that he's stepped into adulthood, the money will be Carl's in the event of his brother's death. How awfully convenient.

And if he died as a result of hooking up with a stranger, their departure captured by cameras inside a gay club, who would have suspected the caring big brother of foul play?

Things like that happened to sheltered gay boys sometimes.

But as we talked, it became clear that Blake really didn't spend that much time in Carl's company. The gifts he received were expensive but rarely tailored to Blake's taste or needs—empty tokens given out of obligation rather than love.

His life sounds very lonely, with only a couple of adults who were paid to keep him safe and content. He had an imaginary friend for way longer than what could be considered normal childhood development, and he would sometimes sink into books for days at a time, consuming one, or even two within a period of twenty-four hours. He used to go on long walks around the property surrounding his house and imag-ine exciting events happening to a different version of him, a version surrounded by companions straight out of Blake's favorite shows and novels.

It sounds like a very empty existence, which ex-plains his desperation to put himself out there during his first-ever time at a nightclub. Be seen. Be noticed. Actually feel someone's hands on his skin.

But now he has me, and I'll give him all the attention he could ever dream of.

My car can deal with the snow-covered road just fine, and as we drive past the old tree that serves as a marker on the road to the cabin, I'm hit by a flood of memories of all the days I spent here with the only other person who knew the real me.

It's so fitting that I introduce Blake to this side of my life.

As the wall of evergreen firs and pines thins, revealing the clearing around the little wooden building, I realize this is the first time I've been here since the summer, and that it looks lonely and cold in the light of dusk.

I imagined this would be a fun trip down memory lane and an introduction to another part of me. Instead, it could have played the role of a murder cabin. Which it kinda is. But I don't want Blake to start overthinking it, so I force myself to smile and stop the car.

"And here we are! Our little safe haven," I say, feeling unconvinced myself when I spot a raccoon jumping out of the window and skittering away. Can't believe those little fuckers got in again!

Blake stretches and opens the door, his green eyes taking in the dull, undecorated building that's surely as cold as a freezer. "Well, there's no way they're gonna track us down *here*," he says, sliding into the snow reaching almost to his knees.

I get out quickly, not even sure where to start. I've been here in the winter many times, but by myself or with Grandpa, I didn't have to worry about impressing anyone.

"Very few people know about the existence of this cabin. Even Owen doesn't because I didn't want to risk him asking if he could use it for a romantic getaway, or something." I approach Blake and pick him up so he doesn't have to wade through the snow. "We'll be nice and cozy as soon as I get the fire going."

Blake yelps and wraps his arms around my neck. He's tense, but as I make my way to the porch of my second home, he leans ever closer, melting against me.

"You're really strong," he mutters, resting his head on my shoulder in a way that lights fires deep in my chest.

"This reminds me of the first body I ever brought here." I sigh as I set him down on the porch. Thanks to the roofing over it, the snow isn't so deep here. "It was winter back then too. And even without a head, it was heavier than you."

Blake stares at me and releases a nervous laugh. "Are you saying I'm too thin?"

"Or maybe I'm just that much stronger than I used to be." I nudge his chin. I want to kiss him, but I'm not sure where we stand after the whole assassin fiasco. He threw me under the bus with that one. Then again, we did hug at the supermarket, and that didn't feel like a gesture between two *friends*, so maybe that nosy lady was on to something. I could, of course, try to make my move and risk getting rejected. It wouldn't be a big deal with anyone else, but I feel so tender about Blake and our budding love story that I'm too nervous to act. This is my opportunity to show him the real me, and I don't want to waste it.

I open the door, and while the house doesn't smell, which is a relief, the main room is messy, dusty, and cold. It's the opposite of Christmas at a time when I want to teach Blake about holiday joy.

"Make yourself comfortable. This place will be homey in no time," I say before dashing outside. Getting firewood is my priority, because the house is a walk-in freezer.

I'm well-versed in getting this place warm, and once the fire is going in both the main fireplace and the burner in the bedroom, I take a moment to assess damage. Fortunately, the cabin is small enough to heat up quickly. The pest came in through a broken window, which I block with a few planks and some paper. It did get into the pantry and broke a few jars, but I can't see any other issues.

Soon enough, our breaths stop creating vapor, but the cabin remains gray as mud.

Blake pulls a chair close to the fire and sits down, watching me work. "Do you come here often?"

"Are you flirting?" I wink at him as I clear the surfaces. This is a disaster. At least I know the bedding is clean and dry. As soon as the bedroom is warm, it'll be ready for us to enjoy a cuddle. "I'm sorry it's such a mess. I don't usually have guests here. The last time I wasn't alone here was with my grandpa four years ago."

Blake's face darkens, and he pulls up his hood, watching me from its shadow. "No, I get it, my brother always has someone prepare our other properties before he actually goes there." He clears his throat as I watch him, struck by the level of wealth we're talking about. *Other properties?* As in more than one? Blake must think I brought him to an absolute dump.

I wrestle my thoughts, wondering how to answer when he speaks again. "You must miss your grandfather. As family but also, you know, as someone who supported you when it comes to—"

Killing. That part of the sentence is silent.

I throw another piece of wood into the fireplace, taking my time with the answer since I wasn't expecting the turmoil in my heart. "I do. But he was so much older, he knew I'd need to be able to deal with his death sooner or later, so he talked to me about it, prepared me for it. For the responsibility of running the shop, for keeping my... *needs* met and secret. And even encouraged me to date. He was sweet like that. But he drilled into me that I can't tell anyone what I do in my spare time. And that's a loneliness I wasn't prepared for."

I've already switched on the generator, which allows us both to see just how thick the layers of dust are on every single surface. Blake swallows as he watches me clean, and I can't help but feel self-conscious about being judged by this pampered boy, who likely didn't have to clean his room once in his entire life.

"I think I get it. There's a difference between understanding things intellectually and actually living with the feeling," he says softly.

I go to the pantry to grab a can of tomato sauce, so I can make us pasta, but the food here won't be as good as what I was able to treat him to at my place.

I glance at his pretty face. He's young, but has strong brows, and his jaw is already quite angular. It's his eyes though that always draw me in, so inquisitive as they follow me through the room. I want to keep him so badly.

"Why did you choose to run your podcast anonymously? Didn't you want to be known? Unlike me, your calling isn't illegal."

Blake shrugs and reaches out for the fire, as if he wants to grab the flames in his beautiful fingers. "Carl thought it might put a target on my back and draw in the wrong kind of people. I mean, even *you* are a fan," he adds with a faint grin and looks up at the shadows on the ceiling, where I'm disgusted to see a whole tapestry of spiderwebs. If I were here alone, I wouldn't have even noticed, but I want him to have a good time in conditions that are appropriate to the season. And Halloween was a long time ago.

"This place reminds me of my treehouse. It had a roof just like this, with beams. I would dry plants by hanging them off there."

I'm so greedy for any little scrap of new information about him. "I hope that's a positive comparison? I'll make this place much more festive soon, I promise. I packed some Christmas lights, and we can dry orange slices."

I decide to sweep the floor before doing any cooking, even though this cabin is more of a hunter's mancave than the setting for a romantic escape. I don't know why I remembered it as much cozier, because it's clearly beneath Blake's standards.

My guest nods and leans back in the armchair, wiggling his feet over the floor. He's biting his plump lip in a way that has my dirty mind stirring, but he's clearly not in the mood, so I focus on my work.

"Maybe it's not worth all this effort?" Blake asks, freezing me to the floor. "We could just follow him to Aspen, have the Christmas Killer be a guest star of the serial murder scene there."

I still, but my mind is racing. He hates it here. He wants out and once I get rid of his brother, he'll be safe to untangle himself from me and my ugly dark cabin, the Christmas shop he hates, and my greedy hands.

I'm not letting that happen.

I shake my head, sweeping with more fervor. "We can't do that yet. It will be much safer to end him when he's back in a place I'm familiar with. And I'd like to prepare. I have satellite internet here so I can do some digging. That assassin he hired was no amateur. I need to know what I'm up against."

Blake lowers his gaze, and his hand tightens on the armrest of the chair as he stares into the fire, likely desperate to convince me that we can't stay here. "But that's also giving them time to track *us* down, and Carl has all the resources."

I put the kettle on the stove, hoping hot chocolate will soothe his fears. "It's been snowing, and I cover my tracks when using the internet or phone. We'll be safe here." I walk up to him and stroke his hair. "You are safe here."

"I'm kinda putting my chances of leaving this place alive at seventy percent," he tells me and follows that with a hollow laugh.

My heart drops. "You don't trust me?"

Blake shoots to his feet. "I didn't say that."

I take off my hat and throw it to the other armchair. My basket with knitting supplies is still where I left it last time I visited. "*What* are you saying then? I know this place isn't like the luxurious getaways you're used to—"

"I'm not used to any *getaways*, because Carl wanted to keep me close to home. I was supposed to start traveling at eighteen. I'm just scared, and unsure, and I don't know what will happen to me in the future so I made a joke," comes out of his mouth as he approaches me. "Don't you see that my life is ruined?"

I step closer and cup his face. When I touch him, it's as if the room lights up with non-existent fairy lights, suddenly cozy. The fire crackles, sharing its warmth with the room, and the fragrance of wood is so unbelievably soothing.

"It's far from ruined. *This* is just a bump on your way to a fantastic life. You will have everything you ever wanted, I'll make sure of that."

Blake's lashes flutter, and he hesitates for only a moment before clasping his fingers on my jacket. "All this just because I'm your type?"

I run my thumbs over his cheeks, now annoyed that the kettle is starting to whistle at me, because I don't want to go deal with boiling water when I have a fire in my hands.

"It's not just that. I feel a connection with you. A bond I made over the muzzle of a gun when you pointed it at me when you *saw* me. And it doesn't matter if you want me. You still have me."

A wave of intense emotion wells inside me, crashing over the jagged rocks of my heart. I don't know where this journey will take me, but I'll just follow Blake's tide.

"I have you?" he asks so quietly I prepare myself for another rejection, but then he's grabbing at my cheeks and pulling me down until our lips touch.

My hands settle on his flanks, then around him, and I wish he was out of his coat already so I can feel him better. I ignore the kettle long enough for the whistle to sing, and it sounds like fireworks to my ears, a colorful explosion above us as I greedily part his lips with my tongue.

I need him to feel the depths of my devotion. My hunger is insatiable but at least I get to taste his lips.

The broomstick drops from my hands, and Blake shivers, pushing into my arms as it hits the floor. I pull him with me to turn the gas off on the stove without taking my mouth from his, and his breath whispers between our faces when we move. He tastes of the sweet tea we got on the way here and of youthful desire, which cannot, and will not, be stopped.

"You smell so good," Blake whispers as I maneuver around the kitchenette, only to stumble against the wall behind the side of the counter.

"So you still want me?" I utter, needy for reassurance after the spat we had after our first time together. I'm selfish enough to slide my hands to his ass, and it awakens so much lust in me, I'm already getting hard.

Blake whimpers, getting to his toes as I squeeze him, and there's no faking the bliss flooding his features. He wants my touch too, and I roll us against the wall, so I have him sandwiched between me and the wooden logs. He trembles and all but submits by showing me his pale throat.

"Yes..."

I kiss his neck, then bite and suck, set on leaving my mark. We'll stay here a while. No one but me will see. "I'd do this even knowing it's another trick," I mumble between one nibble and another, sliding my hands to his front just so I can get the damn coat off him.

"No trick. Just me," Blake says, letting his hands descend my sides. The light is faint, but I still see that his cheeks grow redder by the second as he captures my gaze. "I want to—" He stalls, as if he lost his voice, but moments later, as I'm buried in his sweet neck, I feel him cup my bulge.

I groan like a bear awoken from winter sleep. "All yours. Bed?" My breath is getting raspy and I finally slide my hands under his coat. There are more layers. A hoodie, a T-shirt under it, but I'm that one step closer to his beautiful body.

He meets my gaze, but then he's lowering himself, and I can barely breathe, because in my dreams I've had him kneel for me so many times already, and I can't fathom that it's happening in real life.

"This is how I imagined it," he drawls as his breath tickles me through clothes.

I pull off his hat to slide my fingers into the dark curls on the top of his head. "Oh, you *imagined* it, have you? You could have seen it sooner if you just said the word, sweetie." I unbuckle my belt with one hand, unwilling to let him go. If he wants to see it, I'm happy to give him a front row seat. And oh, *how* he wants to see it.

His eyes widen. He dampens his lips, ready to taste me. And by the time the sharp growl of my zipper cuts through the silence, he's rocking his hips in excitement. "I want it now," he utters, out of breath as if he's sprinted here from the nearest town, just to warm my cock with his mouth.

Heat floods my whole body as if the fire is right next to me. I waste no time as I push my jeans down along with underwear, revealing his prize. I never expected for things to get so frantic within seconds, but I don't want to wait either. We'll have time for more later, but now, my mind is clouded by the sight of my hard cock slapping his pretty face as it bobs out of my clothes.

He whimpers, staring at it like a cat greedy for cream.

"You like what you see?" I ask.

He nods, wide-eyed and full of excitement so pure he almost looks innocent with the hard shaft in front of him. I worried before that he might have given into sex earlier just to appease me, but I'm now confident of his desire being true.

"It's... it's so close," he mumbles, resting his hands on my hips, not yet daring to touch my dick with his hands.

I smirk and stroke my cock in front of him. I need to only lean a single inch forward for my cockhead to brush his lips. My balls tighten at the touch. I want to be inside him so badly, and if he's still too skittish to give me his ass, I'm more than happy with his mouth.

"Show me your tongue," I say, excited beyond reason. This will hardly be the first blowjob I've ever had, but it might as well be because my focus is on Blake only. On his fluttering eyelashes, his beauty spots, his flushed face, and the way his pupils follow my every move. And maybe it's wrong, but yeah, I'm turned on to be the first guy to put that mouth to use.

He obeys me without question and reveals the soft, pink bed I want to rest my dick on. He's trembling, but not in fear. He *loves* this.

His palms are warm on the sides of my hips, then my thighs as he strokes me in rough, circular movements, never looking away. He never closes his lips either, as if he's daring me to act, to take his virgin mouth and teach him how to pleasure me.

"You have no idea how much power over me your mouth has," I whisper, sliding my cockhead over his tongue. The bliss flooding my body manifests in the pre-cum drizzling from my dick. I love how eager he was to do as told. He's so fucking perfect for me. I stroke his hair in appreciation, and he leans into my touch, eager for praise.

I shut my eyes when his soft lips slide over my cock-head, closing just behind it as his agile tongue paints circles on my tender flesh. He squeezes the backs of my thighs, as if he were worried I might try to push him away as he's getting his first taste of cock. I smile, amused by his desperation.

Unprompted, he hollows his cheeks and sucks on my cock as if it were a piece of candy.

I groan in pleasure, meeting his gaze. I want him to see desire painted all over my face. "That's it. So good..." I slowly push farther into his hot, wet mouth, and feel it pull me in. He's ecstatic to be on his knees for me. "Feel every vein with your tongue."

I have to open my jacket, because I'm getting too heated, but his eyes flutter shut as he takes a bit more in, exploring his prize. He's hot and smooth as stones rested in the summer sun. As I'm drawn deeper into his welcoming heat, reality falls apart around us, transforming the dreary cabin into a den of pleasure. I've never brought a lover here before, but now I want to transform this place into our nest, where we can make as much noise as we want without alerting the neighbors.

"Closer," I demand, gently pulling on his head so he can back out if it's too much for him. I wish I could fuck his mouth until he can't breathe, but I don't want to scare him off. I'll ease Blake in so he gets to know my cock first. "Feel it pulsing so hard? I can't wait to flood your pretty mouth with my cum. I wanna see it drizzle down your chin."

I'm so horny I can't help but rock my hips, heat boiling my head, and he answers, opening wider as he leans in. Oh, he's so ready. I bet he wouldn't protest if I decided to switch things up and tried to take him from behind. I still remember how he rocked against my dick in bed, his hole begging to be filled. But I don't have the patience for that when his tongue is a red carpet for my cock, so I roll my hips forward, hitting the back of his throat.

Blake chokes, withdrawing, but when I tighten my grip on his hair, he doesn't fight me and catches his breath while holding my dick on that velvety tongue. For a moment, I worry I've scared him, but when his eyes meet mine again, damp and full of emotion, I know he's still on board, still wants me.

With determination flashing in his gaze, he relaxes his shoulders and moves forward, inviting me deeper into his hot channel.

I plunge in with a short, controlled jab. I want him to feel what he's up against. I'm of substantial size, and I love to see his lips stretch to accommodate my girth.

"Go on, moan. I wanna feel it on my cock," I rasp, pulling back only to stab into his waiting mouth. I wonder if he likes my taste as I spread it all over his tongue. Once I'm done using his mouth, I'll be removing all of those pesky clothes. He must be boiling inside that jacket, but I kind of love how red that makes his skin.

Blake chokes again, but this time he stays put even as tears roll down his face. His breathing is frantic, and I grin when he pulls closer and humps my leg, seeking his own satisfaction while he's struggling to give me mine. His dick must be aching for release, but he's too focused on me to even consider unzipping his pants.

The soft hum he makes resonates through my body and caresses my balls, so I still, just letting myself feel it while the darling at my feet fights the natural reactions of his body to please me.

It's so hot, I lose my cool and speed up my thrusts, plunging my cock into Blake's mouth, and I trigger his gag reflex nearly every time. But a part of him seems to like *that* too. He sucks me with so much devotion I already imagine a ring on his finger. I know I won't last much longer, but I make the final jabs count, gripping his hair as I push deep into his throat.

"Oh fuck! So good. I'm gonna train you to take it. You look so good right now with my dick deep inside you," I babble, flushed and brainless.

When he murmurs something and glances up as if to ask if he's doing a good job, I lose it.

I come so hard I worry he'll choke, but gripping his hair feels automatic when all my muscles tense.

He coughs, trembling against me, but he keeps holding onto my legs, as if he wants to make sure I don't leave him like this. He loves it. He wants to be here, on his knees, in my shabby cabin, worshiping the cock of the Christmas Killer.

I have him now.

He's mine.

CHAPTER 17

BLAKE

I CAN'T CONTROL MY body anymore.

Nico's cock keeps forcing its way down my throat in a rhythm so hypnotizing I'm welcoming the discomfort. My lips and face are stained with his juices, and I'm slobbering like a mindless animal, but every sexy smile, every intense glance he sends my way is like a chain keeping me in place.

He's so tall, so muscular, and handsome. How can I deny him when I know he's put his life on the line for me and would do it again?

Who am I kidding though? I'm not doing this because I'm grateful. I'm doing this because I'm horny. His dick is a thing of beauty, and I want it in my mouth.

Drifting away from everything I used to know and uncertain about the future, I need a new anchor, and as warm, thick cum overflows my mouth and soothes the soreness in my throat, I know I've found it.

The movement of his hips after that first splash of cum becomes languid, and he lets go of my hair to steady himself against the kitchen counter. He doesn't even blink, enthralled by me as much as I am by him. I won't stop sucking until I swallow it all. The taste is salty, a little bitter, but just knowing it's *his* spunk makes it delicious.

I know I can't *really* feel it in my stomach, but I imagine it sliding down my throat and settling inside me, all hot and gooey.

The new surroundings, this old cabin, had made me uncertain, but I have nothing to worry about when I'm on my knees, with his dick softening in my mouth.

He lets out a little moan, and it's almost *cute*. Nico's awakened some kind of demon in me. He has a grasp on it, but even I don't know where this path will lead us.

When he pulls my head away, I don't fight it, even though I already miss his dick. It's still half hard and oh-so-gorgeous, slick with my saliva.

But as I expect Nico to let me go, he drags me back in until my lips are against his balls. "Kiss them for what they gave you."

A full-body tremor goes through me, and I do as he asks, cuddling up to his legs, greedy for any affirmation he's willing to give me. "Thank you," I say, surprised by the hoarseness of my voice. His sac is so very soft to the touch I can't help but caress it with my tongue too. He deserves all my attention, and I want to give it to him.

Nico leans down and once again tugs on my hair, so I look up, and he kisses my lips. "Now let's take care of you," he whispers and nudges my cock with his knee.

My moan is dull and hungry, but before I can get embarrassed, Nico presses me to the wall, his lips dancing over the sensitive flesh of my neck as I try to rub myself against him, my body desperate for release.

"Won't be so fast, sweet thing, I want to indulge in you," he teases and instead of opening my pants, he pushes off my coat, letting it fall to the floor. Then he pulls up my hoodie along with the T-shirt. I'm now glad he got the fire going in the room, but the real heat is inside me anyway.

"But I—" My words are interrupted when he once again rubs my crotch with his knee, and I grab his arms, unable to keep still while the insistent need to come grows ever stronger. The air smells of his cum, our arousal, and I can still see his dick whenever I look down. Maybe the assassin did kill me, because this feels like heaven.

"You what? You don't want to see more of me while I get you off?" He smirks and knows exactly what he's doing when he takes off his sweater and shows off.

My mind is trapped between the insistent arousal thrumming in my pants and the need to see all of him, touch him, admire him with my fingers. He's built like a god among men. A beautiful, wide-shouldered killing machine with veiny forearms I want to *lick*, and snowflake tattoos trailing down his neck.

"I do, yes. Please," I beg and shove his pants lower, all the way to the floor. I follow them and, back on my knees, I press my face to Nico's groin as I clumsily help him out of his clothes and boots. Lust muddles my mind until I can't establish what steps are still separating me from permission to come, so I lick the softening shaft and squeeze my thighs, trapping my own cock between them.

I imagined him naked too many times to count, but in the warm light, he's even more magnificent than in my fantasies. There's something primal in this space. The wood, the fire, his body smelling of lust. His blond hair is in disarray after it's been under a hat, strands of it out of place, but it only makes him seem more deranged, and I fucking love it. I even love his stupid feet, so big and bare against the floor.

Just as I think about also wanting to be naked, Nico pulls me up. At the same time that he unzips my pants, he dives in for a deep kiss that makes my toes curl.

Needing him close, I twist one of my legs around his and rock my hips, desperate for more touch. I'm already in pieces, and by the time I come, my brain will be in shreds, but I want it to happen. I want to let go and be a useless mess who can barely walk on his own.

"Touch me."

Nico grins, and I moan when he licks along my top lip, then under it, over my teeth and gums. My stomach clenches with fear when I have an intrusive thought about him wanting to take my teeth, but my idiot dick only throbs harder. As if the idea of him wanting to use parts of me in his crafting was a reason for arousal. Maybe it's exciting that he'd want to *keep* me.

But I don't get to overthink when he pushes down my pants and underwear, sliding his hot palms over my legs.

My face is on fire by the time he scoots down to untie my shoes, because he's face-level with my cock and I am *so* hard.

"Oh fuck... I just... what do you want to—" I babble, unsure what I am asking.

Nico leans forward and gives the tip of my dick a chaste kiss. "We'll deal with you soon," he says, addressing my cock rather than me, which is fair, because at this point, my brain *is* between my legs, and it's bobbing to the rhythm of my heartbeat.

I squeeze his shoulders, all jittery. "Nico, please... I can't wait anymore."

He helps me step out of my shoes, but just as I think he's standing up, he leans forward, bumping into my legs, and tips me over his shoulder. He wraps his arm around my thighs to hold me, and I dangle from his shoulder when he gets up. I have the perfect view of his back and ass, but it's hard to focus on much when my hard dick is pressed to his hot skin.

"Not too long now, sweets," Nico says as he carries me to the bedroom and nonchalantly kisses the side of my buttock.

"When?" I ask, feeling like a bratty kid when Nico responds by giving my ass a gentle slap that makes my hole throb in ways I've never quite experienced other than last night. He rubbed himself off between my buttocks and creamed them with his hot cum, leaving me breathless.

"As soon as I get my mouth on you. You're leaking on my chest already." He chuckles as I sizzle in embarrassment and lust when I imagine my pre-cum dripping on his skin, but then I hear a smack of lips and my eyes go wide. "Delicious," Nico says and squeezes one of my thighs right before tipping forward and dropping me to the soft bedding.

I can't breathe. Or think. Or move. I'm spread out naked in front of a man who's a killer and who wants to consume me until only dry bone is left. I'm gone the moment he puts his mouth on my cock, as if my orgasm was waiting for precisely that trigger.

Arched on the bed, I moan and grab at the sheets as the contents of my balls pour into Nico's hot mouth. And once it's over, I let my knees fall apart and try to cling to the remains of my sanity while my boiling blood cools.

I look down and see Nico licking my cock and balls in long, slow laps. He doesn't want to miss even a drop, and when he turns to the sensitive skin inside my thighs, I can't help but moan again. He grins when our eyes meet and rubs his stubbly cheek against my leg.

"Sated?" Nico asks, sliding his hands to my ass while the world spins around my immobile body.

I nod, but as my senses come back despite the fatigue I'm feeling, a laugh tears out of my throat. "Never. I want more."

I shouldn't be happy. I'm in bed with a serial killer in his murder cabin, but my body is filled with so many endorphins I feel intoxicated.

Nico chuckles and gives my cock a kiss, reminding me I'm naked with another man for the first time. He crawls up my body and lies on top, stroking me tenderly. He pets my sides, my arms, kisses my neck. I love his weight, and his hot skin is pure pleasure under my fingers.

Right now, I'd gladly wear one of those *The Christmas Killer did nothing wrong* T-shirts his store has in stock.

"That was so good, Blake," Nico murmurs between one kiss and another, and I curl my limbs around him, so very comfortable in those strong arms. I haven't been hugged this much since... well, since forever. Since I stopped being a small child, at least, and his touch burns me in the most pleasant way imaginable.

"You're just saying this to make me easier," I mumble with a grin.

"I'm pretty sure you'll be easy next time I take off my shirt," Nico pinches my side and laughs when I buck under him.

"Nooo, I can't be that obvious. I'm a good citizen, who doesn't give out rewards to famous serial killers," I say, and I can't help the sense of excitement rising in my chest when I think back to him dragging my abductor down the stairs in that balaclava with small ears. I can now reimagine myself on my knees in front of that scary stranger, paying for my life by sucking his cock.

I'm so messed up.

"Are you sure? Because I feel very rewarded, and I didn't even get that cake yet." Nico pulls a blanket over us and nuzzles my cheek. I'm so exhilarated to lie like this with him. Skin to skin.

"Cake?" I ask, still brainless under him, and he offers me a wide grin.

"The one you wanted to bake for me. Are you having cum-induced amnesia now?"

I groan and cover my face, mortified but somehow *still* aroused. "For a moment there, I thought that was some kind of gay slang."

Nico snorts and buries his face in my neck as his hands slide to my ass and squeeze. "I'm yet to eat *this* cake. I hope you'd like that?"

"Oh fuck... I—" My head floats with embarrassment as I worry about him not liking how I taste, or smell, yet I can't help loving the image of myself on my hands and knees while Nico buries his face between my buttocks. "I mean... you're the one with experience."

"But feel free to say if something's not up your street." Despite his size and strength, Nico's so gentle with me I melt on the inside. "I want to know what you like. What you fantasized about when you bit the bullet and went to that nightclub."

This I didn't expect, not after the way he led me through the sex, taking over just like I dreamed he would. But when I swallow and note he's still watching me, I slide my arms around him and soak up the warm weight as I speak. "I thought someone would like me—someone I liked back—and I'd get to go down on him?"

I know I'm making this sound like a question, but a part of me fears there *are* wrong answers to Nico's questions.

He's holding back a smile and strokes my cheek. "Aww, that's almost wholesome. Are you glad I'm your first instead?"

My cheeks are burning, but I force myself to keep looking back at him as I nod. "This was... very hot," I say in a voice so quiet I worry I might need to repeat myself.

"No rush, but I want to fuck you. Is that something you also wanted?" His blue gaze is so intense when he looks straight into my eyes without blinking. As if he's focusing on prey.

That's me. I'm the prey, and that fact is stirring something in my balls again. Am I attracted to danger? Is that it? Maybe that's why I'm so drawn to true-crime, not the intellectual reasons I claim.

"You mean anal sex, right?" I say and imagine it happening on this bed, with me face down in the pillows and him rocking into me.

"Yes." Nico nods, still piercing me with the daggers he has for eyes. Thinking of daggers makes me think about *penetration.* "I want to be deep inside you, make you squirm and moan my name. I want to make you come first so you squeeze your muscles tightly around me. And then I want to come inside you and leave you dripping."

I whimper and attempt to lift him with my hips, only to discover I can't. He grins at me, as if this is a game, and I cross my ankles on the small of his back, excited beyond all reason. "Yes, please, I want that. I want you to take care of me," I say, a bit shy, because I'm showing the very core of myself to a man who, technically, is still a stranger. So I add, "just let me get my bearings first," I add, because no matter how exciting his words are, I do have a brain in my skull, and need to keep some semblance of control.

Nico bites back a smile. "Sure. No rush. Sweets, we will have the best Christmas here," he says as I count the days in my mind.

How long does he intend to stay here?

CHAPTER 18

BLAKE

It's been four days since we arrived at the cabin, and while my thoughts often drift off to Carl's betrayal, analyzing our relationship over the years, it's been an extremely peaceful time. There isn't that much to do so deep in the woods, so I settled on first watching Nico do some repairs, then helping him out. I felt guilty over not offering to help him clean as soon as we arrived. I'm so used to these things just being done it didn't occur to me, but that's no excuse.

We then progressed to making some Christmas decorations, because he insisted, and soon the cabin was adorned with cut pine branches, fairy lights, and paper chains made of magazine cuttings. As much as I detest Christmas, there's no denying that our efforts have elevated the place, making it feel more lived-in. It was also a surprisingly lovely way to spend time together in the evening, just sitting by the fireplace, homemade cake at our side as I cut the paper and Nico glued the pieces together.

Guilt once again poked me straight in the face when during cleaning I found a basket with yarn and a crudely drawn design of a sweater. In an instant, I realized that Nico *made* the piece of knitwear I called the ugliest thing I've ever seen. It must have taken him hours, if not days, and he wanted to give it to *me*. I know it's somewhere in the back of his car, but it would be weird if I started to wear it all of a sudden, accepting his gift out of pity, so I'm stuck in a guilt limbo any time I see the basket of knitting supplies.

There are still moments when I worry that Carl's people will track us down, and I'll find myself with a red laser dot in the middle of the forehead right before it explodes, but Nico's relaxed attitude has rubbed off on me, and the idea of staying hidden until Carl's back from Aspen no longer feels like the slowest of suicides. A part of me detests that he gets to celebrate and have fun with friends he never introduced me to as his last hurrah, but I console myself with the fact that he surely is beside himself over my disappearance. After all, the money won't be his until I turn up dead.

But it's easy to forget Carl's existence when I have a beautiful cock to suck for breakfast, lunch, and dinner. Is it a crass thought? Certainly, but there is something about lewd words that makes my body heat up and long for touch. Nico has been a perfect gentleman about my inexperience, never trying to push beyond what's comfortable for me yet always happy to feed me a steady diet of dirty talk. He's attentive, never fails to make me comfortable, and while the fact that he is a murderer is still present at the back of my mind, it's very easy to ignore in the face of his gentle kisses, passionate touch, and our long conversations over a variety of cakes we bake together.

Is his Christmas obsession strange? Sure. Is he a murderer who likes creepy crafts a bit too much? Yes. But is he also the most caring boyfriend I could ask for? Pretty much.

I haven't actually called him my *'boyfriend'*, but I do like to toy with that in my mind. A lot.

I don't ever feel lonely when I'm with him. He never trivializes anything I say and looks out for me. That's how a good relationship should feel, right? Maybe it's the isolation playing tricks on my mind, but in the face of his attention and care, all the worries I have about being around a killer seem like minor details. In fact, I have a sick fascination with every single murder he admits to me. Am I complicit at this point? I could go to the authorities and make a fuss, discouraging Carl from ever trying to go after me again, but I don't want to.

I will never feel safe until the flakes of his teeth float in Nico's new snow globe.

I don't want to appear like a lovesick puppy, or bare myself to him too much, but reciprocating his attention feels natural, so I applied my new skill and cooked some eggs for him as he forgot all about breakfast, busy planning a way to get his hands on Carl.

He does spend quite some time researching things, learning about the house we have in Aspen, and ways to get there with least possibility of being tracked. I don't know if I should be happy about that or frightened of just how excited he is to kill someone.

Because that's the thing with his morbid and dangerous side. It's all fun and games until it turns against me one day. If he doesn't get his fill of murder because the circumstances aren't right, will his frustration rise? Will it one day overflow to a point where he gets violent with me? It's only reasonable to think about such things. My brother, who seemed perfectly civil, has ordered a hit on me, so how can I not expect a serial killer to turn on me one day?

I think about that any time I get all gooey about Nico and consider if we would work as a couple in real life instead of our la-la land in this cabin. The answer? I don't fucking know. I've never been with anyone else.

But I'm happy when I'm around him. He listens to me and answers requests before I can even voice them, and today is no different. I complained about not being able to publish the next episode of my podcast, so knowing how much that means to me, Nico set me up with a phone and computer for recording. They're not the professional tools I'm used to, but more than enough for my purposes.

"Will it be about me?" he asks excitedly as he adds wood to our fireplace.

I snort. "You can't be jealous of the Zodiac. I bet he attacked couples because no woman wanted someone with his horrible personality."

"But it's December," Nico whines like an impatient puppy. "It makes sense to have another episode about the Christmas Killer."

"There's only so many times I can recycle the same information. There has been no new victim, at least not to the knowledge of the authorities."

"Oh! I know!" Nico paces the room, rubbing his hands. "What if I sent you an *anonymous* letter, and you could have an Interview with the serial killer segment."

Excitement rushes through me like a shock of electricity, but as I imagine the hit that would have been, the amount of things that can go wrong, especially in my current situation, is simply too great.

"That's... so sweet of you. It would do amazing things for my show," I say, watching him grin in self-satisfaction. "But it's too much of a risk. What if they track us down, and then check your place and somehow find out who you actually are?"

His face falls, and he nods, turning his face to the fire with a thoughtful expression. I'm struck by how eager his offer was. I've never worked on the podcast with anyone, and here he is, so excited to be a part of what I love to do. It's touching, even if misguided.

It makes me imagine him as part of my future, which is something I've been trying to avoid in our little bubble of bliss.

Nico finally speaks again. "What if you talked about a theory that the Christmas Killer is a vigilante? Maybe we could reverse engineer some evidence in a way that is plausible that you unearthed it?"

I grin and lean against him, happy to have a collaborator of sorts. We spend the next hour coming up with ways to bring his idea to life, and by the time we untangle the Gordian knot of problems his suggestion brings, it feels like I might just have a future hit on my hands.

Conversation moves from one topic to the other as we drink hot chocolate. I don't remember ever feeling so at ease with anyone and mention that my most treasured memory of my dad is when a snowman I built fell off the sleds I was using to transport him closer to my bedroom window. The figure fell apart and I was inconsolable. My dad took a break from work to help me build another snowman, which I insisted needed to be *identical* to the first one, like the brat I was at the time. And he even put his own tie on the finished thing.

I feel loved whenever I remember that day, and the moment I share that, Nico decided we should build a snowman of our own.

So here we are, getting our boots soaked, rolling snow into balls, which will soon become a head and a torso. The sun sets quite early in December, so it's already getting dusky, but that doesn't dampen Nico's excitement. Nor mine.

He's attractive when he gets intense in bed, but he's just as handsome now, smiling and red from the cold.

"I don't have a carrot for the nose. Any ideas what else to use? Oh! Oh! Just imagine if we still had the assassin's body. We could have used the nose I cut off him." He sighs as if that idea isn't absurdly awful.

"We wouldn't be able to see it from the cabin. Let's just use a piece of wood," I propose and twist on my heel to look at the fallen branches within sight. I come back with a twisted piece of bark and shove it into the snowman's face.

Nico rests his gloved hands on the back of his head, and I notice they're the same red leather he had on when I first met him. Is it wrong to think they're kind of hot?

"It's okay. I guess," he says, but it's obvious he's not impressed.

Stifling a laugh, I approach the snowman and lean against him, with one of his stick arms touching my back. "Well, hello, handsome. Bold of you to just come over and prod me like this," I say but slide my cheek over the snow as I catch Nico's eyes.

Blood drains from his face, and he pins me with a deadly gaze, as if he's really getting jealous over a *snowman*. "Don't do that."

I bite my lip, trying not to grin. "Are you talking to me or *this guy*?"

"This fucker!" Nico says and punches the snowman so hard his head falls off.

I get such a hysterical fit of giggles I have to grab one of the branch-arms to stay on my feet. "You gotta get used to this. They all seem to want me."

Nico reaches into the pocket of his jacket and I stop laughing when he pulls out the black balaclava. He puts it on and stares at the snowman's headless body.

"That's no surprise, but you will have to learn to deal with their flirting if you don't want them dead." His voice is a little muffled through the fabric, and I'm embarrassed what hearing him say such things does to me. Nico leans down to grab the fallen head and I sneak a glance at his ass. He's such a fine piece of man. Lean and strong as a lion, and just as deadly. I'm breathless when he picks up the head and shows me that the bark nose is cracked, twisted out of its original place, and located right next to an imprint of Nico's fist.

Blood floods down my body, and I find myself hot with excitement. "You can't kill people just because they look my way. I'm good-looking. It's gonna happen," I tell him, trying to steady myself on my feet.

Nico places the head back on top of the other balls of snow, but he watches me intently from behind the fabric mask. It's both unnerving and exciting to not see the rest of his face. "I can't? You sure about that?" When he cocks his head, a shiver runs down my back, because I know he's joking (or at least I think so). I also know he's capable of murder, so is it even a joke in this situation?

I once read a study about excitement and fear stimulating the same places in the brain, so if you're afraid of something, you need to tell yourself you're excited, and your brain will align with that. Now I'm not sure if that's such a good thing, because my balls are starting to tingle, and I'm imagining this masked Nico over me, slamming in over and over to teach me a lesson.

"Are you threatening me?" I ask, trying to breathe. At this point, I don't know if this is a game of arousal or if he's being serious, but like the adrenaline junkie I've secretly been all this time, I am provoking him, regardless.

"No. I'm threatening any man who stands too close to you, who dares lay a finger on you or disrespect you," Nico steps my way, and I'm suddenly aware of the crunch of snow under his boots, our darkening surroundings, that we're here alone, and that I can't drive.

My heart beats ever faster. I've not promised him anything. We're just two guys fucking as we plot my brother's murder. Completely normal stuff.

And yet, he's claiming me.

Or joking? Role-playing?

Or maybe this is what I want? To be claimed by someone who can't stand the idea of anyone else encroaching on my personal space? Someone for whom I'm not unimportant or interchangeable. Someone who wants *me* without question.

My heart is burning. And so is my groin.

"I didn't feel disrespected. You don't own me," I breathe out, focused on his blue eyes watching me from behind the mask that takes away all his softness.

"You sure about that?" Nico rasps, and when he takes another step toward me, I back away.

He steps forward, I step back.

Only inches between us and vapor from my mouth in the freezing air.

He steps forward, I step back. Our deadly dance of lust.

He steps forward, I turn around and dash for the house.

Nico follows like the predator he is, boots crunching snow as if it's the bones of his enemies under his feet.

CHAPTER 19

BLAKE

My face is on fire as I burst into the cabin. The heavy stomping of Nico's boots resonates down my spine, so I close the door with the entire weight of my body before locking it with a single twist of my wrist. The handle lowers when he presses it on the other side, and when the entrance remains shut, a wide grin stretches my face. This is just a bit of fun, and I'll let him in soon, but I enjoy the idea of the chase, especially as seeing him in that mask really does something to me.

Overheating, I open my jacket, then kick off my boots and remove my top, because it'll be fun to tease him bare-chested. "I'm sorry, but this is too much. I like the snowman better. He'll treat me right," I call out to taunt him.

A loud bang nearby makes me yelp and jump in terror. I turn toward its source and spot Nico's arm sliding in through the window. He must have punched out the part that was boarded up. It's a moment straight out of *The Shining*. Swift as a wild cat, he reaches the handle and pushes the window open to climb inside.

If I really was scared, I would have grabbed a pan and smacked his head with it, but I don't want to hurt him, so I back out in helpless confusion combined with arousal at the sight of his eyes staring at me from behind the balaclava.

"You can't run from me," he states in a raspy voice and blocks the door with his imposing size. I know the social contract of this game requires me to run so he can hunt me down, but my legs feel like cotton buds and might break under me if I give up on the support of the wall behind me.

My pants feel so restrictive as Nico walks toward me, still in that checkered jacket and winter boots, still in the mask that transforms him into the top predator who will not be denied.

I stumble to the side, but he grabs my arm and presses me face-first into the wall.

"Not even trying anymore? Is it because you know there's no running from me?"

His hold on my arm is so strong I doubt I'd be able to free myself without causing him significant pain. Then he runs his leather-clad hand up my naked side, all the way to my armpit and I let out an involuntary moan that makes him chuckle. His voice is dark, filled with the same passion he has for his kills, and now I'm a fly in his web, about to be consumed.

I make a half-hearted attempt at freeing myself, but he only presses harder against me, trapping me with his heat. The jacket is cold, wet, and makes my skin break out in goosebumps everywhere we touch. I twist against him, mumbling, "let me go!"

He presses his face to my nape and inhales. It makes me feel even more vulnerable, as if he's a cat playing with its prey.

"You don't mean it." Nico presses his crotch to the small of my back. I know his dick very well by now, but sensing it against me doesn't get old.

He's often the big spoon when we sleep and every time we lie like that, I wonder what it will be like for him to just pull my pajama pants down and fuck me. How it would be to wake up to him already hard, lubing me up and pushing his cock inside me before I get a chance to voice whether I want it or not.

Maybe it's messed up to have fantasies such as these, but I can't help myself, not when he's gently twisting back my arms while he grinds against me.

"I d-do! You're scaring me. You kill people," I all but purr, grinding right back.

"Then say my name, and I'll stop. You know I'm not just a dangerous killer about to fuck you. I have a name. Say it if you want me to stop. Say it if you don't want your ass fucked raw."

Sparks erupt in my head. It's happening. He's making *the move*. I've been on edge all these days, asking my-self if and when we'd go in that direction. Every time I've learned the landscape of his body, I've wondered what it will be like to have him deep inside me, and now it's about to happen. He's planning to fuck my ass, and this is my moment to consent or not.

There is no way in hell I would deny him now. Not really. Not when I've been daydreaming about it as if it were an unattainable fantasy. But he's here with me, he knows what he's doing, and I trust him not to hurt me. Of course I want it.

"No, you're a murderer! I don't know your name," I whimper, shivering when he squeezes my hips.

"Suit yourself," he whispers into my ear and slides his hands, still in those red leather gloves that remind me of his dark side, to my pants. He opens them with ease. "I'm gonna have fun with you," Nico says and pushes the fabric down my thighs.

A cold gust of wind from the open window tickles my skin, making me clench my ass, and I throw myself to the side, only to be pulled right back by steel-firm arms. I open my mouth to scold him, tell him it's not a gentlemanly way to behave, but a frantic yelp leaves my throat instead when he swats my ass.

"That mouth of yours isn't meant for speaking, is it?" he asks and drags my clothes farther down, until they pool around my ankles, leaving me exposed. I'm scalding on the inside.

"You know what all of this is for." Nico slides his hand up my belly and I'm left to whimper at his commanding presence. "That's why you already took your top off before I even came in." He steps on the pants and underwear bundled at my ankles. There's something violent about his dirty boot on my clothes, between my legs, and I can't get enough of the threat it represents. "Step out," he orders, and I do what he wants, relishing in the fear that makes my cock ever harder. I can barely stand still with him talking to me like this. It's as if the pleasant, enthusiastic Nico has disappeared, leaving a monster inside his body.

A part of me loves it.

"Let me go," I plead.

"You're exactly where you want to be," he says, and my eyes go wide, my cheeks turning hot as the pits of hell, because he slides his fingers between my buttocks without warning.

He's touched me there before, just teasing, rubbing his cockhead over my sensitive hole, or gliding slippery fingertips over it, but this touch has none of that tenderness. He's pulling one of my hands back, pressing me to the wall while two gloved fingers probe at my hole roughly enough to make me rise to my tiptoes.

"No, stop," I rasp, but my hips are already rolling for him, already trying to get his digits inside. A shiver overcomes me when he rubs his hot, masked face over my nape, and I spread my legs farther. A new sensation awakens inside me, a sensitivity deep within, and while I'm not sure what it is, I know there's just one way to soothe it.

"I'm done playing," he says and picks me up.

I yelp, breath caught in my throat. All he does to lift me is wrap his powerful arms around my waist. I'm no tiny thing, yet in his grip I'm like a baby bird about to be crushed, a feeling amplified by him remaining fully dressed while I'm only wearing socks.

He carries me to the kitchen area. "Hands on the table. Bend over," Nico commands, melting whatever resolve I still had to play the role of a scared boy who doesn't want to get railed.

"I—please, don't hurt me," I moan, though even the act of making such requests is arousing to me as I rest my palms on the tabletop. The air tickling my flesh as he moves behind me is almost too much, so I focus on the patterns of the wood under me, wondering what it'll be like to have him inside. I've been imagining myself in this position for so long, but what if I don't like it? Will calling him by his name work as a safe word? Would he respect it?

He takes his sweet time, closing the window, taking off his jacket.

"Be a good boy, serve my dick well, and you might be alive tomorrow." When he leans over me, pressing his crotch to my bare ass, I feel he's kept his T-shirt and pants on. "Or I'll just keep you here, chained to my bed so I can come and use this hole any time I feel horny." He slides his hand back between my ass cheeks, and *fuck*, he's kept the gloves on, and they feel so amazingly smooth and thick, and I—

"Oh God, don't. Don't do this to me." I'm lying through my teeth, but my body doesn't, and I find myself pushing back so fast the tip of his finger enters my hole. I'm seeing colors at the backs of my lids and reach back, attempting to push him away.

"Hands on the table!" he roars and slaps my ass so hard I'm sure there will be a handprint on my skin as red as his gloves.

I know him. He's Nico. He made paper chains with me, and the paint we decorated them with is still on the plastic sheet folded in the corner of the table. But my body's reaction to him raising his voice is so visceral I instantly put my palms back on the smooth surface.

I'm leaning down like he told me to, and he puts a tube of lube on the table in range for me to see, as if he wanted to inflict yet more mental and emotional torment.

"Spread your legs," he orders, then pushes them apart with his boot without waiting for my reaction. I'm trembling, but my dick is dripping pre-cum to the floor. "What a beautiful ass," he sighs and slips a finger to my hole, this time slick with lube.

The glove makes it thicker as he glides it from my taint to my anus, and back again. Its texture is making me crazy. Smooth and solid, yet still pliable, due to it not being perfectly aligned with his fingers, it adds yet another layer of sensation to my already sensitive flesh.

"What are you doing?" I mumble, lowering my face to the table and inhaling its oily scent.

"Enjoying my captive. Enjoying being your first." And just when he says that, he slides his finger in all the way to the knuckle, spreading my tender flesh as he holds his knee between my legs to stop them from pressing back together. Not that it would help me.

A low moan rises from deep in my chest, and I grab the sides of the table as one of my feet lifts from the floor. Such a strange sensation, so unfamiliar, yet knowing he's the one touching me, and what he intends to do next, has me writhing already. It's not even painful, and I tighten my muscles around his digit before pulling my hips forward, as if I was leading him closer.

The movements of the finger inside me make me press my cheek to the table. I'm in a world of my own where a dangerous killer is forcing me to submit, and there's no other option for me but to give in.

"That's it, open nice and wide for me. I do have a big cock. You need to be able to take it," Nico rasps and presses his crotch to the side of my ass. He's so hard in his jeans, and I know all too well how much stamina he has when I suck him. Will he last just as long when he pushes into my ass, or will he be too excited?

Shivers run down my back as he twists his finger inside me while rubbing my taint and balls as if he were trying to tease me until I truly can't resist him.

"I can't," I say, shaking my head and imagining that hard dick against my hole. I imagine it spraying cum all over my ass, and then Nico's big hands rubbing it into my skin, so not a drop is wasted.

"You 'can't' what?" he asks, as if nothing of significance was happening. "You can't be my sex toy?" His words are accompanied by the rasp of a zipper. The sound makes my ass clench on his fingers. "This feels like you want it."

Snapping my head up, I attempt to throw him back, like a wild horse rejecting its first-ever rider, but my voice is stifled when he grabs my face, blocking my mouth, and pulls my head to his chest. "I might need to teach you a lesson after all."

I try to protest, but three of his gloved fingers sink between my lips, letting me taste the red leather just as he twists another finger inside my ass. The stretch is a surprise, but I try to relax and accept the girth of two digits, which he's determined to prepare me with.

"Oh fuck…" Nico groans. "It's so hot to feel you squirm. I hope you do that when I'm balls-deep inside you."

As if to make that clear to me, I sense his bare dick rubbing against my ass cheek. Hard, hot, pulsing flesh begging to come inside me. I'm not really putting up a fight, but his strong grip turns me on anyway. He's showing me he *could* hold me in place. My cock bobs against the table, and every time it touches *anything* I drizzle pre-cum. I can sense drops of it cooling on my thighs already, but the sensation pales in comparison to Nico's firm touch. It's almost as if he has ten hands and is able to stroke me everywhere, because each press on my tongue, each slick thrust into my anus teases this unfamiliar sensation inside, magnifying it until I'm twisting my hips in anticipation. My skull is a pressure cooker about to explode, and I need more. Faster. But telling him this would have spoiled half the fun, so I do the opposite thing and attempt to climb onto the table, away from him.

Nico pulls out his fingers and grabs my leg to stop me. He laughs. "Oh! You're ready to be my meal?"

I'm not sure what's happening, too focused on the emptiness in my throbbing hole, and then he's pulling on my leg, twisting until I fall to the tabletop, back first, my legs spread for him, my hard dick on show, and my whole body exposed.

Nico slides between my thighs, pressing his dick between my ass cheeks, and I see him in all his terrifying glory. Tight black T-shirt hugging his pecs and lean waist while showing off the muscular arms, pants open, and the balaclava hiding his features save for the intense eyes.

He makes a point of looking down at my crotch. "Looks like this turns you on. Does it, boy? Does it turn you on that I'm about to stuff you full of cock?"

I shake my head but my dick twitches, and I grab the other side of the table, trying to wrestle myself out of Nico's grip. My efforts are for nothing, and he drags me even closer, until my ass is pressed to his groin, and he has me pinned.

What will he do to me now? Will it hurt? Will I like it?

So many questions spin through my head as he steadies himself, a dangerous monster who has no regard for my needs and wants, and will take me because he can.

"I'd handcuff you if I wasn't so horny," Nico rasps, and he doesn't waste any more time. He lifts my legs to his shoulders, and I'm spread open for him. He runs one hand up my body, all the way to my neck, while he grabs his dick with the other and prods at my stretched hole with his cockhead.

My Adam's apple bobs against his hand, and while I know the threat isn't real (or is it?), my body is still frantic with adrenaline. Scared or excited? I might be asking myself that question until the end of my life, but the fact is that when his dick kisses my hole, it seems every nerve ending beyond the place where they meet goes dull. Nico's saying something, but I can't hear him over the thudding in my ears. When he pushes in, I can no longer breathe, and my head falls back as my muscles go rigid with panic. And still, despite the whine I let out in response to the sting, I don't want him to pull out. I might be in pain now but already want *more*.

"Oh fuck... fuck..."

"That's what I want..." Nico murmurs, pressing his dick in relentlessly. The long thrust is languid, controlled, and everything I'm not. "The look on your face when you take your first dick. Look at you... distressed mess, scared of how much you like to be mine."

The breath in my throat is fire, and my eyes gloss over as they meet Nico's. It's heaven and hell all at once, and I know every word he says is true.

I want to be his. I'm a misguided boy who likes the danger of opening his legs for a killer, and I want him to do whatever he wishes to me.

I want to be scared as he pumps me full of cum.

I don't stand a chance against his force, and by the time he bottoms out inside me, my body relaxes, accepting him as its master. The air is fragrant with the sharp essence of his lust, and I close my eyes, savoring it. "Not true. You'll never *really* have me," I challenge him, but my voice turns into a moan when he makes an unexpected jab with his hips, and somehow ends up entering me even deeper.

"You sure about that?" Nico rasps, folding me so that his balaclava-hidden face is just inches away from mine. "I'll keep marking you until you understand that you're mine." He starts rocking his hips against my ass, and I don't understand how it can cause me both discomfort and pleasure, but something about the painful intensity of the thrusts triggers a release of molten hot sensation that soon spreads freely all over my abdomen and up my chest.

The desire bubbling up in my brain makes me relax enough to enjoy his thrusts. I see my legs on his shoulders, and it's a reminder of how open to him I am, my own cock bobbing against my stomach, so very hard I can't deny that I'm loving this moment, regardless of what lies spill from my lips.

Initially, I thought the soreness would be a necessary trade-off for the ecstasy accompanying it and the chance of offering my body to someone else, like I always wanted, but as my insides adjust to being penetrated, I'm treated to pure bliss.

The deep need I've experienced earlier somehow grows until I grab my thighs and hold them open while Nico saws into me. His cock makes a plunging sound each time it enters my hole, and I moan helplessly as I watch him assault me with his tool over and over. I should be embarrassed, I should hide my face and pretend it's not me getting off to this imaginary scenario, but I like this way too much to deny myself.

Nico's blue eyes shine as if he were the devil come to this world only to seduce and corrupt me, and I don't think I ever craved anything more.

He's holding my throat without squeezing as he changes the angle of his thrusts and makes them count. I let out a yelp in response to each, but don't fight it. Sparks explode under my eyelids, because that has to be my prostate he's teasing. I can't imagine anything else inside me feeling like this. The pleasure floods my body in a new wave, filling my already tight balls and making me moan.

And as if it wasn't enough that I seem to be losing my damn mind for this masked devil, he slides his hand to my cock. It's still slippery from lube, and Nico wastes no time, jerking me off, riding me, making me his.

I whimper, overwhelmed and zoning out, but then he presses his forehead to mine, and I'm back with him again, anchored by those beautiful eyes. I reach for his face, cupping it as he jabs into me in a series of rapid thrusts, and there's no more strength left in me to resist. I come, spraying us both with cum and milking the dick inside me as Nico grabs my hips and lets his eyes roll back, plunging into me even faster.

"Yes..." I utter. "Use me."

And oh, does he. He doesn't even say anything, the air between us filled with his grunts and my moans. I'm not even sure if I've stopped coming yet or not. My stomach is covered with my own spunk, but all I can focus on is my throbbing hole squeezing his thick dick as he makes hasty jabs into my body.

I slide my hand to his muscular forearm and feel it tense when he stiffens, his breath hot on my face even through the black fabric. I don't know if I'm imagining it, or if I really feel it, but I swear I sense his hot cum shooting inside me.

I love it.

Nico's jerking over me, his eyes closed as he settles with his hips pressed to my ass, but I'm still in heaven, stroking his chest and shoulders as he relaxes.

I'm exhausted, and my insides feel sore, but the sense of contentment is still glowing in my chest as I peel the balaclava from my lover's flushed face. He's so fucking handsome.

"Hello, Nico."

When a big smile blooms on his lips, it's as if the monster within him is gone. Sated, it's gone back to sleep. I wonder if this is how he feels after killing. I could fall in love with this smile, and it's a thought as lovely as it is terrifying.

"Hey there, sweetheart," he mumbles and rests his weight on me. I slide my legs off his shoulders, missing his cock the moment it slips out, but at least I have his weight to soothe me.

My chest is full of things that need to be said, but I'm not ready yet and very slowly pull myself into a sitting position, so I can slide into his arms. This puts pressure on my asshole, which feels damp and way more tender than it was a moment ago, but when I bury my sweaty face in his shoulder, seeking the tenderness I didn't want when he was roughly fucking me, it's all worth it.

It feels so soothing to be held by him, and Nico leaves little kisses all over my ear. They make my heart flutter, and I know it's probably the high of the orgasm, but I still imagine a life with him where I work part-time in his shop, we live in his tiny attic apartment, and every day is Christmas. For once, the twinkling lights under the ceiling bring me joy not annoyance.

"Was it okay?" he asks, stroking my back so tenderly I could cry.

But I chuckle instead and give him a firm hug. "'Okay'? You're so dumb sometimes, you know that? More like the hottest thing that's ever happened to me."

Nico snorts and nuzzles my ear. "I loved every little whimper and moan you made." He takes off his gloves behind my back, and then slides his warm hands up and down my spine. Every one of his gestures is meant to cherish me. I have never felt so appreciated.

"I liked everything," I admit, hiding my face in his clothes. I love how strongly they smell of him now. "How scary you were. I even liked when it got a bit intense. It was like hot sauce, enhancing the flavor," I tell him and press a kiss to the side of his jaw.

Nico smirks, looking very self-satisfied. "I saw it in your eyes when I put on the balaclava. You're a kinky little thing."

And I'm only discovering how much. He's opening the locks I put on myself one by one. But as I rest in his warm embrace, reality creeps back in, reminding me that we won't always remain in this remote cabin. Sooner rather than later, we will return to civilization, and what then? It's one thing to fuck a vicious killer, but it's not like I would *date* him. People aren't always what they seem, and how far could that potentially go with a man like Nico, a man who enjoys killing and doesn't mind torture to get what he wants? Just a few days ago, I witnessed him cutting off a man's nose, for fuck's sake.

Blinded by desire and my personal interest in the Christmas Killer, I might be unwilling to see him for what he is, but people who appeared way less violent than him have done terrible things. How can I assume I'll be special and never end up on the wrong side of his knife?

Still, it's safest in the eye of the storm, so I hug him, wondering what to do about the future. He's so solid in my arms, and he's made it clear he wants to date me. What would happen if I rejected him for real? I can't live in his Christmas joy delusion while he continues to kill people on the side. It can't work.

My chest squeezes, as if my ribs have tightened around my heart when I imagine never seeing Nico again, but I'm quick to shake it off.

I'll deal with that once my brother is no longer a danger.

CHAPTER 20

NICO

BLAKE IS THE BEST partner and lover I could dream of. It's only fitting that I met him in December, because he's the most amazing Christmas gift. I wish to wrap him with a big red ribbon just so I can unpack him all over again. A metaphor of course, but I'm pretty sure he'd like bondage, so why not do it in style?

I've been working on preparing something special for him too. A present only he will understand and love.

Excitement warms me on the inside as I park outside the cabin. For the first time in years, there's a fire waiting for me on the hearth, and the smoke coming from the chimney gives me an immense sense of calm. I have a good life, yes, but I did know it lacked something—a companion who truly knows me—and the chance to invite Blake deeper into my world feels like the fulfillment of dreams I once considered out of my reach.

But now he's here, he knows my secrets, and he's not running for the hills.

I stomp on the porch to shake off the excess snow from my boots and walk in to see Blake stretched in the armchair with a book in his lap. He looks up and waves at me with a smile so bright my heart shines like a lantern.

"How was it in town?" Blake asks and slots a bookmark between the pages.

"I had to take a detour because of all the snow and I found something interesting. But you have to come with me to see it, so get dressed."

He places the book on a little table next to him and moves up, only to freeze. "Will it be safe for me to be seen?"

"It's in the forest, no one will see you." I walk up to him for a quick kiss because any opportunity is good for that, and I've been away for hours.

I love the way his hands immediately frame my face when he leans into me. His hair smells of smoke, and I find myself burying my nose in it as we hug. "Now I'm curious. What kind of surprise is it?" he asks before meeting my gaze.

I put my hands up and step away because if I stay this close any longer, we'll be going to the bedroom, not outside.

"I'm not saying anything more."

Blake smirks and starts dressing while he excitedly tells me about the book he's been reading, a non-fiction on a serial killer from the start of the twentieth century.

I love that he's as passionate about his interests as I am about mine, and the fact that they overlap makes it even better. I dream of being allowed to see how his podcasts come to life, and I want him to see my process too, until we can share both of those things. Perfect partners in crime.

I grin at the double meaning in my thoughts, but he's ready, and I lead the way into the sunny yet cold air.

"I miss the shop, you know," I say, grabbing Blake's hand and leading him onto a narrow path that starts behind our little love cabin. "But I've been in touch with Owen and I have to admit I'm not worried. He's really got things under control despite the Christmas rush."

"Am I not keeping you busy enough?" Blake asks and leans against me in that almost-accidental way he tries to flirt with me sometimes.

"That's the thing. For the first time, I actually don't feel like I'm missing out, because I get to spend time with you instead."

The sun is shining through the dense woods, snow crunches under our boots, and soon enough, I'll be showing off my big surprise. Could this day get any better? I guess a blowjob is always a welcome addition, but maybe not here. I don't want him to get his jeans all wet.

We talk about plans for the next few days, and he seems set on making me drag him behind me in a sled. He wants to bake another cake, and read a new book on psychopathy, and so many other things we can share now that we're locked in a world of our own, with no dangers or distractions. He doesn't even complain that I'm dragging my feet about going to Aspen. I'm pretty sure we're in a silent agreement about being able to wait, since we're safe here.

"Okay, now we'll be going down," I warn him so he doesn't slip.

At the bottom of the hill, I stop him and push away a few branches obscuring the entrance into a cave. It's such a beautiful day, I'm almost sorry that we have to get out of the sun, but I know he will love my surprise, and I browse my phone, choosing the right app. A moment later, the battery-powered LEDs I installed earlier turn on, and the cave resonates with the soft tones of 'No Time Like Christmas'.

Blake stalls, holding my hand more tightly. "Oh, so you didn't *find* this place, did you?" he asks after a moment and laughs, staring ahead, where the cave bends toward its main chamber. The whole thing is the size of a large studio apartment, but it provides more than enough space for our plans.

I lead him inside to the joyful tune with a spring in my step. The colorful Christmas lights twinkle around us, revealing more of the decorations, including the glitter I've sprayed on the walls, but the surprise is hidden behind the bend, so he won't see it until we're close.

"Guilty as charged," I say with a smirk and glance at his face just before the grand reveal.

His hand slides up my arm as we walk over the uneven floor. "Oh, should I get undressed now or—" His voice dies as we face a large rock resting in the very middle of the cave interior. I've arranged many more lights on the walls around it, but their soft light still leaves the altar-like structure dusky as an old oil painting. I'm very proud of the atmosphere I've managed to achieve here.

"What the hell?" Blake asks.

I move behind the gagged man tied securely to the rock. His eyes widen at us both, and he writhes like a bug under someone's thumb. He's not going anywhere, so I spare him little attention and spread my arms with a smile.

"Tah-da!"

Blake covers the lower part of his face and shakes his head. "What is he doing here?"

I'm a little deflated by this reaction, but I guess he's taken aback with no context. "You love the Christmas Killer, and you have an interest in the nitty gritty of crime, so I thought you'd like to see me at work." I pick up one of the knives I left here earlier as my victim whines and wiggles.

He looks like the perfectly average suburban dad, but I know he's not, so I have no qualms about his suffering.

Blake's hands drop at his sides, and he shakes his head. Is it just me, or is his breathing a little ragged? "I am interested in it in theory! It's not like I watch murder scene pictures for fun! I'm not that kind of person!"

And yet, he's staying put.

I shift my weight from one foot to the other. Have I misjudged this?

"You don't? I...I'm sorry, but I got the impression you were really curious. Like... to an unusual level. You paid someone to hack the FBI just so you could get more crime scene imagery."

"For research!"

I take a deep breath and lean against the rock, fighting my frustration. I didn't want to pull out the big guns, but he's in denial, and I need to make him see reason. "And you stabbed the last guy in the throat for *research*?"

It's dark, but while I don't see his skin paling, I feel the temperature drop by several degrees as Blake focuses on me with a tight set to his mouth. "I was protecting us from an assassin. And besides, he was practically dead after you *cut his nose off*!"

My next victim lets out a whimper, sobs, and thrashes against the rope I used to restrain him. His gaze seeks Blake's help, and my stomach drops when I realize my boyfriend might just want to aid this worm in order to teach me a lesson.

"You don't die from a cut nose," I complain. "And he was already tied down. All you were protecting was your own skin, because don't think I didn't notice you only acted when he started telling on you. And I'm past that, I've come to terms with your little double-crossing, but don't twist it around on me."

Blake stills, and his Adam's apple rolls up and down his neck as he's forced to swallow that truth. "Well, he was there to kill us both, which is pretty unforgivable. What did *this* bastard do?" he asks, gesturing at the writhing man.

He's either being obnoxious or getting on board with the plan. Only time will tell. "Oh, you will like this!" I clear my throat. "Not the crime, his crime is terrible, but that... you know, that he's caught. This little worm," I poke his forehead hard without looking away from Blake, since it makes no difference if I poke the bastard's eye out at this point. He's dying anyway. "Killed his elderly neighbor and suffered no consequences because of a technicality."

Blake's expression softens, warming my heart.

Kurt, because that's our victim's name, thrashes like a dying fish. He keeps trying to scream into the gag I've stuffed in his mouth, no doubt attempting to give me reasons why his actions were justified, but this won't make a difference. I can see Blake believes me, and that's all I care about.

His pretty face sobers. "When you said you were looking for information on my brother and how we can take him down, were you actually watching *this guy*?"

I still, because that's not an angle I was expecting, and my mouth goes dry, because I'm suddenly a kid with his hand in the cookie jar. "I mean... this just fell into my lap. I was also checking the security on your brother's villa and all that."

Blake shakes his head, starting to pace. He's no longer bothered by the fact that I led him to a man I was about to kill, but his shock seems to have been replaced by anger. "*Fell into your lap?* Really? How does a staged murder fall into one's lap, huh? I believed you when you said we need to lie low, but this is hardly that, isn't it? Every night, I worry that I might wake up with a knife to my throat, and here you are, hunting people down for funsies?"

His shouting echoes in the cave, getting so loud I have shivers by the time he's done.

My shoulders sag. "You worry I will hurt you?"

Blake cocks his head, takes a deep breath, and speaks, full of exasperation. "I worry Carl will somehow track us down and send more people after us. More than you can handle. And even if it was just one guy, you are not superhuman!"

"I take offense at that. I said I'll protect you. And this?" I point to Kurt with the knife. "This isn't 'for fun'. This is *justice*." Fuck. Even I don't believe that. The truth is that I had an itch to scratch, and the holiday season always gets me like this.

"Why don't you bring justice to *me*?" Blake asks bluntly.

I roll my eyes. "I just... I like our time in the cabin. Are you not having fun?"

Blake dashes forward and stabs my chest with his index finger. "So you *are* stalling! When you know I'm stuck and worried he'll send someone after me. My own brother is trying to kill me, and you're willing to let this go for now, because you like being with me in the woods and pretending it's Christmas every day? How long did you think this was going to last?"

I spread my arms and don't back down, because my mind is boiling. This was supposed to be a treat for both of us, the loveliest of afternoons.

"I don't know! Until you fall in love with me?" There, I said it, my true intention out in the open.

Kurt howls into the gag, arching off the rock as if he were dying of lockjaw, but Blake ignores him. A storm is raging in his beautiful green eyes, and I know its wrath is aimed at me. "You think I can really trust anyone that much after everything that happened? After my own brother deserted me, then tried to murder me for money?" He steps back with an exasperated sigh. "I don't think I'm capable of feelings like that."

I put down the knife, in case he's skittish, and step closer to him with my heart pounding. "But... I love you," I say helplessly. Those three words can never encompass the depth of my feelings, or what it's like to hold him in my arms at night, but it's all I've got.

He purses his lips, as if he were trying to say something, only to give up. "What the hell? You don't love me. You can't love me because you barely know me," he shouts, throwing his arms to the sides.

He might as well have grabbed the knife at our feet and stabbed me in the heart. I opened up my ribcage for him to see my raw insides, and all he has for me is acid. I stare at him, dead serious. I will *not* back down from what I said.

"I know you better than you know yourself, and that's why I love you. I know you secretly want to watch me take this guy apart," I gesture to Kurt without looking away from Blake for a second. "I know you don't care to go to the police about your brother or me. You want to take matters into your own hands. I also know you claim to avoid sugar, but always put two spoonfuls in your coffee. You say your favorite color is black, but when we do crafts, you always go for shades of blue. You love to say 'no, please, stop' to me when you mean 'give it to me harder.'"

Blake stumbles back, as if I've taken a swing at him, his shoulders so stiff I want to press him against the wall and work on them until they relax. But he shakes his head again, regaining his composure. "If you loved me, you'd make sure I felt safe and gone after Carl instead of wasting your time on some random criminal."

I snarl at him like what I am—a cornered animal. "Fine. Have it your way!" I turn around, grab the knife, and stab it straight into Kurt's heart, because I don't even feel like playing with him anymore.

CHAPTER 21

BLAKE

I GOT WHAT I wanted.

So why am I not happy?

According to Nico's map app, we should reach Aspen after driving for about thirty hours, which is a lot, but we can't risk taking the plane. Problem is, I don't drive, and Nico needs to rest and sleep, which made us settle on a three-day travel plan, which will go to shit if anything goes wrong on the way. My brother's organizing a big party for all his friends on Saturday, and since all attendees are required to wear masks, there won't be a better chance for us to reach him.

But it's the sexy millionaires' kind of Christmas party, so apart from masks, we need clothes that look hot and glamorous. At least when you squint, because that's the best we'll probably get at Corn View Mall, Nebraska. It's also a good place to stock up on bullets and snacks filled with high-fructose corn syrup.

Two days into our trip, the silence between me and Nico is deafening, so for once I don't mind loud Christmas tunes and children screaming about wanting to see Santa in his grotto.

As if to signify how serious he is about our task, Nico's dressed mostly in black, apart from his hat and jacket. Not a festive T-shirt in sight, no reindeer-patterned sweater, and no smile.

Two can play this game. So I refused to show him what clothes I chose in the only occasion wear store we found. I wasn't being unfair about the nature of our relationship. The truth is that, unlike Nico, I am a realist, and see things for what they are. We might share some interests, and we might feel great in each other's company in this honeymoon phase when all faults can be ignored and the sex is always great, but he and I have no future.

Carl's betrayal broke something in me, and whenever I think about growing closer to anyone, all I see are deep shadows waiting to creep out and choke me when I least expect it. I need to learn how to live independently, but that doesn't change the fact that I miss Nico's dumb jokes or his touch. I know he's withdrawn his attention to get back at me for what he surely perceives as rejection, but I'm not a child anymore and will not acknowledge how stupidly he's behaving.

Though I am frustrated that he didn't let me see the outfit he chose either. Because what if he picked out something garish, and we won't be able to blend in at Carl's party? For all I know, Nico could have bought a suit with a snowman pattern all over it, or something. Or I'm just being petty about it because I crave to see him in something hot and refined. As he pointed out, I do deceive myself sometimes, and pretending I don't would only be another lie.

I guess I also miss how excitable he can be. If we weren't stuck in this sour mood, I'm sure he would be chattering about the decorations in the mall, putting tinsel in my hair, making me try the local donuts with the misshapen antlers made of dough, or showing off the tie he's bought.

And then I think of his helpless declaration of love for me in front of a man about to die, and my heart goes all mushy like a marshmallow in hot chocolate. But I wasn't lying. We've known each other for two weeks. Maybe not even that long.

I'm annoyed when I find myself humming along with the melody coming from the speakers and shut myself up with the last gulp of hot chocolate, which I sip from a paper cup on a bench in front of an empty Santa's Grotto. And right on time, because Nico is striding my way, tall, broad-shouldered, and handsome like some Hollywood A-lister. I throw my empty cup into the trash can and promise myself that I will not inquire what he has in the big paper bag he's carrying.

I am not letting him win.

"I think we're all set, unless you want to pick up some sugar-free snacks," he says, standing next to me.

This is cold war on his part, because, as he pointed out, I do actually like the sugary snacks. He's trying to force me to either admit it, or punish me by making me eat the thing I don't want, just so I can keep up appearances. Pure psychological warfare, but what else should I expect from a sociopathic serial killer?

"I don't think they have the stuff I want here," I lie and turn on my heel, so he doesn't have the opportunity to contradict me. There will be plenty of tasty treats at highway stops.

"Are you sure? I think I've seen some that said they're gluten-free, sugar-free, lactose-free, high protein, and with carob nibs. You know, instead of chocolate bits."

Oh, now this is cruel and unusual.

"See, I told you, you don't know me all that well. I'm not gluten or lactose-free," I tell him coldly and see his cheeks flush. I love the way he swallows, making that beautifully masculine throat move. I could lick his neck instead of any candy. But when he opens his mouth, a middle-aged woman in a glittery red sweater stops right next to us and covers her mouth with hands entwined as if she were about to pray.

"I'm sorry to bother you, but would you like to do a good deed, and earn some cash to spend on Christmas?" she asks Nico.

When he turns to her, a wide smile blooms on his lips, and it's infuriating that she gets one and I don't. Even though it's fake.

"Oh, I'm not sure we have the time—"

She puts her hands up. "Just hear me out. I don't see any kids with you so I was hoping you might be more available than some of the dads I asked. Our Santa didn't show up for work." She points to the grotto. "We only need a few hours of your time. And your friend could be an elf helper, if he wants." She beams at me as if that's a good offer. "All paid on the spot, after the job. What do you say? Will you save Christmas?" The lady laughs and pats Nico's arms as my feet freeze to the floor. She said the magic words and I'm already cursing in my mind, because Nico has a hard-on for Christmas, and the fact that he's even considering this is making me want to scream.

I can't cause a scene though and tell him what I think about this. He must know we don't have a few hours to spare, so I let him answer.

He bites his lip and pats my back. "I mean... I can't say no to Christmas. Will you be my elf, Blake?"

I stare at him, lift my brows to remind him how much this will delay us but, in the face of no explicit protest, he offers the woman a wide grin.

"We'll accept. Where can we prepare?"

I can't fucking believe this shit. Not only is he delaying our plans and risking that we won't reach Aspen on time, but also draws me into this clownery?

Unbelievable.

He must truly hate me.

The woman introduces herself as Julia and leads us through a shop with all types of Christmas crap. I have to admit it has nothing on Nico's Winter Emporium. While this place is all plastic, glitter glue, and smells of old donut oil, Nico's shop is the epitome of Christmas magic. All those handmade toys, the miniature train, the local sweet treats, and the scent of pine and orange encompassing it all create a place that really is beyond time and therefore can get away with being an all-year-round Christmas shop.

But I shouldn't be thinking about how amazing his lovely shop is, and what a great atmosphere he has created when he just threw us both into the clutches of Julia's glittery green nails. If Nico thinks I'll be dressing up as an elf ever again, he has another thing coming.

"Thank you for doing this, guys," Julia tells us, leading us past the man working at the pop-up Christmas store's cash register, and into the back rooms. "You are a God-send. The kids would be so disappointed if it wasn't for you."

"How long will this take?" I ask, trying not to sound overtly abrasive as she opens the door leading into a cluttered storage room with piles of boxes and rails surrounding a sparse area close to the entrance. It can't be bigger than my bathroom back at home.

"Oh, just three hours, once you start at midday. Then, after an hour's break, another three hours."

That's it, we are getting out of here as soon as she leaves.

But when Julia closes the door behind her, leaving us in the dim light of a single light bulb swinging from a cable above us, Nico starts undressing to change into the Santa outfit waiting for him on a hanger. Un-fucking-believable.

I swear he's doing this on purpose, because my mouth goes dry at the sight of his chest, and I'm struggling to spit out all the venom on my tongue.

"Why are we going to Aspen if you hate me this much?" comes out of my mouth the moment she's out.

"What? I'm doing what you asked me to, since you claim I can't love you unless I kill him." Nico squints at me and his nostrils flare at a deep inhale.

My face twists. "Yes, and to do that, we need to be in Aspen tomorrow, and not dead-tired. Why would you agree to this job?" I ask, gesturing at the open red jacket he already put over his bare chest, about to hide all that tempting body hair.

To make things worse, we're forced to stand so close in this damn storage room I can smell his cologne, and it's confusing my body when I should be thinking with my brain only. It's like being on a diet and walking past a bakery.

Nico frowns. "It's the right thing to do. Did you see all those kids out there? They'll be disappointed. I can't *not* save Christmas."

He really believes this shit. That he's a decent human being, not a killer on the way to commit *more* murder.

"What about saving *my* Christmas? Since I actually know what kind of person you are? No need for a fake beard and costumes."

"And what kind of person am I, huh?" Nico asks without a hint of a smile left. Instead, his eyes are ice cold. Which doesn't make him any less handsome, but he doesn't need to know that.

I swallow, feeling a bit faint, because I'm sharing a small space with a predator. "Why are you pretending to be Mr. Nice Guy, when we both know you enjoy killing and torture?" I ask, lowering my voice.

He hums, taking his time to think through my question as if it were a tricky one. All I want is to force him out of this room so we can get back on the road. It's really not that complicated.

"I *am* nice. Maybe I want to remind you of that." Nico swallows. "I could be *your* Mr. Nice Guy. I guess the surprise in the cave was a bit of a misfire on my part. You don't need to see any of that if you don't want to, and we can date in normal ways."

What is he even talking about? There will be no normalcy between me and him. He's a criminal I'm unhealthily fascinated by, and there's no pushing the truth back into the closet after I've seen what he is.

I rub my face, because I can't think straight when he's in front of me, half-naked. I've been spending hours in his company, constantly breathing in his scent yet denied touch. At this point, I would lie, steal, and cheat for a taste of him. But he deserves the truth, or we'll never be past this. "Nico, I can't *date* you. You're a serial killer."

My stomach clenches when a darkness settles in his blue eyes. I don't know if it's a trick of light because the bulb above us gives such stark illumination, or just because he's lowered his eyelids, but it feels unnatural. His jaw tightens, and he inhales deeply, which only makes me avoid staring at his pecs, because they're all too close and all too tempting.

"You can't date me, but you *can* fuck me? Fuck a serial killer?" his voice is like a boulder weighing on my heart, and I take a step back, a mouse fallen into a lion's cage.

He can't be so deeply in denial. I'm a normal person, who wants to live a fun, carefree life. I don't want to have to watch my back, or worry for him, or fear what he might do when one day he loses interest in me.

He's a serial killer. What else can I expect?

"That's different."

He stares me down. "I think I get it. You love the danger. You like the Christmas Killer, but not *me*."

It feels like a slap, and I shake my head, because that's not true at all. "What are you talking about? I do like you!"

Nico cracks his neck with a sneer. "*Like* me? How can you like me? You don't even like Christmas!"

I have never heard anything less reasonable in my life! What a wild logical jump to make.

"*You* are not Christmas!"

"But I *am* the Christmas Killer, and *that* is something you secretly love." Nico steps closer, until our boots touch, as if he's daring me to back away. But I can't move. Blood has drained out of my head, and all I can sense is his cologne, all I can see is his handsome face above, and his hairy chest. Even his voice, dangerous and raspy, is keeping me still like an invisible chain.

After having sex at least twice a day since I lost my virginity, the dry spell of the last two days has been a shock to the system, and I can't think straight when he's so close, so authoritative.

"It's... complicated."

Nico shakes his head, and places his hand on my neck, his fingers keeping my jaw still as if he's assessing a turkey to kill for his feast. "It's not, really. You can't date me, but you can fuck me. You hate Christmas, but you have use for the Christmas Killer. You need me to kill your brother, and I want your sweet, tight body as my pay. I think we understand each other now."

I hate the coldness in his voice, because it doesn't suit him at all, but I can't help what his words are doing to me. They're coming straight from my most secret fantasies, and I can't look away even though we're heading straight for a painful crash. "You want me to pay?" I ask, breathless, because saying that out loud sends my flesh into a lusty frenzy. He's so strong, so dangerous, and I'm eating it up.

"Yes," he rasps and just as I'm about to answer, he turns me around so I'm facing a stack of boxes. He's often tender with me, so it always shocks me that he can manhandle me with such ease.

I whimper and grab the edge of the box on top, pushing back against him, because finally he's touching me again. Maybe this uneasy situation can be solved through pleasure, and after the past two weeks, my body learned to crave him with an almost unnatural thirst. I widen my stance and roll my hips in a circular motion, struggling to keep still.

His big warm hands slide under my hoodie, straight for my pecs. He squeezes them hard and pushes against me, already growing hard. I should tell him to wait until we're in a motel, or at least in the car in the middle of nowhere, that the door to this room doesn't even have a lock, but it only excites me more that his lust is so urgent.

I don't understand what's between us now, but responding to his touch is instinctual and doesn't require much thought. Nico's shameless in how he rubs his crotch against my ass, as if this is all I am for him now. I'm not sure how to feel about it, yet it doesn't make me any less aroused.

"W-what if she comes back?" I try, but all and any reasons to protest die in my mind when Nico covers the lower half of my face with his hand, wordlessly telling me to be quiet. And oh, how I long to fulfill all his wishes.

"Then she's gonna find me railing you and either kick us out or call the cops." There's a fresh pack of cleaning sponges resting nearby, and I watch him grab one. Before I can ask him what he wants with it, he unceremoniously stuffs it in my mouth. Leaning over me, he whispers in my ear. "So let's not attract attention with your moaning."

The foam tastes of nothing, but the sound of his voice, so low and commanding, makes me bite into it as he kneads my flesh, already hard against my ass. I look back, only for him to take a handful of my hair and press my face against the cardboard. I can't help myself, and I'm once again overcome by a perverted desire that penetrates every bit of flesh. My body already knows what it wants, and my mind isn't far behind.

In some ways, this is so much easier than the hard conversations we've been having, dealing with who he is, or that I'm intending to kill my brother. With Nico, all sense of past or future disappears, leaving only the here and now, where loneliness doesn't exist.

But lust sure does, along with that pinch of fear that makes my dick hard.

I don't know if this is punishment or if he misses me and doesn't know how else to express his feelings. Either way, when he unzips my pants then pulls them down, exposing me in a room where someone could walk in on us any minute, thinking becomes impossible.

I'm not even sure if we've arranged that I'm his until he kills Carl, or if I'm supposed to fulfill his needs after we're done too. Or if it's a valid arrangement at all.

Nico pinches my nipple, and his cock settles between my ass cheeks as he enjoys kneading my flesh. He shamelessly squeezes my cock too, once more pressing my face down when I try to look back.

I want to remind him we have little time, that we should hurry, but the sponge in my mouth keeps me silent, so I express the urgency I'm feeling by rubbing myself against him with a soft moan. His shaft is such a beautiful fit in my crack, and I twist my hips to kiss it with my hole.

"So eager, huh? Starving for a *violent criminal's* dick?" he asks in an unforgiving voice.

I hate how true his words are. I can't divorce my lust from who he is, and how I criticized him for it. My body doesn't care about laws, and I get goosebumps of anticipation when he backs off a little, because I've no doubt he's getting lube. I've barely started having sex, but I love it so much. I love his dick inside me and how long he can go on for, how strong he is, how confident.

I love it when he puts his weight on top of me and shows me how much in control of me he really is. Deep down, I trust him not to hurt me, but knowing how dangerous he is, how unhinged, makes me harder than anything else. I crave to have him hold me down and fuck me hard on the floor of the cell where he put me that night he abducted me. I want him to scare me until I believe that the upcoming orgasm might be my very last.

Maybe I even *want* to see him kill bad people who would never answer for their crimes otherwise.

I moan into my makeshift gag and spread my thighs wider, hungry for him.

He doesn't waste any more time and spits on my exposed hole despite also following that up with a drizzle of lube. My balls tighten from arousal, and then he's aligning himself with my anus. It's like having warmth explode deep inside me, and I long for him to reach where the sensation originates.

"Come on, relax and open up to me. Give me what I'm owed," Nico whispers, and then his weight is on me again. I want to take him. Fast. Now. But his cock is thick, and I've only taken it a few times. I'm not that used to his girth yet. Still, the raw need wins out, and I twist my body as I push out, relaxing my muscles. It feels almost like my hole is welcoming him with a kiss, and I sob into the sponge, so very desperate to offer him the best I have.

As soon as his cockhead is in, Nico grabs my arms and pulls them back. "I guess this is all you want to be for me..." he mutters before a harsh thrust that leaves me whimpering and shifting my weight helplessly.

Not that I want to escape. My dick is hard, my hole stretched for him, and until he gets his fill, I'm not going anywhere. I missed being under him. He won't leave me behind for as long as he's inside me. I'm so sorry about upsetting him, but we can discuss that later. Right now, our tempers need to mellow out, and as he sinks in balls-deep, spearing my body with his hard shaft, I tremble like a newborn calf.

"Mm... mhm," I hum to let him know how much I love to have him inside me, how deliciously his fingers dig into the flesh of my arms. He has me pinned to the boxes, and I want him to fuck me until he's spent. Once, twice, however many times he wants.

He buries his face against my nape, and his needy grunts turn me on even more as he starts fucking me as if his life depends on the orgasm he's chasing. Fast, animalistic, eager to come. I keep my legs spread wide to accommodate him, and when he bites my neck, all I can do is whimper into my gag. My hole is on fire, but I want his satisfaction. I want him to come inside me and tell me I'm a good boy even though I know I've been a menace.

But am I not being good to him now? Pliant. Open. Once again, I try to look back only to have my face pressed to the box, and saliva dribbles down my chin as he jabs into me harder than before. So far, his thrusts have been controlled and slow, but this was a warning, and I whimper like a lost dog begging for the attention of his master. My skin feels as if it's about to go up in flames. My hole aches in the best way possible. And I want his cum so fucking much.

Nico settles with his lips against my nape, strong grip on my wrists, his hips working like a machine. There's a comfort in knowing he wants me this much despite the turmoil I've been causing.

"Oh, fuck yes..." he mumbles, fucking me with abandon, skin slapping against skin.

He lets go of one of my arms, and when he reaches between my legs to squeeze my painfully hard dick, I'm not sure if he wants to jerk me off or just fondle me for his own pleasure. It doesn't matter. His touch is like oil thrown into fire, and I climb to my toes, presenting my ass to him as he pounds me, filling the small, cluttered space with the sounds of our sweaty bodies.

He's still holding one of my hands back, twisting it almost too firmly, but I love the symbolism of it and moan because each of his thrusts is like a hot wave. His touch makes me feel so damn special, so close to him, so safe from all the evil in the world.

It's as though his dangerous aura is a shield, and as long as I'm within it, serving him with my body, I can't be harmed. I can't deny it. I like it. No. I *love* it. I love when he's inside me, so intense, so needy. Love being the only one who can give him what he wants.

I know he's a cruel monster, yet the strokes of his hand on my cock become fast and insistent. Whether to please me, or to feel my muscles tightening on his cock doesn't matter, because it feels so damn good to be jerked off as he fucks me with that thick tool.

My mind fizzles, and I can almost sense bubbles at the base of my skull as he enters me hard and fast while his hand works my cock at the same speed. I'm overflowing with need. On fire. And if it wasn't for the sponge in my mouth, I would have screamed, begging him to fuck me harder.

Cum shoots out of me almost too fast, and I stiffen, tightening my thighs as he continues sawing into me without mercy.

The little grunt he makes against my skin makes me shoot even harder the second time, even though I already thought I was at my limit. My whole body trembles, throbs with heat as if I'm about to melt, fall apart, and he's the only one who can put me back together.

"That's it..." A few hard jabs later, Nico stiffens on top of me, rocking his hips a little, as if he wants to make sure he's spilled all his cum inside me. I love how his heart pounds against my back. Maybe if we fuck enough times, the frost in mine will melt?

I'm afraid of what might happen if I get swept away by the tide of his madness, but I can't resist his warmth and pull his arm around me as our bodies rest. It's only then that I shove the sponge out of my mouth and breathe freely. "Wow, that was... unexpected."

But he doesn't give me much of a cuddle and pulls back after the briefest moment. "Was it though? You know how much I want you."

I finally get to look back at him and notice he's tying up a condom and throwing it behind a box. I don't know if I should feel complimented or slighted. Because on one hand, it makes sense that he used one in a public space, for convenience, maybe even out of care for me, so I don't have to worry about his cum leaking out of me. But on the other hand, it feels like he wanted a barrier between us.

Still, there will be many other times when I can let him breed me without worry, so I step closer and slide my hand over his side. "Well... I didn't expect us to do it where we could be caught. It was kind of hot."

He scowls at me. "'Kind of'?"

My face falls. "Very," I say in a voice so embarrassingly small I can barely hear it myself.

Nico nods as he takes off the red jacket and puts it back on the rack. It reminds me to pull up my own pants, so I do that after a quick clean up with the damn gag-sponge.

There's a sense of unease inside my chest, and I attempt to extinguish it by resting my face on Nico's bare arm. "Maybe we could... rest?"

Nico looks anywhere but at me. "Nah, you were right, we should go. There's no time for stupid shit." He points to the Santa costume and grabs his sweater, once more standing beyond my grasp.

I can't help the sense of disappointment squeezing my chest, but we are in a public space, and he is right, we've already wasted too much time. I shouldn't be getting upset just because he didn't give me a single kiss. I don't want things to get too serious anyway.

We're having sex again, I said my piece, and there will be no 'saving Christmas' by Nico.

But if I got what I wanted, then why do I feel so bad?

Chapter 22

Blake

IF I'M ATTRACTED TO the darkness inside of Nico, to his dominant demeanor and violent tendencies, then why do I miss his goofy jokes and smiles? It makes no sense, yet because Nico has become so serious, it feels like he's locked me away from a part of himself. And now that I can't have it, I want to stick my hand into that cookie jar so badly I'm going crazy.

But we can't waste time on dealing with the weird mood between us when there is so much on the line. The house is only a short drive away from the large gas station where we've stopped to change for the masquerade.

I shake my head, unwilling to dwell on my brother's impending death, and put on a coat over my checkered suit. It's a nice shade of bottle-green, and while it came off the rack, it fits as if it were made for me. Maybe this is what I should have worn to my first-ever adult outing, not the stupid elf costume?

I step out of the bathroom stall, ready to go, when my gaze settles on Nico's tall, broad-shouldered form.

He's adjusting his tie, so I see him in the mirror and, there's no other way to put it, he's breathtaking. Dressed in black pants and a burgundy jacket with sequin lapels, which make him look as if he's already adorned in blood. This time, he's no bloodthirsty wolf, foaming at the mouth with a hunger for gore, but an elegant monster, hidden in plain sight. His eyes are cold and determined, his hair slicked back.

He turns, putting on a simple black mask that covers the upper part of his face and extends into curled horns decorated with red glitter.

"Ready?" Nico asks as I try not to jump his bones before leaving.

He wouldn't want me to, since I'm reasonably sure he hates me now. After all, I stopped him from 'saving Christmas' which definitely put me on the naughty list.

But a deal is a deal, and he will carry out my revenge before disappearing from my life forever.

I can't begin to describe the emptiness that thought makes me feel at the center of my chest, but the truth is that I cannot date a killer. It just wouldn't work, and as difficult as our parting is going to be, it is the lesser of two evils.

We don't speak on the way to the car, nor as we drive to our destination—an old secret passage into the villa. It was made for the discreet transport of people and goods during the prohibition era so groups of prostitutes could visit the house for lavish parties, and once even provided a convenient exit when the previous owner of our Aspen home was fleeing the cops. Today, the start of the passage looks like a little concrete building with markings suggesting that it contains high-voltage electricity. It's partially sunken into the hill behind it, and it's easy to access with a code only Carl and I know.

Nico doesn't communicate with me as he illuminates the old school lock on the door, which I open after a bit of fumbling with the rust. The passage hasn't been used in a while, but that is for the better, as we won't stumble upon anyone else once we're inside.

"Where will this lead us?" Nico asks, which in itself tells me he trusted me enough to follow me here without question.

"The wine cellar," I tell him as we lock the entrance with a rusty latch and face the narrow corridor leading far beyond the reach of our flashlight. The air here is stale, smelling of damp and wood, but we came here on a mission, and I would crawl over rat carcasses in order to ensure my safety. Though when we actually do stumble upon some rodents that ended their lives in the dark, I feel way less certain about this whole plan. It's as if I'm seeing my future in their dried-out remains, but when I stall, Nico's presence motivates me to go on. He's so tall he needs to slouch and bow his head at all times, which distracts me enough to stop worrying that the old beams reinforcing the vaulted ceiling might collapse and bury us here forever.

We don't exchange a single sentence during the long, stressful walk, but as we reach an iron door that's partially open, relief washes over me as if the whole mission has already been accomplished.

I feel much better standing beneath a ceiling that appears structurally sound for a change, and that fact reassures me so much I almost leave the secret passage without obscuring my face. But Nico is ever-vigilant and pulls on my hand. I'm flustered by his touch and put on the small wooden mask I purchased at the mall. Shaped to imitate a young deer's head, it has small antlers extending to my forehead and a muzzle, which covers my nose yet leaves the mouth bare.

"We need to make sure he doesn't get to his office. It doubles as a panic room and he has an alarm button in there," I say to fill the silence, even though we've already talked about it.

"Anything else com to mind? Something you might have forgotten?" Nico asks and frowns because we've hit a dead end.

Or at least it seems that way, because it's actually a hidden door that will take us from the corridor and into the wine cellar. I can only hope no member of staff is there now.

I'm reminded that we are here on our own, which makes my face flush with intense heat. At least Nico won't notice me blushing behind the mask.

I speak, as if sneaking into a house to assassinate someone was my usual Tuesday. "In the panic room, he has an additional hiding space behind the bookshelf. It opens when someone pulls on the brass statue of an archer."

My hand finds the button opening the passage, and the wall ahead pops back, revealing itself to be a door.

"Follow me," I tell him and enter the cool dark interior illuminated by the light shining in the nearby corridor.

"Just don't do anything rash," Nico says, and a shiver goes up my spine when he strokes the small of my back. "Let me handle things, and if it gets too heated, don't wait up, run."

His touch sends wisps of warmth all over me, but when he takes his hand away, I head toward the insistent noise and heat of the kitchen. With chefs, their helpers, and waiting staff all focused on their duties, nobody pays attention to masked guests who make their way past grills, pots, and huge platters of canapés. Everything smells delicious, but my stomach is tight from the stress of what I'm about to do, and I long to find Carl already.

It's a Christmas party, with plenty of masked guests, so we might be able to get to him without being noticed, but the moment we step among the guests, fear crawls up my throat and tightens around it like a collar with spikes on the inside.

Fine velvets, brocade, and furs surround us from all sides, and I feel underdressed in my off-the-rack suit, but the lights are dimmed to create an intimate atmosphere, so I might just avoid being identified as an impostor. A musical quartet plays festive music, providing the background for easy conversation and wine drinking, but I storm right past the artists, intent on finding my brother. I don't want to be here any longer than strictly necessary.

As I lead Nico into a hallway I used to reimagine as a race track, back when my parents were still around, a faint modern rhythm worms its way into my ear. I head toward a place originally conceptualized as the smoking room, where gentlemen retire after dinner and enjoy conversation uninhibited by the necessity of censoring themselves for the sake of female company. The double doors are partially open, and rays of green and red light coming from inside fall on my Grandmom's portrait hung right across from the room.

I don't think she would have approved of what's going on inside.

The antique billiards table that's as big as some people's studio apartments, is covered with shiny cloth, and two barely dressed ladies dance on top of it for an audience of at least two dozen people.

"Do you think this is where your brother would be?" Nico whispers, stepping inside as I eye two security guards who casually walk past us, staring at glitter nipple tassels attached to a pair of pert breasts.

When the dancer makes them spin, and then steps through a spiraling hoop, I'm certain the view before me will be permanently burned on the backs of my eyelids.

I try acting as if I don't find any of this unusual, but as the two dancers slot together, I'm eaten up by discomfort. Not just because I have no interest in women, but mostly because this is *not* what I expected to see at a *Christmas* Party. And definitely not on the billiards table my dad used to house his toy train collection.

Looks like I don't know my brother nearly as well as I thought. As if *that* wasn't obvious when he sent assassins after me.

When my eyes get used to the relative darkness of the smoking room, I notice that only some of the women present are performers or hostesses. Plenty of ladies within sight wear conventional eveningwear, which offers me some relief, and I clap when the show on the impromptu stage comes to an end.

"I... don't know this side of him," I tell Nico, but as I'm about to retreat and peruse the rest of the house, my gaze lingers on a familiar silhouette.

He's even wearing a suit I've seen in one of his photos. My brother might have a simple mask over the eyes, but he *wants* to be seen and known.

Nico grabs himself a canapé from a passing hostess, seeming perfectly relaxed when I'm about to faint from stress. He's wearing the red gloves, likely to avoid leaving behind fingerprints, but all I can remember is how their leather felt inside me.

Carl seems so at ease when he grabs one of the dancers by the waist and carries her to the floor as she giggles, her bare breasts right in his face.

"That's him," I mumble, leaning against Nico. "My brother. The one hugging the dancer."

I never thought of myself as a prude, but there's something about seeing my older brother like this that makes me long for the safety of Nico's small apartment.

"We have to get him away from people," Nico says and while I consider retreat, he makes his way through the crowd like a snake zeroing in on its prey.

I don't even feel I have a choice, so I follow him, desperate to grab his hand yet too afraid it could draw too much attention to us. Carl stands with his back to us, his arm around the dancer's waist, but Nico seems to have no issue with making himself known. He leans against the billiards table and his gaze lands on the dancer, sticky with lust.

I'm so taken aback I don't even know what I'm looking at anymore. He's like a different man. If pretending comes so easily to him, maybe it's for the better that we will probably part after this ordeal.

The dancer is drawn in by his interest and relaxed body language like a cat to fresh cream. Despite my brother's hand on her hip, she flutters her dark eyelashes at Nico and smiles. It's like a dance. I don't know the steps, but I'm impressed anyway.

I stand nearby, like a tiny fish safe under the shark's belly, so when Nico moves, so do I. He approaches my brother and the girl. While I try to remember how to breathe, he's suave as if he's attended parties like this all his life. In the dim light, I wouldn't be able to tell that his mask is off the discount rack.

"I loved the show," he says to the girl, and extends his hand to her. When she slides her fingers into his, he kisses her knuckles. "I hope I'm not interrupting." He turns to Carl, and while my nerves are already in tatters, they now get thrown into a blender. One of those high-powered ones that can crush ice cubes, only this time it's my ribcage that's being pulverized before the blades can reach my heart.

He's never spoken to me quite in this fashion. But should I be bothered? I know for a fact that he's feigning interest, and I don't expect him to treat me like *a lady*, since I'm obviously not one, but green, slimy jealousy still crawls up my gullet. I fight the urge to clear my throat as the sensation burns.

How can I trust him when I know how good he is at pretending?

Then again, would it matter if he never dropped the act and cherished me forever?

That obviously can't happen, but... in theory, would I care?

Also, I can't believe I'm standing so close to Carl without him knowing. Maybe this doesn't bother a psychopath like Nico, but I'm close to fainting.

Just as my brother is about to answer, his lips twisting, the dancer speaks. "Not at all. We were just about to go find ourselves a quiet little nest, but..." Her slender fingers slide up Nico's arm. "There could be room for more, right Carl?" She glances at my brother, biting her lip.

Nico exhales and stands even closer to her almost naked form. "Illicit. I love it. I can imagine a girl like you craves the thrill. What do you say, Carl?" His smile becomes predatory in a way that makes my stomach twist with nervous desire and my head empty until all I can think about is his touch, and the power his gaze has on me.

I know Nico's gay. I know all of this is a ruse to get Carl alone and murder him in cold blood. And yet I despise that he's smiling like that at anyone other than me. The thought of him going in for a threesome, even if only for the sake of an easier kill later, makes me want to leave, get a new identity, and start a life in his attic, never looking back, just so he doesn't have to stick to this act.

Carl clicks his tongue. "I don't know—"

But the dancer pouts at him and strokes his chest. "Come on, baby, it will be fun. He could keep the mask on. We'd never know who he really is."

Oh. So is this woman... his girlfriend? I know nothing about her existence, and that fact somehow strikes me even more painfully than Carl's betrayal.

Nico raises his hands. "And *we* don't have to touch if that's the issue."

Carl cocks his head at *me* all of a sudden, and I'm a deer in the headlights when our eyes meet. With the mask I'm wearing—literally. "And him?"

My lips dry. He will surely recognize my voice.

Nico pats my back with a smirk. "This is Tommy. Or should I say, Peeping Tommy. He just likes to watch."

His touch burns in the best way, and I long to kill his act by rolling straight into his arms. Maybe I'll even ask him to fuck me on the billiards table, because fuck Carl and his opinion of me.

That's something I only entertain in my fantasies as rage buzzes inside me, a reminder of what my own brother was happy to do to me, to get his hands on all our family's money.

"He's staring," Carl says, making me stiffen. "Is he into me, or something?"

Bile rises in my throat, but Nico laughs off Carl's question. "Nah, he's just shy."

The dancer pulls on Carl's arm. "Come on, live a little, it's gonna be fun." With the way she eyes Nico, I'm pretty sure she's got the hots for *him*, but if she's that keen on fucking my brother over, I'm her biggest fan.

Carl rolls his eyes but smiles and lets her lead him to a door on the other side of the room buzzing with erotic energy. "Ah, what the hell. Let's go."

Just like that? Really?

I give Nico a wide-eyed glance from behind my mask, and when he winks at me, charming and suave like a heartthrob from the golden age of Hollywood, I find myself following his lead like a dog obeying its master.

A guard standing in front of a door on one side of the room nods at Carl, then unlocks the passage and steps aside, letting the four of us through.

The wooden staircase ahead leads to a corridor right next to the master bedroom, where my parents used to sleep whenever we spent time in Aspen. Despite having vague memories of happy childhood moments in this house, my head pulsates with the reality that my own brother, whom I loved, and who I depended on doesn't even recognize me when the upper half of my face is hidden.

How could I have missed how little he cared for me?

"Nothing like a night of debauchery!" The dancer squeals and throws her hands in the air. She twirls and lands in Nico's arms.

I hate it. I hate the way he smiles at her, I hate his hand on her back, I hate that he's not putting a bullet between my brother's eyes yet, and I hate that I'm so jealous, but at this point, just fucking kill *me* already.

How the fuck will I cope with parting from Nico? Knowing that he might be dating someone else? I have not thought this through at all.

"Night of your life," Nico promises and picks her up. When she wraps her legs around him, I'm reeling, not sure who I want to kill first: her or *him*.

"Just behind this door," Carl says, leading us farther. The music is only a low thumping behind walls, and I don't even know where all this is headed, because this woman is a witness in the making. We can't have her here.

An ugly thought rises in my blackened heart. What if this is some elaborate revenge by Nico? What if he brought me here, pulled me into this fucked-up situation, so that I suffer? What do I really know about his cruel, twisted mind?

If he wants to go through with this threesome, could I sit in a corner and watch? Not only would I be watching my brother have sex, which, *barf*, but also Nico with someone else? What kind of fucked up punishment would that be? Watching the man I lo—

"No, this won't do!" The dancer giggles in Nico's arms and before I know what's happening, she pushes up my mask. "If you're watching, I want to see your face. Aw, you're a cutie!"

But my heart turns into ice as I turn my gaze to my brother and our eyes meet.

CHAPTER 23

Nico

Fuck.

Double fuck.

It happened so fast I couldn't stop her, and now here we fucking are. My heart is a boulder in my chest as I let the dancer down to the floor.

"That's my brother," Carl says. He's sobering up fast, his gaze drifting between Blake and me. I've no doubt that he's assessing my size.

The poor girl has no idea what's going on and makes a face at him. "Ew! Carl! What the fuck?" She steps back from us. "That's far too fucked up for me. What next? Is *he* your cousin or something?" She points at me, but all I'm wondering is whether Carl has a weapon on him, so I stand a bit closer to Blake, just in case.

Carl frowns and grabs her by the wrist. "What? I had no idea he'd be here."

The dancer twists her hand away and takes a step toward the door, her earlier playfulness gone. "Are you really trying to convince me you didn't recognize your own brother because of some stupid mask? Give me a break. I'm kinky, but not into some incest shit," she says and strides out, not bothering to spare any of us another glance.

Carl keeps his eyes on me, aware that I might be a predator. "B-Blake. Where have you been? What is this? *Who* is this?"

Okay, so he's playing dumb. Fair enough. It gives me time to count the clicks of the woman's heels. The farther away she is, the better. Preferably, I want her back in the smoking room before I act.

Blake, who's been stiff as an aging tree, suddenly comes back to life. He shuts the double door and leans against it, staring at his brother in a silence so intense I swear I can hear his heartbeat. "You... seem worried," he says flatly. "Distracting yourself with all that music and sex."

I make note of the smaller door on the other side of the opulent bedroom furnished with heavy wooden furniture someone polished to perfection. It's either an exit, or just a bathroom, but when Carl takes a step back, I'm thinking it could be his planned way out.

But no matter the painful rift between me and Blake, I make sure I'm close enough to protect him. This boy might have cut my heart into paper-thin strips, but even as a puppet with a void in its chest I won't let anyone hurt him.

Carl spreads his arms, appearing so shocked I almost believe him. "What? Of course I'm worried! You haven't returned any of my calls. But the party was already planned. You knew about it so I actually hoped you might show up. Come give me a hug!" he says and steps forward, about to grab Blake.

I don't hesitate. I stand between them like a wall so fast Carl bounces off me.

"Stay back," I say, but my voice dulls in surprise when Blake places his palm on my back and lets it rest there, fueling me with the warmth of his body.

Carl tears his mask off in time for me to see his features twitch. He's handsome, I can give him that, but there's a predatory edge to his square face, and as he watches me from under his brows, tense like a trapped animal, I itch to grab his neck and be done with it.

Do I want to play with him? Do I want to see him suffer? Absolutely, but every breath he takes means that Blake continues to be threatened by his very existence.

"Who the hell is this guy, and why is he barking at me, huh?" Carl asks, looking right past me.

The air grows denser with each passing second, but when Carl leans forward, as if he's about to grab Blake, a soft voice resonates behind me like a bell.

"He's the Christmas Killer."

"What? Is this one of your silly podcast ideas?" Carl cocks his head at me. He sneers, but his body language changes.

We're walking a thin line, and I consider pulling out my gun and shooting him on the spot. A much less satisfying kill than it would have been with a knife, but ensuring Blake's safety is more important than my petty desires.

"He said what he meant. Even if you don't know who I am, it won't matter anymore in about... ten seconds," I say and reach for my weapon, but I've spooked him too soon.

Carl pulls out his own gun, eyes wide, and shoots our way while already falling back to the door on the other side.

All I can think of is covering Blake, but he screams out. I hope it's just fear that's made him do so, but he grabs me for balance and blood blooms on the side of his leg.

My throat closes as I envision him bleeding out in my arms, his fingers reaching for my face to touch me one last time, but in the real world he's holding on to me as he sobs with discomfort.

"Fuck. Get him. Get him, please," he begs, meeting my gaze.

"I'm not leaving you," I say with my heart pounding and carry him to the bed. I grab my knife and cut open the side of his pants. Blood is everywhere, all the way down his pale thigh and calf, but I see the wound. It's a graze.

Blake looks at it as well, tears streaming down his face, but his expression changes as he cups my face.

"Go, Nico. Please. You can't let him get to the panic room. It's over if he does."

I barely have two seconds to think, because he's right. Every heartbeat I spend here, on my knees by the bed, takes me farther from the man who already made three attempts on Blake's life.

I nod, press my lips to Blake's in the quickest of kisses, and I'm off, flying over the wooden floor.

In my element, I'm both furious and elated. I already envision the moment I rip into Carl's throat and turn it into a red fountain.

I dash through a bathroom with another exit, this time into a corridor. All my senses on high alert, I can *smell* his fear, so I follow the stench along with the thudding of his shoes on the floor.

He hasn't switched on any lights, but the faint glow coming from outside is more than enough to lead me along the carpeted passage. This is the kind of chase that never fails to get my blood flowing faster, and as I see a door open at the very end of the hallway, I can almost feel blood on my tongue.

I shoot when a shadow passes inside the newly revealed interior, but my mark doesn't collapse and disappears from sight.

Fuck.

I fire several times until my bullets are gone, but I've always been better with knives than with a gun, and shooting while running was a disastrous mistake. The chase is taking seconds, but time stretches out like bloody intestines pulled out of a fresh corpse when I see Carl grab the door, about to shut it.

I ram into it with my shoulder, a human wrecking ball, and while he tries to push against me, it's no use. The sheer force of my collision with the door shoves him back, and just as expected, we're in the office that doubles as a panic room. Carl stumbles back, but as our gazes meet, he dashes for the desk as if his life depends on it.

And the truth of the matter is that it does, because this fucker has Blake's blood on his hands. What kind of monster would care so little about his own family? I would have given my hand if it could bring my grandfather back, and this bastard was not only eager to sell his little brother's life but didn't even care what kind of horror he'd go through?

I wish I had all the time in the world. That I could filet his meat and make his skin into a tent to stargaze under with Blake at my side, that I could pull out all his teeth while he was still alive and could suffer a fraction of what Blake would have gone through at the hands of the pervert who abducted him from the club.

I want to break his bones with my bare hands.

A gun pops as he scrambles to shoot my way, but he also misses, and by the time he pulls the trigger a second time, I'm on him, digging my fingers into his right wrist so hard the firearm clatters to the floor.

Once again, the desire for vengeance fills me like fragrant smoke, but when I look at this pathetic worm and think of my precious boy, I know this kill shouldn't be about the things I want.

My feelings for Blake are real, and I want this murder to be my love letter. He can keep it in his heart even after I'm gone.

Carl tries punching me, but he's got neither the strength nor skill to rival mine. When he reaches for a little elegant box resting next to an open notebook and some pens, a grin widens my mouth, and I pluck the fancy letter opener from its bed of velvet.

Raw fear reflects in Carl's eyes when he tries to scream for help, but I don't give him any more time to secure backup and sink the thin blade under his jaw. A choked grunt echoes in my ears, but there's also a dull, steady noise I didn't hear before, and when I glance to the box that previously housed my weapon, blood drains to my legs. Its base is now lifted, revealing a button which pulses with a red sheen once every second.

"Shit," I utter and jab Carl's throat a couple more times.

Blood sprays my face as it drains out of him, soaking into the bastard's suit and spilling onto the carpet. When I meet his eyes, it's obvious he's no longer all there, and as I pull back, he slumps to the floor. If he's not dead yet, it's a matter of a minute or two.

My head spins as I take several deep breaths, trying to calm down and come up with an escape plan, because I cannot leave the way I walked in. Not with this much blood staining my fancy suit. But as I glance toward the window, wondering if there's some kind of fire escape I can use, footsteps make me freeze.

I hesitate whether I should hide or confront whoever's coming, but when the familiar head of brown curls appears from behind the door, I'm overcome by a wonderful sense of calm.

"It's you..."

CHAPTER 24

NICO

THE AIR IS FRAGRANT with blood, and when Blake steps inside, I feel as though I could move mountains. I have fulfilled my promise, and while he's rejected me, the need to ensure he gets home safely is impossible to ignore. Maybe I'm just torturing myself, but what would be the harm in spending the next three days in the car, collecting our last memories together?

But as he limps inside, the pant leg flopping around his bloodstained skin, I see him staring at the pile of minced meat resting on the floor with a letter opener in the eye socket, and I clench my teeth, offering him a nod. "It's done. He won't ever harm you."

Blake lifts his hands, covering his face, and his entire form shakes, as if this was the start of an earthquake. "Oh God, it's really him... he's dead," he utters in a broken voice.

I dash toward him, restless and needy. But when he fills my arms, when his face is buried in my chest, and his lovely, elegant hands slide to my back, I'm at peace in a way I've never experienced.

This must be what having one's heart full feels like, and I kiss the top of his head, shushing my gentle pet. "It's okay. You're safe."

He shakes his head, and I pull away, hurt that even now he insists on seeing me as a threat. He's staring at the glowing red button Carl had managed to push before his death.

"The security will be here in just a few moments."

My face falls, because this is it—the moment I'm forced to flee and leave Blake to the fresh start he wanted. If he still has the slightest sense of loyalty to me, I'll never hear from him again, unless I tune in to his podcast. Perhaps the next time he discusses the Christmas Killer, I'll hear fondness in his smooth voice and entertain the thought that maybe, just maybe, something about our brief relationship was real.

But now he can wash his hands of me and pretend my bloodstained chest didn't make him feel at home.

"I'll go," I tell him, but before he can answer, a door slams in the distance.

"No," Blake says, squeezing my hands. "You don't have the time. Here," he tells me, dashing toward the bookcase featuring many leather-clad tomes. He twists his hand, so as not to leave any fingerprints, slots it behind the statue I remember him mentioning, and pulls.

The fancy wooden panels below the shelf pop open and he steps away, gesturing at it as numerous footsteps resonate farther down the hallway.

"Mister Augustus?" Someone calls out, and Blake sucks in a lungful of air before screaming.

"Help!"

I sneak into the narrow space in the wall behind the bookshelf. It feels like a coffin when he locks it in front of my face, drowning me in darkness. I wonder if he's enticed me in here to safely pass me on to security or the cops. After all, while I stood close or held him in my arms, I could have snapped his neck at the first hint of betrayal.

What he might not know is that I never would have. I would have taken my punishment like a dog that knows its master is angry.

Instead though, as I stay so still I don't even know if I'm still breathing, Blake has a full-on meltdown on the other side of the secret door, and I have to give it to him that he's a damn good actor.

One of the guards is helping him deal with what he thinks is a panic attack, as other frantic voices discuss calling the cops over.

I bite my lip, trying not to make a sound as Blake shrieks, screams, and calls his brother's name before telling all the guards to leave him alone with his 'beloved brother'.

I admit I might not have been this smart at eighteen.

I'm lost in my thoughts and freeze as the door opens again. Blake's face is tear-stricken as he lets me out, still shaking from his Oscar-worthy performance. "Quick, you need to go before the police arrive," he stutters out, grabbing my hand.

I'm so torn. At this point, I want this room to become my tomb, because I'm leaving my heart behind anyway.

But Blake pulls me along, so I follow him to an adjacent room, which has a sizeable table in the middle, and a television mounted high on the wall. But we go straight to a cupboard, and when Blake opens it, I realize it's one of those kitchen elevators I've seen in the movies.

"In here," he says and urges me with a gesture. "This will take you to the kitchen. Just go back the same way we entered the house. The passage unlocks when you press on a brick with the initials LM."

"Did I do well?" I ask, needy for his approval even though my job here is done, and we both know I shouldn't stall any longer.

He blinks at me, dumbstruck, and his face scrunches as tears roll down his cheeks. "Y-yes…"

I cup his face. I could get lost in his forest green eyes. "I'm sorry if I hurt you in any way. You didn't deserve my silence. I wish you… everything. Just *everything*. That's what you deserve. I understand your choice." Even if I hate it and the monster inside me rattles its cage, itching to take Blake with me, put him in my basement and never let him out.

Blake sobs and hangs his head, squeezing the suit jacket he so obviously liked on me. His voice remains choked, because he doesn't want to alert the security, but I still hear him when he says, "no, I'm sorry. I'm so sorry… and now you need to go. Please," and pushes at my chest.

But the monster wins and I pull him in for a hungry kiss, uncaring that his brother's blood is all over us. It's all teeth, and tongue, and he gives in so pliantly despite the tang of copper. When he pushes on my chest, I let go, but not without one more nip to his tongue for him to remember me by.

There's commotion in the other room as I pack my bulky form into the small cubical compartment, and no more words pass between us. I just stare at him, not even blinking until the door of the dumbwaiter shuts in front of me and I'm sent down.

It feels like a descent to hell.

Where creatures like me belong.

CHAPTER 25

BLAKE

I'M GRATEFUL THE HOUSEKEEPER was there to help me deal with the fallout of Carl's death, because the number of choices and formalities involved in organizing a funeral was way beyond anything I'm used to. It also helped that she didn't harbor resentment toward my brother. If it was up to me, Carl would have been dumped in a hog pen and granted no headstone. But that wouldn't have been the best idea, considering he *was* murdered and that I was the first person there.

As much as I hated Carl for treating me like a pawn rather than family, he's now dead, so it doesn't matter what happens to his earthly remains. In the meantime, Nico has disappeared from my life, and I chose not to message him, since the last thing I want is to send the police on his trail. On the upside, this means I don't need to feign sadness and let everyone interpret my mood as mourning. If that can even be called an upside.

Still, I tried to let him know I want to stay in touch and informed Nico about *my loss*. I didn't tell him that I enjoyed our time together, nor that I'm grateful for the freedom he's given me. He answered with perfectly normal condolences, which didn't include any details that might give the cops the wrong—or right—idea.

There was a night when I wished to write to him about something unrelated to the case—the intense dreams I was having about him, but what would be the point? Nico is a serial killer, and while he does have a code I agree with, a switch inside his head could flip, causing him to turn against me. I find it difficult to imagine him hurting me, ever, but he does have an ease for violence most people don't. Still, looking back, I see how patient he's been with me, how he responded to my needs, and how he put my desires before his own.

But that's not what I should focus on, because the guy is *a murderer*. Even if he were the perfect boyfriend, caring, kind, and selfless, do I want to get involved with someone who might end up tracked down and arrested? People would be asking me 'how could you have not seen it?' and I would have to make the most innocent face while holding Nico's secrets close to my chest. Then, I'd spend the rest of my life visiting him in prison, or worse—

Does our state have the death penalty?

My hands start to shake as I reach for my phone, but it's only a moment of weakness that I quickly overcome. I might not officially be a suspect, but as the person who's gained most from Carl's death, I can't do *anything* that might make the cops doubt me. On my podcast, I've reported about way too many crimes where the perpetrator ended up being caught because of their internet history to make such a rookie mistake myself.

I snap out of my nervous thoughts when a hand reaches toward me.

"I'm so sorry for your loss," says a middle-aged man whom I've never seen in my life.

We're in the same room where Carl hosted the strip show not that long ago, and I find it oddly fitting. Even Grandmom's portrait seems to smile at me through the open door leading into the hallway. I never got to meet her, but I hope she's proud of me.

I exchange a few meaningless lies about my brother being a kind-hearted guy who valued family above all else, and once the man leaves me alone, I sip my coffee and take in the room full of strangers. I do know a handful of Carl's acquaintances and friends, but they're few and far between in the stream of bodies in mourning garb flooding my—*my*—smoking room.

I feel unprepared for managing the vast amount of wealth our family has accumulated over the years, but I'm no longer a child and will get on with the program at the start of the new year. For now, I'll pretend to mourn a brother whom I decided to bury in Aspen rather than close to where I live, just so I can always stay far away from his ashes.

The official explanation for this move is Carl's love for mountains and snowboarding. I'm so full of shit I would make a fantastic PR executive. Maybe he and I shared a comparable talent for lying, because after hanging on to his fake love all my life, I found out that not only had Carl not informed the cops I was missing, but also offered time off to all the staff at my home, so no one questioned my absence.

Joke's on him.

The burlesque dancer was someone he'd met that night, not a girlfriend, so we both commiserated about the masked stranger with dark hair (I made sure to say that several times to implant the fake memory) who might have been the one to hurt my brother. I played the perfectly innocent, inexperienced gay man who got charmed into following the lead of a handsome monster. But maybe that's who I really am, since I'm protecting Nico even now.

The somber atmosphere, the parade of guests I don't know, and the endless stream of bite-sized snacks on silver platters is getting all too much, so I walk out of the room and onto a balcony.

From my vantage point, the expanse of the snow covered-forest seems endless, and it reminds me of that week in Nico's cabin. The conditions there were so far from what I was used to, but even though I had to use a crappy eco-shower, wash dishes, and sweep the floor, I felt I had everything I could ever want when Nico smiled at me. And when he held me at night, the sense of loneliness that accompanied me since my parents died was gone.

I was so... content with everything that the perspective of going back home later tonight and being greeted by empty rooms rather than Nico's touch is borderline painful. But what's the alternative? Willingly flying straight into the web of a guy who enjoys killing?

For a moment, I consider looking for love on dating apps, but how could that compare to the way Nico saved me from rape, torture, and murder, then slowly got under my skin with attention and enthusiasm? Maybe that's what it feels like when a spider crawls into one's ear at night? Yeah, no, bad comparison, ew.

Nico's presence felt good, and when I stopped being fearful of him, I craved for him to consume me, until I belonged to him wholly, body and soul.

I shiver, imagining him watching me now from one of the trees close by, and I can't even describe the sense of peace this gives me. It's the relief I need during a party filled with strangers Carl never bothered to introduce me to.

"Hey, Blake..." Someone steps onto the balcony behind me, and I turn, all too aware of the journey my body would make if this guy were to push me off here.

But it's only Mike... or Misha? I've been introduced to him in the past by Carl, but I don't know much about him, other than the fact that he makes my gaydar buzz.

"I'm so sorry for your loss. Carl was such a great guy," he says the most generic thing he can with a hurt expression on his handsome face.

He looks good in a black suit, I have to give him that, but it's nothing when compared to the burgundy outfit Nico wore the night we parted. I'm still upset I didn't get to suck him off while he stood over me, majestic and mysterious in the mask he was wearing. I should have lured him into it in that gas station bathroom.

"Yeah, he will be missed," I say, responding with an equally cliché phrase and step away from the railing, just in case.

In case of what though? In case Misha/Mike (I'll go with Misha) was my brother's secret gay lover, in on the scheme to kill me?

"I'm here, if you ever need someone to talk to. I know you're not a kid anymore, but everyone needs a shoulder to cry on sometimes."

More like, Misha needs a free place to crash in Aspen and doesn't want to miss out on that just because Carl is gone.

"Thanks. I appreciate it," I say, briefly glancing at the French door behind Misha as I rub my shoulders. "Starting to get chilly out here."

I was hoping he'd get the hint, but my eyes go wider as he takes off his coat and, without asking, puts it over my shoulders. Which also means he ends up standing much closer to me than I'd expect, given how little we know each other.

Misha smiles. "There. I always really liked you, Blake. You know that, right? I just... didn't think it was appropriate to let you know before."

"Let me know what...?" I let my unfinished question hang in the air as the scent of his herby cologne surrounds me from all sides.

Misha places his hand on my shoulder and squeezes it with a sense of familiarity that feels *wrong* on so many levels. Misha might be trying to woo me, and while there isn't anything inherently wrong with that, guilt bites my insides, making me pull away. This is an uninvited touch. I don't want his scent on me, and his hands anywhere near me, because his proximity makes me feel as though I'm cheating on Nico.

"I did hope we could take the plane back to Vermont together. Get to know each other. I imagine it must be hard to be alone now," Misha says and rubs his thumb along the side of my hand, making anxiety simmer at the pit of my stomach.

Abort! Abort!

I step away, sliding out of the reach of his arms. Is this a normal way to act among gay guys, or is he eager to get together with the *naive gay brother* now that Carl isn't in the picture? I barely know him, and if I wanted company, it would not be his.

Not dissuaded in the slightest, Misha sighs and glances toward the snow-capped mountains, no doubt thinking he makes a pretty melancholic picture. "Carl talked about you a lot. It really is a shame that we often only realize who and what's really important when Death knocks on the door."

My thoughts were already with Nico, but when Misha said that pretentious sentence, the missing puzzle pieces of my mind slotted into place, leaving me with a sense of purposeful contentment.

Maybe the sentiment Misha expressed wasn't really so pretentious after all?

I *do* want company, but not Misha's, nor any other handsome stranger's. There's already someone who's burrowed deep in my chest and I can't get him out of there no matter how desperately I try to convince myself he and I can't work as a couple.

Because we *did.*

Nico has shown me more heart than any of the people who *ought to* care for me, and he's been gentle, patient even, when I betrayed his trust. He might be a killer, but he is so much more: a vigilante, a gentleman, a Christmas enthusiast, and an artist.

As I offer Misha a smile to soften the blow of rejection, my heart blooms, beating for someone else.

"I'm talking to someone. Sorry," I say, and hand him back the jacket. My thoughts are already back in Vermont, with the man I rejected despite deep down knowing it to be a mistake. Oh, I have been so blind!

Disappointment washes over Misha's face, but at least he's not getting pushy, I have to give him that.

"Sure, but just know you can hit me up anytime. I'll leave you my card. There are some serious predators out there."

"Definitely. Carl always made sure I was careful," I say, walking past him on my way inside. He smells nice. He looks nice. He is polite. If it wasn't for the fact that he's clearly trying to get with me for the wrong reasons, I might just be interested in him. But while I'm technically single, my heart doesn't feel that way, and as I step into the warmth of the smoking room, the longing for Nico's arms around me feels like a lead blanket.

There hasn't been a day, or even an hour when I didn't randomly start thinking about him, and instead of relief, all I feel is an ever-growing emptiness, as if he's left his knife inside me, and the wound refuses to close. There was such an endless void in his eyes when he told me he understood my choice, as if he wanted to say he was unlovable, when that's so far from the truth.

I can't run from my true feelings any longer.

CHAPTER 26

NICO

THIS HAS GOT TO be the saddest Christmas Eve I've ever experienced. Even worse than the first one after my grandpa's death. I have to fake my smiles for the customers rushing around the Winter Emporium, but at least work keeps me busy and not mulling over what I could have done differently to gain Blake's love.

The disappointing reality is that there's probably nothing that would have saved our relationship. It was doomed from the moment I took off my mask and revealed myself to him for what I am. Blake could have found me exciting to fuck, sure, emotionally enticing, *maybe*. But not someone he'd want to spend his life with. I should have known my dreams of becoming someone special for him were always just a delusion.

I didn't even feel like treating myself to a Christmas kill this year and instead punished myself with endless hours of work at the shop. It's something I usually enjoy, but given the circumstances, I know I'm doing it to avoid spending every waking hour worrying about Blake and how he's coping with the massive change in his life. I wish I could be there to hold his hand through it all, but he doesn't want me to, so I have to suck it up and move on.

In the last few days, I've even been toying with shutting down the whole Christmas Killer operation and locking away that part of me forever. How else will I ever find love? So those are my options, either live a lie with my partner, or stay alone and misunderstood.

The problem is that deep down, I know the itch will come back. I'm already more snappy, and I sulk in my apartment watching Christmas romcoms while entertaining myself by imagining ways in which the main characters could die. How long will I be able to stay away from my secret basement, my weapons, and the need to find a victim?

A hand closes on my shoulder, and Owen looks into my eyes, the pile of orders he brought from the stockroom resting behind the counter.

"Are you okay?" he asks, as if either of us has the time for coddling my feelings when the shop is bursting with Christmas Eve activity. As predicted, all the forgetful husbands who didn't get their wives presents are either at the jewelry store or here. And that's on top of the usual clientele and those picking up baked goods and other food last minute. All our temps are rushing around, and even Adam, Owen's boyfriend, is here, helping out so they can both drive off to visit his family as soon as the doors close.

I take a deep breath. "I guess I'm not, but don't worry about it. It's gonna pass. I just wish things would have worked out with Blake." I can't afford to be falling apart in the middle of the shop. I have to pull myself together, because no matter how much I love Christmas, right now the cheerful songs and bright colors remind me of everything I can't have.

Owen hesitates. "Are you sure you don't want to visit Adam's family with us? I kinda talked to them ab—"

I shake my head and force myself to smile. "I appreciate that, really, but I'd rather get some rest at home. It's been a... challenging month."

My dark side, the one excited about cutting someone's head off, spills in my heart like a drop of the blackest ink, making me ponder the option of abducting Blake. He will most likely be alone tomorrow, I know where he lives, and I could talk my way into his proximity. Just imagining his unconscious weight in my arms gives me a shiver of pleasure, but none of that would satisfy my true cravings. Even if I kept him in my basement for the rest of our days, I can't make him love me. If anything, his presence would be torturous for *me*, and he'd grow to resent me, causing both of us pain.

At the end of the day, I don't want him in a cage. I'd rather he was free and happy, even if his future doesn't include—

The sharp clang of a bell makes me snap my head up, and as the customer on the other side of the counter turns back to also see what this is about, I spot a familiar face in the middle of the shop.

Everything stills, and as Blake lowers a bell he must have borrowed from the Santa charity collector working outside, my heart thumps, accelerating. Last time I saw him, he was wearing formal clothes that showcased his body shape, but with his curls in a mess and a flush on his pale face, he's somehow even more handsome than I remember.

More confusingly though, I recognize the sweater he's wearing, and my heart stops pumping altogether.

It's the one I made. Red, oversized, adorned with crocheted Christmas treats like gift boxes and Santa faces, as well as plastic candy canes. The big white words in the middle spell out *Oh what fun!*

And Blake is wearing it. In public, not just discreetly bringing it to me in a bag so no one sees what he called the most hideous thing he's ever seen. I'm not sure what to make of this, but my feet slowly guide me to him like he's a snowflake I have to catch with my mittens.

Most of the customers haven't yet gotten the memo that something's going on, but when the music dies, I can sense all eyes on me and the scared boy with the bell in one hand and a gift-wrapped box in the other.

I can't believe he's here. Shouldn't he be in New York, skating by the Rockefeller Center? Or back at his home, far away from the Christmas cheer he claimed to detest? Instead, he's at the very center of it, and when I come closer, about to ask him to follow me to the backrooms, he opens his mouth and... sings.

Disbelief makes my stomach drop, but I stay still, meeting his eyes as his voice trembles. He's an average singer, and the tune he chose is Mariah Carey's 'All I Want for Christmas is You', which always kinda makes me tear up, even though it's so cheerful. Hearing the words from his mouth, in the odd silence of the store filled with people melts the ice that's grown around my heart since our parting.

I don't know what's changed his mind, or what he's trying to achieve, but I don't even wait until he's done, and approach him in quick strides. He's still singing the last chorus when I take him in my arms.

The customers don't know about my plight, but a few still clap and whistle.

The crushing realization of what this might be about, settles on my heart, then squeezes as if it's barbed wire.

I have to take a deep breath so my voice doesn't tremble, but I manage to whisper into Blake's ear. "There's no need for this, sweetie. You have nothing to fear from me." Because a normal person like him must have had sleepless nights worrying about the monster who killed his brother. I imagine him terrified that if he doesn't appease me, I would come after him one day.

I expect him to pull away, happy, if uncomfortable with the situation he's put himself in, but as the cheers around us die down, he puts the bell away and presents me with a meticulously wrapped gift.

When he confirms that he wants me to open it, I rip into it like I'm a greedy kid. The smell of fruit and cinnamon makes my mouth water.

"I made it myself," Blake adds quickly. "Because I know how much you love fruitcake... Can we... talk? Please?"

I swallow, looking into those soulful green eyes. "Sure, I—Owen, will you be okay—"

Owen is right by my side with a wide grin and nods. "Of course. I can handle this, easy. Take all the time you need."

"Let's go somewhere private, hm?" My face is on fire as I lead him to the stairs so we can get to my apartment. I'm sizzling just thinking about him being at my place again, and I try to ignore all the joyous comments flying my way. It's too much to handle, and I'm relieved the moment we are out of everyone's sight. Blake grabs my fingers and lets me lead him to my door, and then inside.

I have so many questions. Why did he choose to come back? Why now? Was the song a way to express his honest feelings, or is this just me reading into things again?

"Fuck. It's a mess. Sorry," I grumble and nervously start clearing up the empty pizza boxes, and the stack of used tissues from yesterday's cry-fest. I'm glad I'm presentable because of my work in the shop, or he could have walked in on me in a fleece onesie with stains on it.

But as I move to put away the trash, he stands in my way and takes the boxes from me before dropping them to the floor.

"I don't care. Just…. listen."

I force myself to not avoid his gaze anymore. "Yes? Is everything okay… in Aspen?" I ask because my mind is doing the craziest twists now about the possibility of him wearing a wire. But would he sell me out? After everything we've been through? Just looking into his pretty eyes is enough to mess with my head.

"Nico… I flew back last night, and I knew I needed to see you. Have you…" He swallows and stares at our feet as his sweaty palms tighten on my hands. "Do you want me to go?"

"No!" I say in an instant and squeeze him back. "Tell me what you need."

Blake nods, massaging my hands as he twitches in front of me, opening and closing his mouth several times. "I just… I wanted to say sorry. I was confused, and scared, but I didn't want you to go."

A storm erupts in my chest. Is it possible that there's still a future for us? I don't dare blink in case he is only a figment of my imagination and will disappear as soon as I close my eyes.

"I had to leave. You don't have to worry about me. I get your reasoning even if I don't like it." But he's holding my hands, wearing my sweater, he baked me a fruitcake, and even sang me a romantic Christmas song. It has to mean what I hope it does, or he would have chosen a more non-committal tune, like 'Rudolf the Red-Nosed Reindeer'.

"Yes, but now I'm back and..." Blake inhales and shakes his head before resting his forehead against my chest. "It's all I wanted. To come back and see you."

I take him into my arms, and for the first time in two weeks, my heart steadies. He fits in my embrace the way he fits in my soul. "That's a lovely sweater you have on," I tease, melting into him.

The breath he lets out is soft and sweet as cotton candy, and so full of relief my blood thrums with joy. "It's not actually ugly. It's soft, and warm, and I love it," he mutters, and something in his voice tells me he isn't speaking only about the garment. But as I pull back to kiss him, he reaches into his pocket and presents me with a little square box wrapped with a velvet ribbon. "Merry Christmas."

I rub my eyes because they suddenly itch. "For me?" Stupid fucking question, since he's giving it to me, but I'm a mess. "Thank you. Should I... put it under the tree? For tomorrow?" Am I getting ahead of myself with my hopes that he'll stay the night?

"No, I want you to see them now," he tells me and shoves the gift at my chest.

I'm not sure what to make of it, but I unfasten the ribbon and open the box. I'm now glad he didn't give it to me downstairs because it's filled with... teeth. And I've seen enough of them to know they're human.

Blake swallows and pushes back his locks, fidgeting under the weight of my gaze. "They're Carl's. I got him cremated but saved the teeth... for you. You didn't get the head and you deserved to. I know it matters to you, and this way, if you want to, you could make a new snow globe. With miniatures inspired by this kill. And maybe... the two of us could feature in there?"

His eyes glisten, and I put away the box on the counter, because the need to hug him is overwhelming. "This is the most thoughtful gift anyone has ever gotten me." I squeeze him tightly, but then lift him and spin him around, feeling as though we're already in the most romantic of snow globes.

He yelps and clutches at me, but as I stop and lower him back to the floor, he grabs me by the collar and tugs me down until our lips clash. Gravity goes haywire, and I stumble against the wall, clawing my fingers into his buttocks as he raises one knee and tries to wrap his leg around my hips.

I love him. I love him. I love him.

I've been trying to wean myself off this feeling in the last two weeks, but now it's back with full force, and I can hardly breathe, too overwhelmed by the need to never let him go.

I lift his legs for ease and carry this baby koala into my bedroom. Maybe I'm getting ahead of myself, but I'll be happy even if he only wants to cuddle. All I need is to be close.

"I missed this," Blake rasps, and as my knee hits the unmade bed, we both topple onto the mattress with a soft sigh of relief. His thighs tighten around me, and he arches his back, kissing me even harder, pushing his fingers into my hair, holding me close. Like I'd be going anywhere when I'm on top of him. "Missed you. I just... I only want you," he whispers, stroking my face.

He's pouring hot chocolate all over my marshmallow heart. "You did? You *do*? Blake, sweetness, I'm going mad without you." And while my feelings for him might be soft and gooey, my dick is most definitely responding to my presence between his legs. It would hurt, but if he says he wants to be friends-with-benefits, I'll probably agree to it anyway, because he could stab me a hundred times and I'll still slide myself onto his blade if it only gets me closer to his lips.

Blake exhales, stroking my skin in desperate swipes. He's still nervous. I can see it in the way he keeps swallowing, but in the end, he covers his eyes with his forearm and whines. "You'll think it's silly, because it's been such a short time, but I'm thinking about you all the time. I think... I love you."

With those three words, he lit up all the Christmas lights inside me. I pull away his arm to look into his eyes and smile. "It's not silly. Sometimes you meet your person, and you *know*. Just like when I first saw you, so scared but so determined to live. So beautiful with your green eyes, dark curls, and sweet lips. You're the only item on my letter to Santa," I say and kiss him again, still not believing that he's here.

Blake chuckles and throws his arms around my neck, nuzzling my face with his cute little nose. "You're such a cheese sometimes."

"And you love it." I grin and slide my fingers under his sweater. His body is made to be worshiped. One of my hands goes up his spine, while the other delves into his jeans to squeeze his perfect ass.

I groan and press harder against him. The need to connect physically is overwhelming. Like I'm a beast in heat at the end of the season, and if I don't rut *now*, I might die. He must be feeling the same thing, because as we kiss, he grabs the front of my jeans and unzips them before pushing his nimble fingers inside. His touch is like fire, and I rock against his hand as he watches me, eyes wide with focus.

"Yes.... and many more things."

"Yeah? Did you dream about me breaking into your house? Just because I couldn't stay away?" I murmur and pull away from his lips so I can slide my tongue along his neck. "You're such a naughty boy deep down." As I say that, I rock into his hand to show him how much it excites me, and he bends into a deep arch. His body stews under the warm clothes, but I want to sample him before getting to the main course. His skin tastes of salt, soap, and desire, and as I bite his shoulder, making him shudder, I feel like a beast about to sate all its needs.

"Yes... I'm sorry, but I can't help myself. You're so tall, and strong, dangerous, and when you look at me like this, I dream of you on top of me, your cock inside me," Blake whimpers and unzips his own pants too, already pushing them down, as if he can't wait to feel me on his bare skin.

"Keep the sweater on. I'm gonna fuck you in it. You know I made it, right? Makes me feel like you're marked as mine when you wear it." I grin to myself when I imagine him in nothing but that. It's barely long enough to cover his ass.

But as he wiggles under me to slide his jeans all the way off, I notice he's wearing colorful underwear, and I'm instantly filled with so much arousal I press harder into my boy's hand. It's a jockstrap. And not just any jockstrap but the kind he snickered at when I took him shopping in my store. The bright-green fabric featuring snowflakes and candy canes stretches over his hard cock, but when I squeeze one of Blake's buttocks, lust shoots through my veins so fast and hard I get lightheaded.

"You like it?" Blake asks with a smug smile.

I press my head under his chin and take three deep breaths to steady myself. "Fuck... Blake... what are you doing to me? I want you to wear these all the time. I want to see the outline when you wear pajamas—No. I want you in only these and a T-shirt in bed so I can just touch you there whenever I feel like it." I'm losing my mind with lust. I denied myself such thoughts about him for two weeks and now they're all flooding back.

I pull away just to flip him over like a damn pancake, and I take a good long look at the pert ass framed by white straps. With a happy groan, I squeeze his buttocks then pull them apart.

He's beautiful everywhere, so it's not a surprise that his lovely pink hole beckons me closer as I rub it with my thumb, making Blake shiver and arch his ass toward me. "Yes... touch me. I want to be yours. No one else is good enough."

White-hot rage boils in my brain, and I cover him with my body, settling my weight on top, and my hard dick in his crack. "You haven't tried to check that, have you?" I slide a hand under his sweater, all the way to his neck and give it a gentle squeeze.

He shakes his head so hard he smacks me with his hair, moving under me like a cat in heat. "No. This one guy tried to 'get to know me better', but he didn't feel right at all. It's you or no one, Nico."

I'm gonna have to keep a close eye on my precious boy. No one's making a move on him on my watch. I kiss his nape much gentler, rocking my hips so my cock glides over his pucker. "You're so sweet I want to suck you, but I need to be inside you more."

He nods and presses his back to my chest, legs spread. I can't imagine a more obvious invitation and squeeze his bare thigh, resting my weight on top. His breathing quickens, and he glances over his shoulder, nipping my lips.

"Yes. Please. Come inside me. I need it so much," he rasps and rubs his groin against the mattress.

"Can't think of anything better than creaming your tight little hole," I murmur and grab the lube from my bedside table. As soon as I'm nice and slick, I press my cockhead to his pucker, turned on by being so openly invited to. He loves a bit of role-play, getting pinned down and taken, but it seems that today he's eager to show me his love like a good boy.

He thrashes in anticipation the moment my slippery shaft arrives at his entrance, and I blow hot air on his ear, eager to give him all of my affection. We are perfect together, and when I press inside, breaching his body, that fact becomes as obvious as baubles on a Christmas tree. He lifts his head with a breathy rasp, pulls close my pillow, and then rises his ass ever so gently, sucking me in.

"Oh... oh... that feels... so good."

He's speaking for me too, because the way he arches to take more of my cock is heaven. I hug him, kiss the back of his head, but don't hold back. I'm far too excited about my Blake to think about anything other than the tight muscles of his channel squeezing me so delightfully.

"Feel this? You're mine now. No going back." I pump my cock into him at increasing speed. It turns me on that he was so horny he didn't even care if I got undressed as long as he got my dick in him. He's just in the naughty jockstrap and my sweater while I ride him almost fully dressed. That's how much he couldn't wait to get back under me. My balls feel so tight I might blow any second, and as I tighten my hold on him, following my instinct and sawing into him over and over, he rubs his head against my chin like a cat.

"Never... never felt like this... this is so, so intense," he mumbles, stumbling over words, greedy for my touch and attention.

I'll give him all of that and more. "I'll give it to you hard and often so you always have me in the back of your mind. You're gonna be my soft little mattress." I groan when he squeezes his ass on my cock. His scent is delicious as it goes to my head causing a natural high. "Oh, fuck, Blake... My cock needed this so bad. I'm gonna come."

"Yes, yes, yes, give it all to me," Blake rasps and changes the angle of his hips to one that somehow makes him feel even tighter. "But that's the only hole you can fuck from now on. I'm so greedy for you." His words turn into a moan as I slam into him harder, overcome by fantasies of filling him with my seed.

"All yours..." I moan out as I come so hard my eyes roll back. "Feel it? You'll be the only one ever getting my cum," I mutter, rocking into him a few more times as I catch my breath. All the tension mounted up for painful days now slides off my shoulders, and I'm where I belong. His needy little shivers only make it better.

I'm a sweaty mess, still panting, but I remember he's a horny bunny and can't be sated with my cum alone.

Helpless little whimpers escape him as he attempts to fuck the bed, and when I pull out, I allow myself a moment of indulgence and watch my cum between his buttocks, around and inside his lovely swollen hole. But he needs more, so I flip him back. Hair sticks to his sweaty features, but he doesn't seem to care that it makes him look lewd. The moment I pluck his stiff cock out of the jockstrap, he produces a litany of filthy begging, and slides his hand into my hair.

"No need to ask, baby," I tease him right before taking his dick down my throat in one go. So hot, hard, and delicious. I suck around it with my eyes closed as he clenches his fingers and moans. He is everything I've ever wanted, and came back to me even knowing what I am. What else could this be if not true love? He is my own Christmas miracle.

As he explodes in my mouth, closing his thighs around my head, I briefly feel intoxicated as visions of a happy future float through my head. Him, waiting for me with dinner as I return from my latest kill. Drinking chocolate by the Christmas tree. Long walks, and other beautiful things that I always feared might not come true for me. But they will. With Blake, they will.

A soft sob makes me look up just in time to see my love covering his face.

I swallow his load, keeping my eyes up, then turn to licking the insides of his thighs for dessert. "You okay, sweetness?"

"Y-yes," he whispers and wipes his eyes before sobbing again. "I just... I never thought anything could feel like this. It's so much..."

I crawl up his body and settle on top of him like a sated lion. "And I can't believe you came back to me. You're the only one who knows all of me, and I'm so honored to know all of you as well."

Another tear escapes Blake's eye, and he rubs it away with the back of his hand before rolling against my chest. "I was cold for so long, but you unlocked all those feelings in me. And it's scary but also feels so, so good. I love you so much."

"I won't let you down. I promise. I love you. No matter what, you'll always have me." I entwine our fingers then kiss his hand. "Merry Christmas? Can you now admit it's the best time of the year?"

Blake laughs, sweet and carefree in my arms. "Let's see... Christmas is when I met the most amazing guy in the world, who fights evil and demands nothing in return, who always takes care of me, and who never disappointed me, even when I was being a horrible brat." He exhales and rubs himself against me as our bodies cool. "I think I have no other choice but to love Christmas."

EPILOGUE

BLAKE

One year later.

"This is one of our most popular products," I say, pointing to the T-shirt stretched over the headless mannequin. It's definitely not a bestseller at this time of year, but Christmas Killer merch is one of the things that keeps the Winter Emporium afloat over the other months.

"I don't know," the elderly lady says, biting her lip as Owen passes behind her in a full Santa costume. "Seems kind of extreme."

"It really is just a joke that people make. Nobody actually thinks that a murderer 'did nothing wrong'. I always see it as a conversation starter, and if your granddaughter likes true-crime, then she might really appreciate this gift. You can only get this design through our shop, so she couldn't have bought this one all the way in Florida.

Besides, did you know that many people theorize that the Christmas Killer is actually killing other serial killers?"

It's a spruced-up version of the theory I've been pushing in this year's edition of my podcast's Christmas special, and while I did receive some backlash for it, I cannot stand strangers slandering Nico's name, whether *he* cares about it or not.

He is the best boyfriend, a talented artist, a fantastic cook, and deserves nothing but love and praise. Call me brainwashed, but that's my reality. I even fell in love with Christmas thanks to him, so I happily work in his (or dare I say 'our'?) shop part-time, and push the products with genuine excitement.

The lady seems a bit unsure, but my sales pitch worked, and she's buying the T-shirt. Whether I've convinced her, or she's just too uncomfortable saying no to me doesn't matter.

As I make my way through the busy shop, answering questions as I go, my gaze settles on the lone sandwich resting on a plate behind the counter. It's been over an hour since I made it for Nico, but only one or two bites have been taken while he's busy by the register, offering smiles to people who are taking far too much time choosing between two baubles.

My man is so hardworking—one of the many things I love about him—but this won't do. I baked the bread myself, adding sunflower seeds, because Nico loves them, and while it's sourdough and therefore doesn't get dry too fast, I want it fueling my boyfriend, not starfishing on the table.

I get behind the counter with the sweetest smile, and just as Nico is about to serve the next customer, I offer her a little apology and pull him away.

"Your lunch. Finish it, and I'll take over while you eat," I tell him, gently stroking his shoulder.

He opens his mouth like a fish on dry land but doesn't try to argue and grabs the sandwich. One kiss later, Nico scurries off to the storage room while I focus on the customer.

The woman is buying a whole set of plates hand-decorated with a mistletoe pattern, and it makes me think back to the tiny apartment I share with Nico upstairs. We have mistletoe hanging in there all year round.

While I don't miss my grand, yet empty, mansion, there's no denying that our space is cramped. At least thanks to Nico owning the building, I was able to set up a little office for my podcasting at the far end of the storage room downstairs. I would have done so in the murder-basement but we try not to use it all the time, to avoid suspicion.

Living with Nico has been surprisingly easy. I like my alone time, but he's also often busy with research, the shop, or working out, so I never feel crowded by him. And then we get to cuddle in bed or on our tiny sofa to watch TV. He's never bored watching true-crime documentaries with me and loves playing hypotheticals of what he would have done differently to avoid getting caught. Some of his ideas are pretty original, but I have to proudly boast that thanks to my knowledge, he's incorporated a few new safety measures to his routine as well. After all, I need to make sure my man *never* gets caught.

I try not to think about that too much, so I redirect my thoughts to the surprise I plan to reveal to him later tonight. I know Christmas is only next week, but I can't wait to share the good news. I'm in the middle of selling a teen lesbian couple a pair of holly-themed rings when Nico squeezes my shoulder, still chewing on his food.

"With the bakery next door closing, it's lucky you got so into baking. I can't live without good bread and cake."

I grin and accept the money before tying a little rainbow-striped ribbon on the box containing the jewelry. "I am still accepting Christmas time wishes, if you want me to make anything specific."

"Oh yes! Please make your fruitcake. With extra apricots and pecans." Nico's blue eyes glaze over.

"You're the only person I know who is this excited about fruitcake, but your wish is my command," I say graciously.

We leave the counter to Owen and go together to fix the miniature train that seems to be stuck. Nico could do it himself, but I love his company, so I want to hang out with him now that the rush of customers has died down.

"Fruitcake is extremely underrated," Nico says with full seriousness. He looks up at me with a frown. "Would fruit*bread* be just a different type of fruitcake? Would it depend on the ratio of ingredients?"

I match his expression, because I have never thought of that myself. "I'll get back to you on that, but it's a gray area, isn't it? Like with banana bread, it's in the name, but I always thought it was more of a cake. I'm sure there's some professional baker or food historian who has strong opinions about it."

Because that's what I do now—subscribe to YouTube channels on baking and collect cookbooks.

I used to think that I'll be traveling the world, wild and free, and instead I'm shockingly content with barely leaving the state and making my man sandwiches. Weird how life goals can change when you meet the right person. Though Nico has agreed to a long vacation in France at the peak of summer next year, when business in the Winter Emporium grinds to a standstill.

After our first Christmas together, I did consider telling him that with the money I have he could simply retire. He could employ another manager and only pop into the store when he feels like it, but it only took me a few weeks to understand that Nico's heart is in this shop. It's great that we have my money to fall back on, but he wants the Winter Emporium to thrive and loves talking to people about Christmas traditions from around the world, choose items from local artisans, and champion handmade decorations by holding workshops.

His passion only makes me love him more.

Maybe it's selfish, but I also love that his other passion is something he can only ever share with me. I'm the one person who understands his need for violence and the art he creates from the outcome. It makes me feel special. We are special to each other, and no matter how much I hate Carl for caring about me so little, I know that I wouldn't be in this amazing relationship if he hadn't made the terrible decisions he had.

And I certainly wouldn't be as happy as I am now if I fulfilled my original dream of traveling the world and hooking up with all the hot guys I wanted. Nico's warmth managed to melt even the ice on my stunted heart. And isn't that what life should be all about?

I watch him oil the wheel of the toy train, all focused, and I smile at a family watching him through the shop window, because this makes me remember that he's the source of joy for so many more people.

And yet, he's mine. I've seen men (and women) hit on him more or less discreetly, and he's always so proud to say he has a boyfriend. It makes me feel appreciated.

We spend some more time discussing what bread I should try making next as Nico fixes the train. Once he gets it going, a few people come in to see the miniature town and clap. Even though it's time to close the shop and I'm itching to show off my early Christmas gift, I let Nico finish the day at his own pace, because watching him share festive joy with a kid is priceless. He lets the boy push the button responsible for the train's whistle, and I smile at the absolute glee on the kid's face.

Nico ends up gifting the boy a pin marking him as *Santa's Express Train Conductor*, but in the end, the family leaves, we close the shop, and I wonder how incredible it is that I'm so happy sweeping the floors while Nico polishes the counters.

I know he's tired and wants nothing more than to settle on the sofa and rest, but I hope the surprise I have for him will recharge his batteries. I slide my arms round him just as he places the cleaning supplies back in their usual spots. He still smells of his cologne, but there's also a note from the cinnamon aroma of the coffee he had right after closure. I love it so much.

"Soo... how about a very short walk?" I offer.

He squints at me, then peeks through the window, but it's not snowing like it had earlier. "How short?" Nico asks even though I already know he can be convinced.

"Extremely. You might not even need a coat," I tell him and wink. "It's a surprise."

"Okay, but *you* are taking a hat," he says and grabs the beanie he knitted for me from under the counter. It's brown, has small ears, and makes me look silly, but I love it anyway, so I don't complain when he puts it on my head. "I won't have you ill again. You're a very miserable patient."

"Guilty as charged," I tell him and get to my toes so we can kiss. But then I grab his hand and pull him toward the exit as excitement explodes inside me like fireworks.

He says nothing, no doubt trying to show some enthusiasm for my sake, but I know he will love my Christmas surprise. As soon as we lock up after ourselves, I take the ten steps separating us from the closed bakery next door and open it with a key I've been hiding from him for two weeks now.

"Merry Christmas," I say, pushing him out of the frosty street and into the empty shop.

"Wh-what?" Nico asks, throwing me a suspicious glance. "You didn't..."

"Yes, I did!" I slap the light switch and make a little dance in front of the counter, which not that long ago held so many breads and pastries. "Think about it. It was the best bakery in town. We could reopen it, expand the shop, since you said you need more space, have some sort of customer loyalty program for both places. Aaand, maybe host baking workshops and stuff like that?"

Nico runs his fingers through his hair, looking around the dusty space. "And you *bought* it? This isn't rented?" he asks in disbelief as I nod.

"Yep, the whole building."

"This is incredible, Blake." Nico's smile widens and he turns to me. "We could knock down this wall, connect a cafe to the shop, and serve Christmas-themed treats all year round!"

"And expand our apartment," I add, since that was the first thought in my head when I found out Mrs. Sally was selling her place and moving south to be closer to her daughter and grandchildren.

I love Nico with all my heart, but I want another damn room up there.

Nico picks me up and twirls us like I'm some Disney princess. "Yes! A massive open-plan kitchen, just for you and your recipe experiments."

It's so sweet that he thinks of me first that I have to lean in and kiss him or I might just cry.

We're perfect together.

The end

If you'd like to read a bonus chapter about Nico and Blake's future together find the bonus chapter at http://kamerikan.com/freebies
And if you're keen for more stories about murder on Christmas, read on.
If you'd like to stay in touch, you can find us in our Facebook group, the Merikan Playroom.
Please, review this book on your favorite platform:)

K.A. MERIKAN
FESTIVE
FUGITIVE

Festive Fugitive

K.A. Merikan

I didn't expect my Christmas gift to be six-foot-two, a trained killer, and obsessed with me.

Eli

One bullet. One dead man. And now my wreck of a life is spiraling out of control.

The bastard deserved it, but I'm just a regular guy. I botched the escape, and since I killed him while wearing a Santa costume, they call me the Festive Fugitive. Cute.

Too bad I'll be spending Christmas behind bars or in a body bag.

Then he appears. Cesar.

My dark salvation. A trained killer who looks at me as if I'm his personal miracle. I killed his boss, yet he says I did him a favor. He wants to protect me, claim me, cage me in his arms, and God help me... I let him.

Because what's falling for a monster when there's a manhunt hot on my tail and a target on my back?

Cesar

Taken as a child, I was turned into a loyal weapon. I killed, tortured, burned, and bled. I was respected and needed. Until I wasn't.

When I lost an eye, my master pushed me aside, but as I waited for my 'one last job' so I could retire, Eli pulled the trigger.

I never expected some half-starved, grief-drunk civilian in a Santa outfit to free me, but that's what happened.

Eli is everything I am not—fragile, impulsive, untrained. And yet he killed the man I was bound to. He doesn't know it, but he owns me now.

He thinks I'm his protector, that I've taken him under my wing. But it's more than that.

He's mine. My obsession. My purpose. My beautiful, reckless mess of a man, and I'll burn the world before I let anyone take him from me.

I guess Christmas came early for Eli this year.

"Festive Fugitive" is a standalone M/M dark romance where a trained killer takes an amateur vigilante under his wing and gets increasingly obsessed with his new ward. (+Christmas crafts!)

Themes and tropes: Size difference, trained killer, snowed in, on the run, only one bed, hurt/comfort, revenge, loneliness, possessive hero, past trauma, brainwashing, dark humor, disabled hero, morally gray heroes, touch starved, free use (within the couple)

Warnings: Violence, strong language, PTSD

Available on Amazon

K.A. MERIKAN
ALL I WANT FOR CHRISTMAS IS
REVENGE

All I Want for Christmas is Revenge

K.A. Merikan

"I will kill the men who murdered your family...
for a price. You will be mine."

Saint

Being a hitman is the loneliest of jobs. We don't have many friends. Some don't even have family. Lovers? Try explaining to your boyfriend why there's blood on your shirt.

Christmas is the worst time to be alone, but this year, love is on the cards for me. All thanks to a letter I found in the street.

It reads, "Dear Santa, all I want for Christmas is revenge..."

At first, I'm intrigued by the words, the grisly details, and the rage steaming off the page. The author doesn't know it yet, but we are a perfect fit. His bloodthirst is equal to mine, his creativity in coming up with ways to kill is admirable, and when I track him down, I instantly fall for the wrath in his dark eyes.

His wish is my command, if he's ready to pay the price - being mine.

Rowan

My therapist always tells me I should let go of my pain and rage. But I don't want to let go. I want the men who attacked my family dead.

I just never thought I'd get my wish granted. But there's a catch. The handsome monster who abducts me to his lair wants me as his payment.

Me, the strange loner filled with bitterness and sarcasm. Me, who never even had a boyfriend. Me, with my cane and irrational fears.

But I'd sell my soul to the Devil for revenge, so I might as well offer my body to a seductive assassin. After all, he cooks well, kills people, buys me bath bombs... What else could I want in a boyfriend?

"All I Want for Christmas is Revenge" is a standalone M/M dark romance where an obsessive hitman desperate for love zeroes in on a young man willing to trade his life for revenge. (+Cute Christmas dates!)

Themes and tropes: Size difference, assassin, mistrust, snowed in, small town, revenge, loneliness, illicit arrangement, possessive hero, past trauma, dark humor, abduction, first love, soulmates, age gap, disabled hero, morally gray

Warnings: Kidnapping, violence, gore, stalking, strong language, and steamy, explicit scenes

Available on Amazon

ABOUT THE AUTHOR

K.A. Merikan is a duo of queer writers who don't believe in following the well-trodden path. In their books you can dip your toe into dangerous romance with mafiosi, outlaw bikers and bad boys, all from the safety of your sofa. They love the weird and wonderful, stepping out of the box, and bending stereotypes both in life and in fiction. Their stories don't shy away from exploring the darker side of M/M romance, and feature a variety of anti-heroes, rebels, misfits, and underdogs who go against the grain.

Be prepared for shocking twists, dark humor, raw emotions, and sizzling hot scenes.

e-mail: **kamerikan@gmail.com**
http://kamerikan.com

More information about works in progress and publishing at:

Facebook: https://www.facebook.com/groups/1817541075240882

Patreon: https://www.patreon.com/kamerikan